WHAT WAITS
IN
THE WATER

WHAT WAITS IN THE WATER

KIERAN SCOTT

Scholastic Inc.

ISBN 978-1-338-19291-9

10 9 8 7 6 5 4 3 2 1   17 18 19 20 21

Printed in the U.S.A.   40
First printing 2017

Book design by Christopher Stengel

*For Amanda, who waits patiently
for this book even as I type*

WHAT WAITS IN THE WATER

Dear Future Me,

This morning was the first time I was actually happy we moved here. It's the end of April already and I honestly thought spring was never going to come. Like, maybe in Michigan that's not even a thing—you just go straight from fall to winter to fall again. But when I walked outside with my coat all buttoned up to my chin, it felt warm. And I heard this exciting drip, drip, drip coming from the corner of the porch roof. The snow was MELTING. I mean, I honestly can't even believe I just wrote that. I really couldn't remember what grass looked like before today. I even saw these teeny tiny leaves pushing up from the ground. Mom says they're crocuses, but I wasn't ready to believe that yet. I'll believe flowers are possible when I see them.

On the way to school, people were walking around with their coats open. They were shouting and smiling to each other. Waving. NOT WEARING HATS! Tires shushed through shallow puddles formed by MELTING SNOW! (Writing that might never get old.) As I walked past the coffee shop, I started giggling. I couldn't help it. It's possible being inside for so long has made me delirious. But then P strolled by and looked at me like I was a crazy person, so I forced myself to stop.

Anyway, it was the first time I started to think that maybe life could be cool here. Maybe living in a tourist town could be fun. I bet business will start picking up for Mom and Dad once all The Summer People get here. And I bet once the lake warms up, it'll be kind of exciting. The other day, A promised to show me the sunniest spots for tanning. I am SO pasty. I can't wait to get a little color. Plus there will be lots of boys from out of town hanging around—just like at Christmastime, when they all came for the skiing. Not that I'm ever going to get up the guts to talk to them or anything, but still. Eye candy, you know?

When I got to school I was in such a good mood that when N said hi to me in the hallway I said hi back—and SMILED. Maybe spring in Michigan will turn me into a not-shy person. I mean, N has been so nice to me since we moved here. And he's kind of shy himself. Who knows? Maybe we can learn to be not-shy together. It sounds cheesy, but tonight, writing this with my window OPEN and a warmish breeze coming through, I sort of feel like anything can happen.

ONE

"Seriously, Hannah, can you drive any slower? By the time we get there, the weekend's gonna be over."

Hannah Webster clutched the steering wheel of her new RAV4 and tried to restrain herself from grabbing her stepsister's phone and chucking it out the open window. Ever since they'd pulled out of their driveway in Oak View, Ohio, five hours ago, Katie had been complaining. She'd whined about the air-conditioning being too strong. She'd whined about Hannah's road trip playlist being too dorky. She'd whined when Hannah had stopped at a rest area to use the bathroom. And then Katie had bought a large coffee and whined about how *she* had to use the bathroom until Hannah had to pull over at the *next* rest stop. And now, she was whining about the fact that Hannah was doing the speed limit. But what did Katie expect? Hannah had just gotten her license and her new car a month and a half ago. She wasn't trying to get a ticket.

What made it even worse was that the entire time Katie was complaining, she was also texting. With Jacob Faber. Hannah's Jacob. *Her* best friend. Any time Katie wasn't grumbling, she was giggling. And sighing. And shaking her head like Jacob was oh so adorable. And to top it all off, she refused to tell Hannah what they were texting about.

"We're almost there. The GPS says we're five minutes away,"

Hannah replied, barely keeping the fed-up tremor out of her voice. Right then, five minutes sounded like a lifetime.

She pushed a stray strand of hair behind her ear and glanced in the side mirror. They had just hit the downtown area of Dreardon Lake, Michigan—all quaint shops and family-friendly restaurants with blooming flowers bursting from window boxes and colorful flags flying everywhere.

Jacob had been talking about Dreardon Lake for years. Hannah had seen pictures of the town, but the photos didn't do it justice. Main Street was a bustling hub, full of people carrying trays of coffees, toting squirming toddlers, texting while walking. Hannah tried to concentrate on the sun shining outside the car, the pair of kids skipping down the sidewalk with ice cream cones, the shoppers swinging bags as they hopped from boutique to boutique. She tried to absorb the happy-go-lucky vibe. This weekend was going to be fun. Right?

It was mid-August—the last Thursday before school started next week—and she was going to spend four whole days with Jacob and his family at their summer house. Jacob had promised lake swims, cookouts around the fire pit, board games and movie marathons, and Jacob's mother's famous chocolate chip brownies. It would be perfect. The perfect end to the summer.

Katie snorted a laugh and sighed, shaking her head adoringly at her phone.

Or it would be perfect if she *wasn't here*, Hannah thought.

"Is Jacob waiting for us?" Hannah asked.

Katie's thumbs tapped at her phone screen. She laughed again at Jacob's reply, then sent another text, marked by the *swooshing* sound Hannah had been listening to the entire drive. If she never heard that sound again it would be too soon.

Hannah paused at a stoplight, allowing groups of fresh-faced tourists to cross the street. She glanced at her stepsister. From the moment Hannah had met Katie Chen a little over two years ago, the girl had never looked anything other than impeccable. Today, she had her black hair up in a sleek, high ponytail, and was sporting the exact opposite of what Hannah considered to be good road trip clothing. Between the pink miniskirt, the white off-the-shoulder top, and the high platform shoes, she looked like she was ready for a poolside brunch, rather than a long haul on the highways of Ohio and Michigan. Her eyeliner was painted into a perfect cat eye and her lip gloss matched her skirt. Her appearance was, in a word, photo-ready. Which was good, since Katie's favorite pastime was taking selfies. She was taking one right now, as the light turned green, her mouth fixed in a ridiculous pout, her chin tilted down, her phone poised above her head.

"Katie," Hannah said sharply, gripping the steering wheel so hard she pinched the flesh of her own palms.

"What?" Katie rolled her eyes.

"I said, is Jacob waiting for us at the dock?" Hannah asked.

"Oh. I'll ask him."

Katie sent off another text—*swoosh*—and Hannah eased through the light. She didn't want to think about what Jacob's reaction would be when he saw Katie's outfit. Or when he compared it to Hannah's own loose sweatpants/faded T-shirt combo. Hannah's wavy dark brown hair was tied into a messy side braid and she wore five-dollar Old Navy flip-flops left over from last summer. But at least her toenails looked good. She'd painted them red on a whim last night—something she'd never done before—and they hadn't come out half bad if she did say so herself.

The thing that was really disappointing about Katie was that Hannah had always wanted a sister. Her mother had passed away when Hannah was only two, and Hannah didn't remember her at all, though she cherished the many photos of herself as a baby in her mom's arms. It had always been Hannah and her dad, and she'd been fine with that. Her dad took her swimming, and cooked brunch for the two of them on lazy Sunday mornings. He could even make errands like grocery shopping fun. She'd never really felt as if she *needed* a mother, because her dad was everything. But a sister—a sister would be awesome. A sister would be someone to share secrets with and play in the backyard with and try on makeup with. A sister would be an automatic bestie—a person who knew her better than anyone and always had her back.

Then, a couple years ago, Hannah's dad had gotten serious with Mylin, who had two kids of her own—a daughter, Katie, who was Hannah's age, and a son, Fred, who was three years younger. Hannah had been all in. A sister! With a bonus little brother! It was like a dream come true.

After a few group outings with their parents—to play mini golf, eat pancakes, see a movie—Hannah had taken the plunge and invited Katie, via text, to hang out with her and her friends at Sweet Retreat, their neighborhood cupcake and candy shop. Katie's response had been instant and curt:

No thanks. I don't do sweets.

Well, okay, Katie *had* ordered an egg-white omelet on their pancake date and refused snacks at the movie theater. So Hannah had tried again, including Katie on her birthday movie night evite.

Katie had never even replied.

Finally, Hannah had decided that maybe Katie was just nervous about hanging out with a group of people she didn't know and had invited Katie to chill by the town pool with her. She'd almost fallen over with excitement and relief when Katie had said yes. But Katie had spent the entire day lounging on the pool chair alone, texting her friends and answering Hannah's every question with one-word replies.

By the time the wedding rolled around, this past January, Hannah had come to dread the new family arrangement. Mylin, Katie, and Fred moved into their house, and Katie started at Hannah's high school, where she instantly made friends with Felicity Felix, who was basically Hannah's archnemesis. So that, as they say, was that. Hannah and her "sister" were never going to be friends. No matter how much their parents tried to throw them together.

"*In half a mile, make a left on Lone Dock Lane,*" the GPS lady directed, bringing Hannah back to the present. Hannah blinked and drove onward.

"He says he's there, gassed up and ready to go." Katie made a face after reading Jacob's latest text, like she wasn't quite sure what it meant. Hannah didn't respond. She found that the less she opened her mouth around Katie, the better off she was. Everything she said seemed to annoy her stepsister in one way or another.

In truth, Hannah felt that *she* was the one who had every right to be annoyed. Annoyed that Katie was along for the ride this weekend, and ruining everything. Because news flash: Katie hadn't even been invited. Jacob had called *Hannah* out of the blue last week and invited *Hannah* up to his family's lake house for a four-day weekend. Not Hannah and Katie. Just Hannah.

"I'm so bored, H," Jacob had groaned on the phone. "My parents are getting on my nerves. I need my best friend or I swear I'm going to commit patricide."

"Wow. Big word," Hannah had joked. She'd tried to play it cool, but her insides had been doing cartwheels—not just because Jacob wanted to see her, but also because Hannah had always wanted to visit his family's lake house. Plus she secretly loved spending time with Jacob's mom, Frida, who had been Hannah's mom's best friend from college. Frida was full of fun stories about Hannah's mother that Hannah never got tired of hearing. It made the beautiful, gentle-looking woman in the old photos and videos that much more real.

"They're making me play Dictionary!" Jacob had blurted, incredulous. "They're making me *learn* things. In the *summer*! You have to come help me."

Hannah had laughed and felt flattered and wondered if maybe, just maybe, there was something more behind the invitation. Was Jacob really missing her in a best friend-y way, or in a different way? Could he have finally realized he had feelings for her? That they were meant to be together? The thing Hannah had known with every inch of her heart since she was five years old?

A light up ahead turned yellow.

"You can make it," Katie said.

Hannah stepped on the brake.

"Ugh! It's like driving with my grandmother! Next time we do this, I'm totally driving."

"Look around! There are people everywhere. Do you want me to run them over?" Hannah snapped. "Sheesh, no wonder you didn't get your license."

The second the words were out of her mouth, Hannah wanted to swallow them back down. But it was too late. Katie's cheeks were already turning pink.

"Oh. My. God. I can*not* believe you just said that!"

Hannah's face flamed, too. "I'm sorry. I didn't mean it that way."

Katie was super sensitive about the fact that Hannah had passed the driver's exam on the first try. Katie had done fine on the written test, but flunked the road test. Katie's sixteenth birthday was a month after Hannah's, so she had already been a few weeks behind, but now she had to wait another week before she could retake the test. Meanwhile, the car Mylin and Hannah's dad had bought for Katie—a red RAV4 almost identical to Hannah's blue one—was parked in the driveway back home undriven. It looked incredibly lonely and depressing just sitting there, and Hannah didn't blame Katie for being testy about the situation. The car was so shiny, Katie probably felt like it was mocking her every time she walked out of the house.

"I know you're perfect, all right?" Katie grumbled, crossing her arms over her chest. "You don't have to be such a jerk about it."

"I'm not perfect," Hannah protested. "And I hate it when you say that. I'm just living my life and you act like I'm doing it to offend you."

"Oh, so what you're saying is you're perfect without even trying." Katie pulled her movie-star-huge sunglasses out of the tote bag at her feet and slipped them on. "Awesome."

Hannah bit down on her tongue. Katie had it all wrong. True, some might see Hannah's straight-A average and the fact that she was captain of the swim team as marks of success. But Katie was a kickass softball player and the most popular girl in school—a school she'd started at only seven months ago, and that Hannah had been attending her *entire life.* There were different kinds of perfect in the world. But Hannah didn't feel like pointing that out now. *Silence.* It really was the best—the only—policy.

As she turned into the parking lot for the Dreardon Lake docks, Hannah wished she could turn back time just a few clicks to the day she had asked her dad if she could go to Jacob's house. Her father had come up with the brilliant idea for Katie to join Hannah on this trip so that the two of them could "bond." If Hannah could go back to that moment, she'd throw herself on her knees and beg her father to have mercy on her and let her go to Michigan alone. She'd definitely put up a fight, but not nearly a big enough one. In the end, when her dad had asked her to do this "one little thing" for him, she'd capitulated and said, "Sure, Dad. Why not?"

Why not? I have about a billion reasons why not, past self, she thought now, as she eased the car into one of the few empty parking spots alongside the lake. The dark blue water stretched out ahead, the sun shimmering on the tiny waves moving across its surface. Normally, the very sight of water would put Hannah at ease, but as Katie typed furiously on her phone—probably complaining to Felicity and her friends about Hannah—she couldn't seem to make herself unclench. In the distance, the sky was cloudy, and a breeze ruffled the trees around the lake. Storm coming. *Fantastic*. Now they'd all be rained in together for the afternoon.

Hannah turned off the engine, pulled out her phone, and texted her father, just as she'd promised she'd do when they'd arrived.

We're here!

The reply was almost immediate.

OK! Have fun!

There was also a text waiting from her friend Theo, the fastest guy sprinter on her summer swim team.

We'll miss you this weekend!

It was accompanied by a pic of Theo and two other teammates in their swimsuits by the town pool, sticking out their tongues at her. Hannah turned the phone a bit to hide the screen from Katie, who teased her every time Theo so much as breathed in Hannah's direction. Katie's theory was that Theo was head over heels in crush with Hannah and that Hannah should "wake up and smell the hottie."

But Hannah and Theo were just friends.

And Theo was no Jacob.

Right back atcha, Hannah typed in response. Then she stuck out her own tongue and took a quick selfie. Katie rolled her eyes at Hannah. *What?* Hannah wanted to snap. Katie was the only person on earth allowed to take selfies?

Hannah sent the photo to Theo. At that same moment, someone knocked on her window, and she was so tightly wound, she jumped.

It was Jacob.

"H! You're here!" he said as Hannah opened the door and got out. He wrapped her up in a hug and she basically melted. His long arms were taut and strong and he smelled of woodsiness and fresh air and mint gum. Hannah loved how he was just a touch taller than her, enough that she could rest her chin right on his shoulder without standing on her toes or bending her knees. His brown curls had grown out a bit, and were a little wet from a swim or a shower. He was tan, and this somehow made his incredible, welcoming smile stand out more, along with his stunning green eyes.

"I'm here!" she replied, grinning.

"*We're* here," Katie corrected, sauntering around the back of the car.

Great, Hannah thought, trying not to cringe.

"Katie! Hey!"

Jacob hugged Katie, too. Hannah felt a pang as she watched the embrace last a few moments longer than was strictly necessary. For the millionth time, Hannah wished that Katie and Jacob had never met. But the only reason they'd met was because Hannah's dad had married Katie's mom and Jacob and his family had, of course, come to the wedding. So wishing they'd never met would be like wishing her dad and Mylin had never gotten married. And being married to Mylin made her dad really happy, even though living with Katie made Hannah fairly miserable. It was really complicated and extremely difficult to balance the positives against the negatives. But at the moment, the negatives were tipping the scales big-time.

"It's really good to see you," Jacob said as he pulled back. He looked Katie up and down, and Hannah seethed. She walked past them, purposely bumping Jacob to divert his attention, and opened the back of the car to get their bags.

"Here. Let me help," Jacob said.

"I'm fine," she said, hoisting her Oak View Swimming duffel onto her shoulder. The straps were decorated with pins from all the meets she had swum in over the years, and they clinked together in a familiar way as she adjusted its position.

Katie made no move to pick up her own bag—a red rolling suitcase with heart stickers all over it—and Jacob popped up the handle to pull it across the parking lot.

"Um, guys?" Katie said, looking up from her phone. She seemed to notice where she was for the first time, and was clearly confused. Her phone beeped with an incoming text and she didn't even glance at it. "Where're we going?"

"To the boat."

Jacob paused at the end of the dock and Katie stopped short. "The what?"

"The boat," Hannah repeated. "The house is on the west side of the lake."

Hannah took a deep breath of the fresh mountain air and relished the tinge of the water's crispness around the edges. It really was beautiful here, and she couldn't wait to see the Fabers' cottage. Four days hanging with Jacob and his family on the lake in the sun? Not even Katie could spoil that. Maybe Hannah could chill with Frida all weekend and ignore Katie's existence. It was a thin plan, but it was something.

"So let's drive there," Katie said.

"Can't," Jacob replied, squinting one eye against the sun. Behind him, on the lake, a water-skier whooped and there was a huge splash. "The house is only accessible by boat."

"Yeah, right." Katie gave a disbelieving laugh, like they were messing with her. When neither Hannah nor Jacob joined in, her jaw dropped. "You're joking. I have to get in a boat? Like, right now?"

Hannah bit her tongue so hard that this time she tasted blood. But really, Katie couldn't be serious. Hannah had *just* asked Katie if Jacob was waiting for them *at the dock*. Jacob had told her he was *gassed up and ready to go*. She'd turned on Lone *Dock* Road and into the parking lot for the *Dreardon Lake docks*. How dense could the girl be?

"Is there a problem?" Jacob asked.

"Uh, yeah! Hannah didn't tell you?"

Jacob was starting to look miffed. "Tell me what?"

Hannah sighed. *This* was the reason she should have given her father when he'd insisted that Katie should come along. But she hadn't even thought of it at the time. She'd been too fixated on the fact that she was losing out on her chance for alone time with Jacob. Too lovesick to see the perfect argument right in front of her.

"Katie can't swim," she said finally, when it seemed that Katie was never going to get up the guts to do it herself. "She's afraid of the water."

Beside her, Katie shivered, and Hannah got the sense that Katie was more than afraid of water. She was terrified.

TWO

The lake was oddly quiet. Aside from a few fishing boats in the shallows, there was no one else in sight. The singsong conversations of the birds in the trees played like a peaceful soundtrack in the background as Jacob steered his small motorboat across the flat water. But it wasn't just the serenity of nature that made everything feel so still, Hannah realized. It was that Katie had finally stopped complaining.

"Are you okay?" Jacob asked.

They both looked over at Katie, who sat on the front bench seat with her back toward the bow of the boat so that she was facing them. Her knees were locked together, both arms splayed out to grip the sides of the boat. She wore a bulky orange life jacket over her dainty clothes. The vest was inflated so tightly it was pressing against her chin. Their bags were next to her on the bench, propped on either side to balance the weight, and she sat with the stiffest posture imaginable. She looked like some wealthy nineteenth-century heiress unused to primitive modes of travel.

Jacob's skiff really was pretty flimsy—just a low, metal fishing boat with no frills. Hannah could reach one hand out and skim the water with her fingers, no problem. When it came down to it, this wasn't the sort of vessel that made a person who was scared of the water comfortable. Hannah felt a small swell of guilt.

"M'fine," Katie lied.

Hannah took a deep breath and tasted the metallic scent of the boat at the back of her throat. "Don't worry. I'm sure it's a short ride. Five minutes?" she asked Jacob hopefully.

"More like ten," he said, and Katie moaned.

Hannah shot him a look like, *really?* And Jacob shrugged, then grinned. Hannah couldn't help it—she smiled back. Was it wrong that she was glad Jacob was amused by Katie's misery? Jacob, in general, was a fan of practical jokes and had a thing for throwing people off their game—making them feel ever so slightly uncomfortable for his own amusement. He wasn't cruel, exactly, he just liked to test people. And he never did it to Hannah, so she found this quality endearing rather than obnoxious—which was what his mother had once called it. He did like to rib her, but she had a talent for ribbing him right back. The banter was just part of their relationship.

"So what've you been up to since the season ended, Champ?" Jacob asked her then.

Hannah blushed and curled her toes against the well-worn pads of her flip-flops. Her summer swim team had taken first place at their regional meet two weeks ago, with Hannah winning both her sprints and acting as anchor on the victorious 400-meter medley team as well. Jacob had come back to Ohio for the weekend to swim with his own team, which had taken third place.

When they were all home during the year, her family and Jacob's lived only three small towns apart, and their high school teams competed against each other. Their summer teams, however, were invitational, and she had snagged a spot on the much-coveted Sharks, while Jacob—who was a fantastic long-distance swimmer—

had made the Hurricanes, which was still a good team . . . just not as good as the Sharks.

"Oh, you know, it's tough being the queen," Hannah joked, lifting her chin. "It's been all autographs and photo ops . . ."

Jacob reached across to shove her shoulder, which tipped the boat slightly, and Katie yelped.

"Sorry! Sorry," Jacob said, momentarily raising his hands.

He pulled the corners of his mouth back in a private grimace for Hannah, and Hannah shook her head. Why would Katie insist on coming to a weekend on a lake when she didn't even know how to swim? What did she expect to do for the next four days? She should have just stayed home and finished her all-important back-to-school shopping with her friends. Getting their outfits perfectly Snapchat worthy was of huge importance to Felicity, Katie, and their crew, after all. But instead, here Katie was, clearly miserable.

Then Hannah caught Katie looking over at Jacob, and he looked back at her. Hannah had a sinking feeling. Katie had come along so she could see Jacob, of course. Hannah knew that the two of them had hit it off at the wedding. Hannah wondered, swallowing hard, if something was going on between them. And the idea made her want to shove Katie right over the side of the boat.

Not that she'd ever do that.

She cleared her throat. "Actually, I've been volunteering at the Y," Hannah told Jacob, reclaiming his attention as the boat rounded a small, eerie island at the center of the lake. Hannah paused, momentarily distracted by the strangeness of the trees. The island was covered by them, but the trees on the south side were all black and charred and jagged, their gnarled, bare branches jutting out at odd angles. Some of the trees had fallen or were tipped sideways at such an extreme angle they looked as if one stiff breeze could crack their will and send them tumbling into the water. Dotting the rocky shoreline were several black-and-orange NO TRESPASSING signs, some of which were splashed with mud, while others had been marked by black spray paint, haphazardly covering the NO. On the north side of the island, though, the trees were fine—lush and green and majestic. The whole thing put together gave the impression of a bizarre yin and yang symbol. Life and death coexisting on the same hunk of rock.

"What happened there?" Hannah asked, interrupting her own story.

Jacob glanced over his shoulder. "That's Mystery Island," he said. "Or that's what the local kids call it anyway. People used to camp out and party over there, but there was a fire one summer and it's been off-limits ever since." He smirked. "Not that the signs actually stop anyone from going out there."

"It's freaky," Katie said with a shudder.

"No arguments from me," Jacob said, then turned to Hannah. "So you were saying? About the Y?"

Hannah glanced away from a family of turtles that was slipping from a rock into the water near the green side of the island. When she looked at Jacob, she managed to put the burnt trees in her peripheral. "I've been teaching a Little Swimmers class."

"That's cool," Jacob said. "I bet the kids love you."

"They are fairly worshipful," Hannah conceded. "But I think that's just because I give them Hershey's Kisses at the end of each swim."

"Ha! I knew there was an evil mind lurking beneath that innocent act of yours," he exclaimed, his green eyes dancing.

Hannah laughed and tipped her face toward the sun, ignoring the cloud that crept across and doused the light. "You know me well," she said. "But honestly, it's been really cool. It's fun to watch them progress from barely being able to float to swimming across the whole pool."

"You should teach Katie to swim," Jacob offered. "I mean, since you're clearly such an excellent instructor."

"What?" Hannah said, at the same moment that Katie protested, "No way!"

"Wow." Jacob let out a low whistle. "So I see the ice hasn't melted at all."

Hannah clenched her teeth, irritated by Jacob's non-filter. She had told him about the coldness between her and Katie in confidence. He didn't have to blurt it out as if it were common knowledge.

Unless . . . had Katie told him about it, too? What had she said to Jacob about her? She glared at Katie, who turned her head and stared pointedly over her shoulder toward Jacob's house, which was just now coming into view.

"Yep," Jacob said. "This is going to be one interesting weekend."

"Finally," Katie mumbled as Jacob slowed the boat to a *putt-putt-putt* and let it drift toward the long, low, wood-plank dock in front of his house. Hannah's skull hurt from the effort it took not to roll her eyes.

"I can't believe I'm really here," Hannah said, gazing up at the cottage. "It looks bigger than it does in pictures."

"That's home sweet home," Jacob said. "So, listen, the boat's gonna rock a bit when we get out," he warned Katie, turning the engine off entirely, "but I promise it'll be fine. The water's only a couple of feet deep here anyway."

Katie made a sound somewhere near a whimper. When she saw Hannah looking at her, she cleared her throat and shook her ponytail back off her shoulder. "Okay."

Jacob tossed the tie-off rope over one of the metal cleats—a fixture screwed into the dock for securing boats. He stood up and jumped off his skiff, which did rock back and forth drastically enough for water to splash over the side. Katie squealed and her knuckles turned white as she tightened her grip.

Hannah stood up next and got her balance—more rocking, more whimpering from Katie—then passed their bags to Jacob one by one. He offered his hand, which she took, and she hopped out next to him. His palm was warm against hers. She reluctantly let go and unclasped the three latches on her life jacket. Then she tossed the vest onto the dock at her feet, looking around.

It seemed like something was missing, and she realized it was because Jacob's skiff was the only boat here. She knew the Fabers had a larger speedboat they used for fishing, water-skiing, and tubing. She'd been looking forward to trying out water-skiing for herself if Jacob's dad, Jim, would teach her. But the boat wasn't docked. She was just about to ask where it was when Jacob faced Katie.

"Your turn."

"Uh-uh. No way. Not moving," Katie said. Her skin looked rather green.

"Okay, that's fine by me. But you should know that if you don't get off the boat, then you have to stay on the water *all night long*," Jacob teased. He looked at Hannah. "We could serve her dinner out here, right? I mean, burgers under the stars . . ."

"Sure. That'd be nice. But I think it does get pretty cold in the mountains overnight, even in summer," Hannah added, bringing a fingertip to her chin. "Would you happen to have a Snuggie on hand?"

"LOL," Katie said. She lifted her butt off her seat half an inch, then dropped right back down again when the skiff shimmied beneath her. She blew out an annoyed sigh and looked up at Hannah. "A little advice here?"

Hannah was actually surprised. Katie had never asked her for help before. Not once. Not ever.

"Okay, slide over to the middle bench. You'll feel safer there," Hannah said. "Then just stand up quickly, like ripping off a Band-Aid, and we'll lift you out."

Katie shot her a skeptical look, but did as Hannah instructed. She raised herself up slightly, turned, and sat down on the next bench, which Hannah had recently vacated. Jacob leaned over and offered Katie both hands. Katie looked around, clearly trying to find a way to get out without actually standing up, but she didn't find it. Tentatively, she lifted herself to a sort of bent crouch, and grasped Jacob's hands so tightly she basically started to pull him toward her. The boat dipped and Katie let out another screech as Jacob started to teeter. Hannah stepped forward at the last second, grabbed Katie around the waist, and awkwardly dragged her up out of the boat and onto the dock. Katie careened into Jacob, and clung to him. Conveniently.

Somehow, all of this resulted in Hannah tripping and falling on her butt.

"Ow," she said, checking her palms for splinters.

"I am *never* getting on a boat again," Katie said, yanking open the latches on her life jacket. "You're just gonna have to figure out another way to get me home."

Now Hannah did roll her eyes. She shoved herself up and grabbed her duffel bag off the dock.

"Where's your mom and dad?" she asked Jacob, turning toward the house. It was a small but beautiful cottage with blue shingles, white trim, and a wide, raw-oak front porch. There were two rocking chairs and a porch swing and a triangular pile of fire wood stacked near the wall, as well as a stone fire pit surrounded by three flat benches close to the shoreline. It was all so familiar to Hannah from Jacob's descriptions and pictures, it almost felt like home.

Jacob didn't answer; he was busy helping Katie with her giant suitcase. Hannah sighed and strode up the dirt path to the front porch. When they were halfway up the hill, the screen door creaked open and two people stepped out. But they weren't Frida and Jim; they were two kids Hannah's age—one guy and one girl. Hannah stopped, uncertain.

"You made it!" the girl said, as if she knew Hannah and Katie. She was tall and broad-shouldered with curly black hair, brown skin, and a gap-toothed smile. She wore short shorts and an off-the-shoulder sweatshirt that read BOOK NERD.

The boy smirked and leaned sideways against one of the porch pillars. His dark blond hair was tousled over his forehead, and he had freckled skin and light brown eyes. He wore a weathered gray T-shirt with frayed jeans and sandals. He looked directly at Hannah in a way she wasn't at all used to, and it made her both nervous and a tiny bit intrigued.

"Meet my friends Alessandra Ellison and Colin Barnes," Jacob said, coming up behind Hannah with Katie's bag. Colin lifted one hand in silent greeting. "They're here for the weekend, too."

"Nice!" Katie said, clearly recovered from her boat trauma. "The more the merrier."

Hannah's throat tightened. Were these friends of Jacob's from his school back home or something? Strangers made her feel uneasy in her own skin. It took her at least a half dozen times hanging out with someone before she felt comfortable around them. Which meant that this weekend was shot. Right around the time she was set to go home, she'd probably start to relax.

"You invited other people up from Ohio?" Hannah asked Jacob under her breath.

"No," Jacob replied, just as quietly. "They have places in town. They just like to crash here because of the direct lake access."

"Oh."

"Guys, this is my best friend, Hannah," Jacob called out, reaching an arm around Hannah to give her a squeeze. She was still inwardly preening over being singled out when he announced, "And *this* is Katie." Like he was presenting some sort of fantastic door prize. Or like he was showing off a person he'd told his friends all about and was excited for them to finally meet.

Hannah almost gagged.

"Come on in," Alessandra said, with an expansive wave of her arm, as if she owned the place. "Lunch is ready and we're starving. Jacob made us wait for you because of his twisted need to be in charge of everything."

Colin and Jacob both laughed, and Katie jogged up the steps to chat up Alessandra. Of course. Katie was *great* with strangers, probably because she lived in a world in which popular people flocked to her like she had her own YouTube channel. She loved parties and unfamiliar situations. She thrived in them. This had just become Katie's perfect weekend.

Meanwhile, something prickled at the back of Hannah's neck. She had the oddest feeling that something else was going on— something Jacob wasn't telling them.

"They're staying here?" Hannah asked Jacob under her breath as they mounted the stairs.

"Yeah. Don't worry, Your Shyness. You're gonna love them," Jacob said.

Hannah walked inside and saw sandwich fixings—bread, turkey, cheese, tomatoes, pickles—sitting out on the long, oak dining table, along with bags of chips and a few bottles of soda. Colin and Katie were already digging into the food as Katie peppered Colin with questions like how long he'd known Jacob (*a while*) and where his own house was (*in town*).

Hannah looked around. The house was small and cozy. The first floor contained both the living and dining room, with a few plaid couches, the long table, and tons of lake-related knickknacks like carved wooden boats, a lamp shaped like an oar, and an embroidered pillow that read YOU'RE ONLY HOME IF YOU'RE AT THE LAKE. The little white kitchen was off to one side, and at the back of the first floor was a screened-in porch and bathroom. Upstairs, Hannah knew, there were only two bedrooms and one more bath.

"So where is everyone going to sleep?" Hannah asked, tossing her bag near the stairs, where the pins clattered against the bottom step.

"I'm on the couch!" Alessandra said, raising a bottle of soda.

"And Colin and I are bunking in my room." Jacob rolled Katie's bag up next to Hannah's and turned to her with a grin. It was a mischievous grin. A grin that made her insides clench and heightened the suspicion she'd had outside. "And you and Katie have the master."

"Wait. We have to share a bed?" Katie said, her mouth half full of a turkey sandwich.

But Hannah had a better question. "If we're in the master bedroom, where are your parents sleeping?"

"That's the best part." Jacob's grin widened. "My parents are away for the weekend," he announced, making Hannah's stomach sink to her toes. "Surprise!"

Dear Future Me,

*I did it. I went to my first surprise party and it even turned into a
sleepover!!! The whole afternoon I kept going back and forth over
whether or not to go—chickening out and then feeling brave. But it
wasn't until A showed up at my house to pick me up that I knew
there was no going back. I was going to have to be social. Of course it
helped when A told me I looked "drool-worthy in that dress." (The
black one with the skinny straps and the long flowy skirt. Plus Mom
let me wear her vintage gold ring for the first time, and she's never
getting it back. LOL.) After that, my mom only had to give me a
SMALL shove out the door. Honestly, if it wasn't for A I know I
wouldn't have gone at all. I guess I'm a person who needs a
wingman. Wingwoman? Wingwoman.*

*I blame my parents for moving us around so much. When have I
ever been in one place long enough to make real friends and get
invited to a real party? Never. Until now.*

*But anyway, I'm SO GLAD I WENT because I spent almost the
entire night talking to N. It turns out we like almost all the same things!
He loves watching vids of service people surprising their families—his
dad was in the army—and he thinks chocolate cake is the only food
worth eating (I have to bring him Aunt Jerry's famous triple layer. I
mean, eventually. Not yet. Because if I gave it to him now that would
be sort of stalker-y, right? Or pathetic? Or needy? Or all three?).*

I'm probably being stupid anyway because school will be done in a little over a month and then I'm sure I won't see him all summer. I mean, unless I go visit him at work or something. It's not like he's going to come visit me. But maybe we'll bump into each other on the lake beach or something. He said he's getting a two-seater WaveRunner this summer and sort of hinted that he'd take me out for a ride. Who knows? Maybe he'll follow through.

So, P was having a bunch of girls sleep over after the party, even though everyone else was going home. And she asked ME to stay, too. I didn't have a bag or anything, but she lent me pajamas and A and I got to stay in the upstairs guest room with a couple of other girls. P's house is sick. It's totally modern and huge and has three guest rooms! So a lot of girls got to stay. It was so much fun, and this morning her dad made these insane multigrain pancakes that were so good I got the recipe for Mom.

The only bad part was the ghost story P told us before we went to bed. The story totally freaked me out and then A said that it was TRUE! IT ACTUALLY HAPPENED IN THIS TOWN AT THAT VERY LAKE! After that, I couldn't sleep for hours. I kept hearing things outside and feeling like someone was watching me. I'd write the story down here, but if I think about it too much I think I won't sleep again tonight and that would suck because I have a trig test tomorrow. Monday tests are the worst!!!

I should probably go study now and then go to bed. I never know how to finish these things so I guess I'll just say, "Good night, Future Me!" xoxo

THREE

"No parents?" Katie said, her dark eyes bright as she nibbled on a potato chip. "This trip just got interesting."

"Are you kidding?" Hannah said. "My dad's gonna freak."

Katie pulled a face like Hannah was dense. "So . . . we don't tell him."

"Please. He's going to find out," Hannah said. "All he has to do is call Jim or Frida to check in and we're toast."

"Not if you text him first and tell him everything's fine," Katie said, rolling her eyes. "And if you keep texting him with details, he'll have no reason to call Jacob's parents."

Clearly, Katie had done this kind of thing before. Hannah, however, had not, and she instantly began to sweat. She never lied to her dad.

She turned away from the others, not wanting to see their expressions, which she knew would be judgy and mocking. In her lifetime, Hannah had been the rule follower often enough to predict the very curve of people's frowns and sneers down to the millimeter. Pulling her phone out of her pocket, she headed back outside to the porch, feeling overwhelmed by irritation and uncertainty. This was the way she felt whenever she was confronted by a situation that forced her to decide between what was right and what other people considered cool. Why couldn't it just be considered cool to do what was right? Would that be so awful?

The screen door smacked shut behind her. Hannah stared out at the lake, watching a large bird chase a dragonfly across the water, the bird's wings skimming the surface before it took flight again. The clouds had crowded out the sun now, and the entire lake was in shadow. Out on Mystery Island, the leaves on the healthy trees turned upside down in the wind, indicating rain was on its way. The blackened, dead trees creaked and swayed. It was eerie how the noise they made carried clear across the water.

Hannah unlocked her phone. Inside the house, Katie was telling everyone what a lame, goody-goody loser Hannah was. Not that Hannah could hear her, but she could imagine. And Colin and Alessandra and Jacob were all having a good laugh at her expense, she was sure.

Her dad had always been strict, and had always expected the best out of her—the best grades, the best behavior, her best effort. This was exactly the type of scenario he was always railing on about. "If you ever find yourself at a party and there are no parents there"—because that happened all the time to Hannah, ROFL—"call me right away and I'll come get you. It's better to be safe than to end up with a record . . . or worse."

Her dad, an ER surgeon, had seen every horrible, life-altering, deadly accident imaginable, and sometimes it seemed like he spent his nights imagining each gory, horrifying one of them happening to Hannah. If he found out that Jacob's parents weren't here and she didn't tell him, she would be grounded for life.

Yes, he was overprotective, but still. Hannah kind of liked it. She liked that she was her father's number-one priority. At least she had been until recently. It wasn't that she begrudged her dad h relationship with Mylin—not at all—but it had definitely changed things a bit. There was no denying that.

She had to be honest and just tell him. True, he would probably order her to come straight home. But at least she wouldn't be hiding something.

Hannah dialed her dad's cell, but when she lifted the phone to her ear, all she heard were three low beeps and then nothing. She looked down at the screen.

CALL FAILED.

Hannah tried again. Same exact thing. Except her phone didn't even try to dial out this time.

The door opened behind her. It was Jacob, and he was wearing an apologetic look.

"Your phone won't work out here. There's no signal."

Her heart sank. "What? Jacob, come on."

"I'm not kidding," he said with a shrug. "With the Wi-Fi you can send email and text, but no calls. I could program your number into the signal booster, but it only takes six numbers at a time, and you have to be on the same network as ours. Plus my dad might have programmed his fishing buddies' numbers in there last weekend, so . . ."

Hannah swallowed a frustrated groan. "It's okay. I'll just use yours."

She held out her hand for Jacob's phone. Before he could give it to her, the door opened again and Katie came striding out.

"Uh, can I talk to you?" she said to Hannah, cocking one hip.

Yeah, right. She could just imagine how *that* conversation would go.

"No, I'm going to call my dad." Hannah's hand was still extended, but Jacob made no move to offer her his phone.

"No," Katie said. "You're really not."

Katie stormed across the porch, grabbed Hannah's arm, and dragged her down the three steps to the dirt path, then farther away from the house. Jacob didn't follow. He pushed his hands into the pockets of his cargo shorts and watched.

"First of all, you're making us both look like losers," Katie said quietly. She cast a glance toward the house, and Hannah saw that Colin was at the window, watching them, too. She felt a little thrill that she couldn't explain. The guy hadn't said a word to her since they'd arrived. That was weird, not attractive. Right? And Hannah was in love with Jacob. *In love* with him. She had been as long as she could remember. Unlike some people who'd swooped in last winter and started flirting like it was a competitive sport.

"Secondly," Katie continued, "if your dad tells us to come home, *I* am not leaving."

She crossed her arms over her stomach and raised one eyebrow, as if that would intimidate Hannah into taking her side.

"Okay, *first of all*," Hannah mimicked, "it's my car. And we're in this together. If I decide to leave, you're coming with me."

"How many times are you gonna rub it in that you can drive and I can't?" Katie snapped.

Hannah could barely contain a screech of rage. "That is *not* what I'm doing!" She took a deep, calming breath and blew it out. "Katie, come on. Can we just be real for one second? If . . . no . . . *when* our parents find out we were here alone, with no adults, and with a strange *guy* staying over . . . they're going to murder us."

Katie shook her head. "Okay, yeah, they'll be pissed. But we'll still have had an awesome weekend. Isn't, like, a week of grounding worth that?" she shot back.

"Try a month. If not more," Hannah muttered, hugging herself.

"You're such a—"

"I have an idea!"

Hannah and Katie both jumped. Jacob had somehow gotten right up next to them without either of them seeing or hearing him approach.

"What?" they both snapped.

Jacob was unfazed. He turned to Hannah and lifted his chin. "What if we race for it?"

Alessandra and Colin walked out onto the porch, both munching on sandwiches. They kept back, but were definitely close enough to hear the conversation, which made Hannah feel like she was participating in a spectator sport.

"Oh, please. You're gonna try to make me swim out to the island or something," Hannah said with a scoff, not wanting to call it by its silly name in front of the others. *Mystery Island.* Her underarms prickled under the strangers' scrutiny. She tried to scoff casually, but didn't exactly pull it off. "You know I'll never beat you in a long-distance race."

"So we'll do a sprint." Jacob lifted one shoulder like it was no big thing. "You set the course and pick the stroke. I win, you don't call your dad. You win, you can call him and feel free to leave and I'll even convince Katie to go with you."

"Hey!" Katie protested, and Jacob laughed.

Hannah's heart skipped a beat, and she felt her ambition kick in. Was he serious? Jacob had never beaten her at a distance shorter than 400 meters. Not once. She glanced over at Colin and Alessandra, who were looking on with interest. Surely they had already pegged her as a downer. If she could beat Jacob, at least she'd win some points. She had no idea why she cared, but she did. She hated that people judged her as less-than just because she wasn't a party animal.

"Fine." Hannah yanked her hair tie out and undid her braid, getting her long waves ready to coil up on top of her head. "Two hundred meters, free."

Jacob stuck out his hand. "Deal."

They shook on it, then headed toward the house to change into their bathing suits. Hannah felt a stiff breeze. The sky was darkening and the temperature was dropping noticeably. She figured they had maybe ten minutes before the storm rolled in.

FOUR

Hannah shivered in her bathing suit as she stood on the edge of the dock, and she focused on the lake ahead of her. Clouds filled the sky. Hannah tried not to look at the ominous island in the distance, but she had the weirdest sensation that the island was somehow watching *her*.

"To the first buoy and back, yeah?" Jacob said, standing beside her, looking gorgeous in his swim trunks. His green eyes were bright with a confidence that Hannah couldn't wait to squelch. "That's two hundred meters, give or take."

Hannah snapped her swimmer's cap into place and adjusted her goggles above her nose. Katie thought she was a dork for packing the goggles, but Hannah needed them; she always felt so disoriented when she opened her eyes underwater without her goggles on. So she brought them everywhere she went—as long as there was going to be a place to swim. Jacob had brought his goggles along, too, which made Hannah feel entirely vindicated.

See? Jacob and I have so much in common, she told Katie silently, hoping she could communicate entire sentences with a glance. *Even things you think are lame.*

Katie just glared at Hannah from where she stood behind her on the grass, along with Alessandra and Colin.

Hannah turned back around. "That's the plan," she told Jacob as she stretched out her shoulders. "Enjoy watching my backside."

Jacob smirked, and Hannah's blush was nuclear.

"I didn't mean . . . I was just trying to . . . I couldn't say *eat my dust*, so I—"

"I got it, Webster." Jacob pulled his own goggles down. "You're cute when you're flustered."

Hannah's heart ping-ponged around inside her chest and she felt like she might throw up. Had Jacob really just called her *cute*?

"Are you ready?" Alessandra called out from behind them.

No! No! I'm actually having a stroke!

"Get set!"

Jacob gave Hannah a triumphant look, like he had this in the bag. What was with all the cockiness?

This is a sprint, dude, she thought. *A sprint! Get ready to suck my wake.*

Suck my wake. Why hadn't she thought of that before she'd said—

"Go!"

Hannah flung herself into the lake. The second the cool water parted around her, she understood that her breath was all wrong. Jacob had thrown her off with his comments and his attitude. Was that on purpose? Had he been trying to mess with her head? Screwing with her just so he could win? Dang it. Hannah never let herself get psyched out by anyone. That was part of her strength as a swimmer. Even Junior Olympian Annie Snow, with her entourage and Team USA bathing suit, hadn't intimidated her at their meet back in June.

But then, if Jacob *won*, that meant she had to *stay*. So maybe he was psyching her out because he wanted her to stay. The very idea sent a thrill down her spine even as she kicked and stroked. Jacob wanted her to stay.

She felt Jacob pull ahead and a switch flipped inside her—the competitive switch. Her adrenaline kicked in.

Get out of your head, she admonished herself. *Get into the race.*

If she won, she could still change her mind and *decide* to stay, but if she lost . . . well, that would suck on a number of levels.

Hannah focused. She tuned into her shoulder muscles and felt them fire. The water ahead was murky and she couldn't see the buoy yet, but she could sense from years of experience swimming these distances that it should be coming up any second. She brought herself up even with Jacob and, after three full breaths, felt herself pulling ahead. She saw the buoy, made the turn, and Jacob wasn't even there anymore. He'd definitely fallen behind.

That would teach him to challenge her to a sprint.

Now she really dug in. She felt her rhythm normalize and knew it would be a cake walk—a cake swim?—from there. She could even hear Alessandra and Katie screaming and cheering and . . . was that Colin? That deep, thrumming voice? It was hard to separate it out from the beating of her own heart in her ears.

Hannah was just about to turn on the last-leg speed when she felt a tug on her ankle. Startled, she shook it off, assuming it was some sort of lake vegetation. But then it tugged again. And whatever it was, it was solid. It didn't feel like a weed or a reed. It felt like . . . a hand. Like long fingers snaking around her flesh.

Was it Jacob? Was he messing with her? Trying to cheat?

She looked back, throwing off her rhythm entirely, and saw nothing but dark lake water. Even though her eyes told her there was nothing there, she felt the tug again, and this time it didn't just pull her back, but *down*.

Hannah stopped swimming and kicked as hard as she could, kicking *at* the thing—kicking out. Her pulse was in full-on panic mode now. What *was* it? A fish? What kind of fish had fingers?

Finally, Hannah burst up out of the water, gasping for breath. There was water up her nose and she sputtered, then screamed . . . just as Jacob passed her by.

She felt another tug.

Hannah kicked as powerfully as she could and hit something hard. A rock? No. She tried to stop herself from thinking the next thought that swirled to life at the back of her mind. Because it made no sense. It couldn't be a . . . a *skull*?

On the shoreline, Katie, Alessandra, and Colin cheered for Jacob, who was plowing closer and closer to the rocky beach next to the dock. They weren't even paying attention to her.

"There's something in the lake!" Hannah screeched, swimming like crazy toward shore, forgetting about form and function and just moving. "There's something in the lake!"

Jacob waded up onto dry land and began jumping up and down with his arms raised above his head in triumph.

"Help!" Hannah shouted, struggling to catch her breath, terrified at every second the thing was going to grab her again. "Hey! Help!"

Colin turned, his expression concerned. He said something to the others, but Hannah couldn't hear what it was between the distance and all her splashing and sucking wind. Jacob finally stopped gloating and rushed back into the water. He waded toward her, grabbing her arm and pulling her up to standing. Her feet slipped on the algae-covered rocks.

"What's wrong? Is it a cramp?" he asked.

"No!" Hannah gasped and coughed. "There's something out there! Something tried to grab me!"

There was a moment of silence during which all Hannah could hear was her own ragged breaths.

"Come on, Hannah. Don't be a sore loser," Jacob finally said, shrugging her off as he waded back out of the water.

Hannah followed him, her toes squishing into the soft, mushy lake bottom, tiny weeds sticking to her skin. Whatever was lurking beneath the surface of the lake, it hadn't felt at all like this. It had felt solid when she'd kicked it, and when it had grabbed her, it had felt like it had . . . a *purpose.*

"I swear to you, Jacob, something pulled on my leg," Hannah insisted, brushing water off her face. "I'm not lying! And I'm not a sore loser. You know that. There's something out there!"

But even as she said it, she heard how insane it sounded. Something had *pulled on her leg*? What? A lake trout? Nothing in that lake had hands. A mouth, maybe. Teeth even. But not fingers. Not a skull as hard as stone.

Had she imagined it? Had her subconscious realized she was going to lose and made the whole thing up?

But no. *No.* She knew what she'd felt. And she'd been in the lead when it had happened.

"Wow, I can't believe you want to go home so badly that you'd make up a lake monster," Katie said, laughing as Hannah and Jacob joined the others on the dock. "I swear, Hannah, it's like you're allergic to fun."

Alessandra guffawed at that, and even Jacob let out a chuckle at her expense. Hannah couldn't believe he was laughing at her. It was as if he was breaking their lifelong, unspoken pact. Hot, humiliated tears sprang to her eyes. She could handle Katie mocking her, but Jacob?

"You guys, back off." It was Colin who spoke up. He had a low, sonorous voice that did strange things to Hannah's heart, even as upset as she was. It felt as if someone had lit a little fire inside her chest. He looked at Alessandra. "You know she's not the first person to think there was something weird out there."

Alessandra stopped laughing. In the distance, thunder rumbled.

"What do you mean?" Hannah said.

"Yeah, what are you talking about?" Katie asked. Colin and Alessandra continued to stare at each other. "Jacob." Katie changed tactics. "What is he talking about?"

"I have no idea," Jacob said, and scratched his nose.

But he was lying. He always touched his nose when he was lying.

"Jacob—" Hannah started.

"Okay, fine," Jacob said. "There are these stupid stories about the lake being haunted."

Hannah's heart thunked. She felt the fingers around her ankle all over again. "Haunted?" she repeated in a whisper.

"And some people have seen things," Colin added, putting his hands in his pockets. "Or, you know, *said* they saw things."

"Things?" Katie echoed.

"Monsters," Alessandra clarified, then rolled her eyes. "Or, monst*er*. One. One lake monster . . . type . . . thing."

The thunder sounded again, closer this time, and the wind kicked up, sending a chill down Hannah's wet spine. She hugged her bare arms, teeth chattering.

"You're—you're kidding, right?" Hannah asked. "This is, like, a joke to mess with the outsiders."

"Yeah." Katie laughed. "Ha ha. Very funny."

But no one else laughed. And Hannah had the oddest feeling that the island behind her was creeping toward her—like one of the trees was going to reach out a blackened claw of branches and snatch her back into the water.

"Okay." Hannah held up her hands. "Anyone gonna blame me for wanting to go back to Ohio *now*?"

"Hannah, come on. It's just rumors, right? And there's no such thing as, like, a . . . lake monster." Katie tried to sound unaffected, but her eyes were wide and Hannah could tell she was a little freaked.

"Exactly," Jacob said, taking Katie's side, of course. "Do you really think my parents would have bought this house, or kept it, if there was a frickin' monster out there?"

He and Katie cracked up, and Hannah scowled at them. Why did it feel like Jacob kept mocking her?

Colin shrugged. "Look. If Hannah wants to go home, we should just let her go home. It's her choice."

Everyone fell silent. Colin's voice was so authoritative, and so unexpected, it was like no one knew how to respond. *Hannah* certainly didn't know how to respond. When had a hot, confident, likely popular-at-school guy like Colin ever taken her side on anything—ever defended logic instead of doing everything in his power to seem cool? Hannah could have kissed him—if she were an entirely different person and this were an entirely different universe.

The thought made her blush. Colin's brown eyes looked through her, almost as if he knew what she was imagining. He gave her a knowing smile and she just about keeled over.

"Thanks," she mumbled, wishing she had the fortitude to utter more than one word. She was still trying to wrap her brain around the fact that it was Colin who had spoken up for her and not Jacob. So much for that whole *best friend* thing.

It began to rain then, in quick, stinging droplets. Colin, Alessandra, Jacob, and Katie made a run for the house, whooping. Hannah followed them more slowly, pulling her swim cap off and letting her hair tumble down over her shoulders.

As suddenly as it had begun, the rain now started to come down in sheets, and the wind howled. It was a downpour. Just as she reached the house, Hannah paused and snuck a glance back over her shoulder. The rhythmic timpani of the rain surrounded her, and she breathed in that particular scent of freshly soaked earth. And in the distance, the misshapen outline of the half-dead island loomed.

FIVE

"Right hand, blue!"

Hannah emerged onto the upstairs landing with her bag, hearing the laughter waft up from the living room. She looked down over the banister.

Katie screeched as she reached for the blue circle on the Twister board, contorting her body around Jacob's. Colin was reading the spinner, and Alessandra was basically doing downward-facing dog over Jacob's head, her pose like a rock. Jacob was laughing, trying to hold his position, and Hannah wanted to scream. None of them even cared that she was leaving, and suddenly she started wondering if there really was something wrong with her. Why couldn't she just relax and have fun like them? Why *did* she always have to be such a daddy's girl?

After showering and putting on dry clothes, Hannah had spent the last fifteen minutes staring at her phone. She hadn't been sure what to do. Even though she'd lost the swim-race bet, she *could* still reach out to her dad and tell him that Jacob's parents weren't there. Hannah knew her dad would insist she and Katie come home, or he'd drive to Michigan to retrieve them himself. And if he did that, Katie would freak out on her, call her a loser, accuse Hannah of making decisions for her. In the end, Hannah had decided she would just show up back home—with or without Katie—and explain everything then.

Mylin would probably hate her forever for leaving Katie behind (Hannah was assuming the ever strong-willed Katie would hold her ground and stay), but it wasn't as if she could kidnap her step-sister and throw her in the boat and then the car. Katie had to make her own (bad) decisions.

Outside, thunder rumbled and rain battered the windows. Hannah tromped down the staircase and dropped her duffel on the wood floor with a loud *thump*. Jacob looked up from the Twister game and lost his balance. He fell sideways, toppling Katie and Alessandra like dominoes. Alessandra let out a peal of laughter.

"Jacob!" Katie cried, laughing so hard tears squeezed from her eyes. "Foul!"

"Hang on! Hang on! Time out." Jacob jumped to his feet and made a T shape with his hands. "We'll have a do-over."

He clapped Colin on the shoulder as he crossed the room to Hannah. Colin leaned against the back of the couch and sipped water from a plastic bottle. He had the Twister spinner in his other hand, and Hannah couldn't help noticing how the sleeves of his T-shirt clung to his biceps. Ridiculous. Her brain was ridiculous.

"H, listen. Please don't go," Jacob said under his breath, tugging Hannah aside. He ducked his chin and looked at her with those soulful green eyes. "I'm sorry I didn't tell you my parents weren't going to be here, but my mom had this business trip at the last minute and my dad decided to go along. They didn't tell me until yesterday and I knew your dad wouldn't let you come if he knew, and I really wanted to see you."

Hannah felt a pang in her chest, but wouldn't let herself indulge it. She lifted her chin and crossed her arms. "You mean you really wanted to see Katie."

A light blush spread its way across Jacob's cheeks, and Hannah's heart broke a little bit. "No. Well, yes. I wanted to see her, too. But come on!" He reached out and awkwardly squeezed her elbow. "You've always wanted to come up to the lake."

Hannah blew out a sigh.

"Hey, when your dad finds out . . . *if* your dad finds out, I will take one hundred percent of the blame." Jacob shot her his most charming smile. "And you know your dad loves me."

It was all she could do not to laugh. "It's not just my dad, Jacob," she said as quietly as possible. She glanced back toward the others. Colin was still drinking from his water bottle, and Hannah wondered if he was listening in. Over on the Twister mat, Katie and Alessandra scrolled through feeds on Katie's phone, leaning into each other like they were old friends. "I'm not . . . I'm . . ." Hannah paused.

There was something on the tip of her tongue, of course— something she'd never have the guts to say. But Hannah was scared. Whether or not lake monsters were real; whether or not something had really tried to drag her under the water before . . . she still felt jittery in her own skin, and she didn't like it.

Finally, Hannah brushed the feeling off and stood tall. She didn't need Jacob's permission.

"So, are you gonna take me back to town or do I have to swim for it?" she asked with a smirk.

Jacob reached up and back, lacing his fingers together behind his head so that his perfect arms stuck out like wings. "I hate to have to tell you this, but there's no way I can take you across the lake right now."

"Jacob—"

"No, I'm serious. Look outside."

She did. Raindrops sluiced down the windowpanes, and beyond that there was nothing but gray. And the occasional flash of distant lightning.

Right. Hannah groaned. The storm.

"We could get killed out there in the middle of the lake," Jacob said, dropping his arms to his sides. "Especially since the boat is basically made of tin. What do you think your dad would do to me if I took you out there and got you fried by lightning?" he added, stepping up next to her and giving her an annoyingly endearing, teasing smile.

"What do you think my dad's gonna do to *you* when he finds out you tricked me into coming on a weekend when your parents weren't here?" she shot back, but there wasn't much strength behind it.

Jacob tilted his head winningly. "We'll go in the morning?"

"Fine," Hannah muttered.

So she was here for the night. That meant she'd have to share a room—share a *bed*—with Katie. She could only imagine what that would be like. At home, Hannah knew that Katie stayed up until two o'clock in the morning, switching between Instagram and Snapchat on her phone, texting, and watching YouTube videos. Hannah was sure that Katie would mock her to the ends of the earth if, heaven forbid, she actually tried to go to sleep. Sleep was probably only for dorks.

"Great!" Jacob said, giving her a quick hug. "Why don't you come play with us?"

"Twister? I think I'll pass."

Hannah knew she was being lame, but she felt too awkward to join in all the touchy-feely fun.

"Your loss," Jacob said with a shrug, and rejoined the group in the living room.

Hannah crouched to unzip her bag and pulled out the book she was reading—the latest from her favorite mystery author. She plopped down on the couch with it.

"Oh, hey. I saw that movie. It wasn't bad," Colin said, noticing the cover.

"The movie?" Hannah said. "Please. The book is so much better."

"Have you even seen the movie?" he challenged her.

Hannah shook her hair back and settled deeper into the comfy couch cushions. "I don't have to. It's just a given."

Colin gave her a half smile and was about to say something else when Jacob interjected.

"All right, man. We're starting over. Spin the spinner."

"Sir! Yes, sir," Colin said. Then he rolled his eyes so only Hannah could see. Hannah smiled to herself. Colin hit the arrow, making it spin so fast she thought it might never stop.

"Left foot green," Colin said eventually.

Hannah opened to her dog-eared page in the book, but couldn't seem to concentrate. She kept reading the same sentence over and over again. Every time Colin shifted position, her heart would do a twirling dance as she wondered if he was about to talk to her again, but he never did. He just kept reading out Twister directives until, finally, Alessandra shrieked and fell over.

"Oh!" Jacob cried. "That was some spectacular fail."

"Whatever." Alessandra shoved herself up and dusted herself off. "This game is stupid anyway."

Releasing her spiral curls from the ponytail she'd tied them into, Alessandra strode over to the couch. She lifted Hannah's feet up, sat down, and then put Hannah's feet back down in her lap.

Okay. That was weirdly familiar.

Hannah curled her legs, pulling her feet back onto the cushion.

"Sorry," Alessandra said. "I just didn't want to mess up your reading flow." She narrowed her eyes in an attempt to see the cover of the book until Hannah finally held it up for her. "Oh, I loved that one! It's so much better than the first two."

"You read the Dark Heart trilogy?" Hannah asked.

"Hasn't everyone?" Alessandra said.

"Hannah hates the movie," Colin put in, turning around to join the conversation. "Which makes you a total snob, by the way," he added jokingly, throwing a look at Hannah.

"Please! They should never have hired Taylor Tommaney to play Becca. She can't do melancholy. It's all wrong on her!" Hannah protested. "And don't tell me I need to see the movie to understand, because you can tell from the frickin' trailer that she's a disaster."

"Girl has a point," Alessandra said to Colin. "The casting was subpar."

"That's just because you girls spend so much time obsessing over the books and imagining exactly what the characters look like that no actress in the world could possibly be good enough," Colin said.

Hannah was about to argue that he was wrong, but instead caught Alessandra's eye, and she knew they were thinking the exact same thing.

"Yeah, you're totally right about that," Hannah said sarcastically.

"Score one for the male person," Alessandra added.

She and Hannah laughed, and Colin smiled sheepishly.

"Okay, okay," he said, holding up his hands.

"Hello?" Katie called from the Twister mat, still frozen in her pose. "Are you gonna spin again anytime this decade? I'm about to pull a hammie over here."

"Right. Sorry about that." Colin turned and hit the spinner. As he called out the next directive, Hannah reached for a bag of SunChips on the coffee table.

"So, you finished the whole series?" she asked Alessandra.

"I read all three books in one weekend," Alessandra replied, grabbing a chip from the bag. "Why? You wanna know how it ends?"

"No!" Hannah cried with a laugh. She crunched into a chip and went back to reading.

She realized she was starting to feel comfortable. Maybe she was being silly before . . .

Bam!

A loud crash of thunder sounded and the whole house was lit by a flash of lightning. Hannah and Alessandra jumped, and Jacob and Katie tumbled over onto the mat.

"Well," Colin said flatly. "That was loud."

Everyone laughed, and Hannah, still smiling, slowly turned the page.

Dear Future Me,

Okay, I have to write the scary story down. Maybe if I write it down I'll stop THINKING ABOUT IT ALL THE TIME!!! Which is what I really can't stop doing. Like, I missed five questions on the history test today—just completely SKIPPED THEM because my mind wandered and didn't come back until the bell rang.

So, at the slumber party, P decided that we should tell scary stories because that is SO original, and she also decided that she should go first. And of course everyone just went along because it was her party. But whatever. Her story went like this:

Back in the '90s, her brother's best friend's mother's sister committed suicide in Dreardon Lake. One day the girl was happy— nominated for prom queen, girlfriend of the hottest guy in school, bound for Michigan State—and the next, she was dead. None of her friends or her family saw it coming. It was like one day she was perfect and happy and FINE and the next she was gone. She didn't even leave a note. Just walked out in the middle of the night and drowned herself.

Yes, you read that correctly. She DROWNED HERSELF. This is what I can't stop thinking about. According to P, this girl walked up to some lookout point over the lake, tied her father's 25-pound dumbbells to her legs, and JUMPED OFF! The police, who found her body, like, five days later all bloated and veiny and NIBBLED AT BY FISH, said she must have dropped like a stone and never resurfaced. AND ALL I CAN THINK ABOUT is this poor girl, tied to these weights at the bottom of the lake, sucking in all that water, realizing what she was doing was insane and wanting more than anything to get free and not being able to see anything because it was all dark and terrifying and panicky and heart pounding and gasping for air and—

I can't. I'm crying. Even right now I'm crying just imagining it. And I can't stop imagining it. And I don't know if it's my stupid brain and I can't shut it off or if it's that P spins a really good yarn, as Grandma would say, but I wish I'd never heard that stupid story. Because I don't think I'm ever going to stop reliving it.

SIX

Hannah woke up before everyone else, which was always the way. It never mattered what time she went to sleep—she was up with the first sunrays of dawn. At home it could be irritating, because she often didn't know what to do with herself until everyone else got going. If it was nice out, she would sometimes go for a run to get her cardio in, but then ten minutes away from her house she'd remember she hated running and stop, breathless, achy, and irritated, and drag herself back home. Sometimes she'd read or watch TV or do some extra homework, but she could never do the one thing she wanted to do that early, which was swim. The Y pool didn't open until eight a.m. and the swim club didn't open until nine, so even now that she had her driver's license, doing laps was not an option at six or seven a.m.

But here at the lake, she could swim whenever she wanted.

Hannah rolled over quietly, not wanting to wake Katie, who was snoozing beside her in the king-size bed. Katie must have been exhausted from the whole boat ride trauma of yesterday, because she'd pretty much crashed as soon as they got upstairs last night. Hannah had been surprised that she'd fallen asleep easily as well. The thunder had died down in the night, which definitely helped.

Hannah automatically picked up her phone from the bedside table, but the screen was black. She remembered that she'd turned it off last night, after shooting a few texts back and forth with

Theo about car-pool plans for the first day of school. She'd also texted her father to say good night. She hadn't even waited for him to reply, worried that she'd be tempted to tell him what was going on.

Instead of turning the phone on now, she placed it back on the table facedown and jumped out of bed. She knew she couldn't avoid her dad forever, but she could avoid him for now. He was probably still asleep anyway.

Hannah grabbed her Speedo and went to the bathroom to change. The whole house was quiet; Jacob and Colin must have been dead to the world, too. Hannah's footsteps creaked on the stairs down to the living room, but Alessandra didn't stir on the couch. Her face was planted nose-first into a cushion and she had one leg elevated behind her while her arm trailed to the floor. So maybe Hannah had lucked out bunking with Katie after all. Smirking, Hannah slipped outside, keeping the screen door's squeal to a minimum by barely opening it wide enough to slide through sideways.

The morning air was cool, and a fine mist clung to the lake's surface after last night's storm. A tremor ran through Hannah's body from her toes to the top of her head as she remembered the race yesterday and the hand that had tried to drag her down.

Yes, it had felt like an actual hand—she could at least admit that to herself now.

But she had decided to pretend it had never happened. Because it couldn't have, really . . . right? The lake monster stories, she was sure, had been made up by bored locals with nothing better to do.

Hannah snapped on her swim cap and goggles and walked to the edge of the dock, swinging her arms front and back to loosen up her shoulder muscles. She kept her eyes averted from the island. The water lapped quietly against the dock posts. Everything was so . . . completely . . . silent.

It's just a lake, she told herself as she did some quick butt kicks to warm up her thighs. *There's nothing out there but fish and turtles. Maybe a few frogs. Nothing to be afraid of.*

Shaking her head at herself, Hannah let her toes curl over the edge of the dock. She stared down into the dark blue water. Nothing out of the ordinary.

She took a breath and dove straight out. The cold shocked her, but she shook it off. The lake had been chilled by the rainstorm and the sun hadn't gotten strong enough yet to warm it up. Hannah surfaced and swam away from the shoreline freestyle. *Stroke, stroke, stroke, breath. Stroke, stroke, stroke, breath.* She lost herself in the rhythm of her movements until she started to feel her muscles warm up, then she paused and treaded water.

She'd swum out pretty far. If she had to guess, she'd say she was about halfway between the dock and Mystery Island. She glanced at the side of the island with the creepy burnt trees, wondering what had happened out there. Had someone lit a campfire and carelessly, but innocently, forgotten to douse it? Or had it been more sinister than that? Maybe someone had gone out there with the explicit intention of ruining the island. She couldn't imagine why, but people had done more awful things than that for reasons she could never understand.

Yesterday, the island had seemed ominous and threatening, but now, with the trees on the healthy side stretching overhead against the rapidly brightening sky, it wasn't so bad. It looked more injured than anything else. More sad than scary.

Breathing deeply in and out, Hannah tried to measure the span of lake between herself and the island. No, she wasn't a long-distance swimmer, but she could make it there no problem if she took her time. Maybe she should give it a try. It could be kind of cool to explore Mystery Island. And there was something about doing it on her own—ignoring the NO TRESPASSING signs and breaking the rules—that sent a rush of adrenaline through her. She'd show Jacob and Katie and the others that she wasn't completely lame—that she could be daring and fun. She was about to go for it when the front door of the house opened. Hannah turned around in the lake and saw Jacob stepping outside in his pj's.

Jacob. Alone. My Jacob.

With one last glance at the island, Hannah started swimming for the dock. Now her heart was pounding harder, more in anticipation of having Jacob all to herself than from any exertion on her part. Her body was used to this sort of exercise, and she loved how strong and confident she felt in the water. She swam faster and faster, both wanting to get to Jacob before anyone else woke up and sort of wanting to impress him with her speed. Her pride refused to let him believe he'd actually won fair and square yesterday. She was faster than him and they both knew it.

In far less time than it had taken her to swim out, she was touching the dock again, flinging her arms up to hang off the sides. Jacob walked over, a big, fluffy beach towel in his hands.

"Nice form," he said, rubbing the sleep from one eye.

She squinted up at him. The sun was rising just behind his head, casting his face in shadow. "Thanks."

She reached a hand up and he hoisted her from the water. She tripped into him, and his T-shirt was still warm from being cuddled under his covers. Jacob wrapped the big towel around her and gathered it together at her front. She expected him to release her then, but he didn't. He held her there, just inches from his chest, his shoulders, his face. There was no breath inside of her. In the distance, birds chirped. Hannah's skin prickled.

He was going to kiss her. He was going to *kiss her*!

And then, the screen door slammed.

"Woooo-hoooo!" Alessandra shouted, running for the dock. Colin was right on her heels. Both wore swimsuits, and Colin's hair stuck straight up in the back as if he'd just rolled out of bed and into his swim trunks. They barreled right past Hannah, knocking her into Jacob again, but this time her forehead bumped his chin and he took a step back, rubbing at the spot.

Moment officially crushed.

Colin and Alessandra both cannonballed into the water, splashing Jacob and Hannah from head to toe. Jacob ripped his shirt off, then followed.

"Cowabunga!" he shouted as he threw himself off the end of the dock.

Colin and Alessandra screamed and screeched as he splashed them, and Hannah stood there, watching, feeling like she could cry.

It was going to be her first kiss.

Her first kiss, from *Jacob*.

So close. She'd been so very close.

"Come back in!" Alessandra shouted, splashing Hannah's feet.

Hannah shook her head. "No, I'm good. If I stay in any longer I'm going to prune."

"I thought you were a swimmer," Colin said matter-of-factly.

"I am, I just . . . don't feel like swimming right now," she lied.

Hannah turned and walked back toward the house, suddenly wanting more than anything to be alone. She needed to think. She needed to figure out what, if anything, had almost just happened.

Hannah only paused when she saw Katie on the porch, scowling at her in her pink boy shorts and white Oak View Softball sweatshirt. Hannah scowled back. What exactly had Katie seen?

Whatever. It didn't matter. There was no way Hannah was going to let Katie get to her. Not now. It wasn't as if Katie had some claim on Jacob. If anyone had a claim on him, it was Hannah, who had known him since they were both in diapers. Her stepsister opened her mouth to speak as Hannah walked by, but Hannah just kept right on walking, letting the front door slam behind her, completely cutting off whatever it was Katie had to say.

Hannah could feel herself blushing as she headed back into the master bedroom. The sun streamed through the windows, cutting long swaths of light across the hardwood floor. She sat down on the messy, white duvet and the bedsprings squeaked beneath her. The air felt close and warm. She hugged the towel tighter around her damp skin.

He almost kissed me. He really almost kissed me.

She realized then that Jacob hadn't mentioned anything about taking her back into town for her car.

And she realized that maybe that was a good thing.

Her fingers fluttered up to touch her lips just as Katie sauntered through the door.

"Oh my God. What're you doing?" Katie demanded.

Caught, Hannah immediately stood up. She yanked her duffel off the floor and unzipped it. She started to pull out the hastily folded clothes, keeping her back to Katie.

"Nothing," she said. "Unpacking."

"Unpacking? I thought you were leaving," Katie said with a sniff, taking a few steps into the room. "Don't tell me you're going to stay just because of that pathetic little show out there."

Hannah whipped her favorite plaid shorts down on the bed and turned on Katie. She hated confrontation with every fiber of her being, but if she didn't say something right now, she was actually going to explode.

"You're just jealous," she stated.

Katie's jaw dropped. Hannah noticed she had a tiny bit of dried saliva next to her mouth—she must have been drooling in her sleep—and decided not to say anything. A tiny revenge.

"Jealous?" Katie snapped. "Are you kidding me?"

"Jacob and I have been friends forever." Hannah was shaking as she continued in her task, ripping out underwear and tank tops. "You're jealous because we know each other so well and we have something the two of you could never have."

"Oh, please. Who's the one he's been texting with until two a.m. every night?" Katie shot back. "The only reason he doesn't want you to go home is because he knows you'll have to take me with you. Jacob doesn't want *me* to leave."

Hannah tossed her now empty duffel into the corner with a clatter so loud it startled even her. "You are *so* conceited!"

"And *you* are so selfish!" Katie replied. "You don't get to have everything, Hannah. Your school, your house, your friends. What about me? Why am I the one who has to leave everything behind?"

Hannah stared as tears—real, shining tears—filled the usually cold-as-ice eyes of her stepsister. Katie had never said anything like this to her before, and if Hannah was being honest with herself, she'd never really thought about it. When Katie's mom had married her dad, it was just obvious to the world that Mylin, Katie, and Fred would move in with Hannah and her father. Hannah and her dad had more space. Hannah went to the better school. And their house was closer to the hospital where both her dad and Mylin worked.

For weeks, Hannah had silently ruminated and occasionally outright complained about having to change up her habits. About sharing her bathroom with Katie and Fred. About the Wi-Fi slowing down because their devices crowded the signal. About her dad having to split his time between Katie's softball games, Fred's karate matches, and Hannah's swim meets.

But she'd never really thought about everything Katie was giving up. She'd had to move in the middle of her sophomore year. Leave her friends, her team, her home. Clearly, that had sucked for her. But still . . .

"I'm not being selfish," Hannah said quietly. "He's *my* best friend. He always has been. That shouldn't have to change just because my dad got married."

"Ugh!" Katie threw up her hands and stormed out of the room, slamming the door so hard the windowpanes shook.

Hannah took a deep breath. She felt bad for not empathizing with Katie back when their parents had gotten married, sure, but that didn't mean she was wrong now. Katie couldn't just sweep in here and steal the guy she liked and expect Hannah to be happy about it. Did she expect Hannah to—what? Call it even? *I get to keep my school so you get to take the love of my life?* That didn't make any sense.

Hannah heard the screen door bang shut, and she went to the window to see what her stepsister would do. Katie walked over to the dock, a rolled-up magazine in her hand, and sat down on the edge, dangling her feet into the water. Maybe her fear of the lake was abating. But instead of reading, she shouted something to the others and they replied, splashing her until she screeched. The sun shone down on the water, making it glitter like a blanket of diamonds.

It was all so idyllic, and Hannah was struck with the sudden sensation that Katie belonged here, and she didn't. She tried to shake this feeling off, but she couldn't. There was something about the way Jacob was looking at Katie that Hannah didn't like.

Then, Hannah saw something move in the corner of her vision, far from where Jacob and his friends were swimming. Behind them and off to the right, something rose up out of the water. At first Hannah thought *seal*, but that was impossible. There were no seals in mountain lakes. As the—*thing*—showed a bit more of its body, Hannah saw that it was wrinkled—black and gray and mottled—but it was too far away to make out any actual features.

What is it? Hannah squinted. It was too big to be a turtle, too slow to be a lake trout, and it hovered there for far too long, like some sort of alien being.

That thing wasn't natural. Whatever it was, it didn't belong out there.

The answer came to her then.

Lake monster.

Hannah's blood was roaring in her ears. She grabbed for the

window latch, but it wouldn't budge. She wanted to bang on the pane and scream.

Katie! Turn your head! Hannah thought, wishing she had psychic powers. *Turn around!*

But Katie wouldn't. Because she was too busy flirting with Jacob.

Hannah's palms started to sweat and she fumbled with the window lock, which seemed to have been painted shut. It finally cracked and opened, and Hannah fought to throw up the window. She was ready to yell down to the others, but when she looked out at the lake again, the thing was gone. All that was left of it was a series of tiny ripples in the water.

She stared at the spot where the strange creature had surfaced, both desperate to catch another glimpse and terrified that it would return. Had she really just seen the lake monster Colin and Alessandra had talked about? The longer she stared, the more her head began to pound, and she started to wonder if she'd simply imagined it. Maybe it *had* been a turtle. Or a piece of trash surfacing? An old, sunken boat bobbing to the top of the lake? But then, where had it disappeared to?

With a deep breath, Hannah turned from the window and began changing out of her bathing suit. One thing was for sure— she wasn't going swimming in that lake again anytime soon.

SEVEN

"So if you want to buy a cute top or a pair of vintage jeans, go to Suzie Lee's," Alessandra explained. She was walking backward down the busy sidewalk and somehow not tripping over the barrel planters, decorative light posts, or random benches. It was like she had a sixth sense. Hannah was impressed. "But avoid Dreardon Styles at all costs."

Hannah, Katie, Jacob, Colin, and Alessandra had all come into town for the afternoon. Katie had braved the boat ride across the lake, white-knuckled, while Hannah had kept her eyes peeled for the *thing*. But it hadn't appeared again.

Now, Alessandra was giving them a quick tour while Jacob and Colin strolled along behind the girls.

The town was as busy as it had been when Hannah had first driven through it yesterday. Motorists drove slowly to avoid shoppers and strollers and bicyclists. Half the cars on the road towed a boat, or had kayaks or mountain bikes tied to their roofs. Little kids trotted along beside their parents, struggling to eat huge ice cream cones as streaks of chocolate and colorful sprinkles melted down their arms.

"Dreardon Styles is a total tourist trap," Alessandra continued knowingly. "Crappy quality, high prices."

"What about that place?" Katie paused in her texting to point out a cute little house with a hand-painted window sign that read GINGER'S PARADISE.

"*Love* Ginger's," Alessandra said, and spread her fingers wide. "Best selection of sandals in the summer and boots in the fall."

Hannah paused to look in the window of an antiques store. The display was artfully arranged to look like a shabby-chic kitchen, with doilies under mismatched china plates and an old *Hannah Montana* lunch box next to a Spider-Man umbrella. She moved out of the way as a couple walked by her hand in hand.

"Watch it," Katie admonished Hannah. Hannah blinked, looking down and realizing that she had accidentally stepped on Katie's heel.

"Sorry," Hannah muttered.

The argument they'd had earlier lingered between them. Hannah couldn't really focus on the charming town tour. She kept thinking back to the hostile exchange with Katie in the bedroom. *And* to the moment when Jacob had wrapped Hannah in the towel while they stood on the dock. What had he been thinking? Did he really want to kiss her? Or was he crushing on Katie like Katie claimed?

And then there was that thing she had seen in the lake.

Glancing around and seeing that no one was paying any attention to her—*shocker*—Hannah tugged her phone out of her cross-body bag. There was service here in town. Maybe she could Google "Dreardon Lake Monster" and see what came up. She pressed her lips together, her thumb hovering over her keyboard, but then her phone lit up with a text from Theo.

Current situation?

Hannah smiled. It was a game they sometimes played. It meant she had to take a picture of whatever she was doing at that second and send it to him. She snapped a photo of the antiques-store window and sent it to him with the message:

Antiquing.

His reply was instant.

I've always wanted a Spider-Man umbrella!!!

Hannah laughed and was about to type something back when Alessandra nudged her.

"Boyfriend?"

"What?" Hannah asked, startled.

"Texting your boyfriend?" Her expression was perfectly innocent, interested, open.

"Um, no." Hannah shoved the phone back in her bag. "I don't have a boyfriend."

"Then why are you blushing?" Alessandra teased.

"I'm not!" Was she? "I'm just . . . hot."

"If you say so." Alessandra cocked her head to one side.

Hannah noticed that Jacob and Colin had caught up to Katie and the three of them were walking ahead in a bunch. She tried not to feel offended, but really—why was Jacob so adamant about Hannah not leaving, when it seemed like he barely even remembered she was there?

"Everything okay?" Alessandra asked, her brow knit.

Sheesh. Am I that transparent? Hannah wondered. Rather than answer, she decided to change the subject.

"Does it bother you that all these people crowd up your town every summer?" she asked.

Alessandra shrugged, falling into step beside Hannah. Jacob, Colin, and Katie were crossing a side street now, all of them looking down at their phones as they strolled along.

"Not really," Alessandra said. "Without all these people, I swear my mom's bakery would go under. We have a few regulars, but it's the tourists who are crazy for her cupcakes. It's like they've never experienced buttercream before."

Hannah laughed.

"And the summer is a little busier than the rest of the year, but really we have tourists all year round." Alessandra bent to grab a discarded paper cup off the ground, and deposited it in a trash can at the corner. "We get leaf-gawkers in the fall, skiers in the winter, and campers in spring. Sometimes you barely remember who belongs here and who doesn't."

Up ahead, Hannah saw Katie and the boys duck into a sporting goods store called Sports Stuff. Hannah and Alessandra headed in that same direction. But suddenly a woman about Hannah's dad's age stopped Alessandra on the street.

The woman had light brown hair pulled back in a low ponytail and wore no makeup. Her frame was wiry and frail and she wore a pair of shorts and a large sweatshirt.

"Ali! Honey! How are you?" the woman said.

The woman lifted onto her toes to put her skinny arms around the much taller Alessandra, and Alessandra hugged her back, tightly and unselfconsciously, closing her eyes as if the hug really mattered.

"I'm doing well, Mrs. Caldwell, how are you?"

The woman's blue eyes seemed to tear up as she tilted her chin back to look at Alessandra. "Fine, you know . . . okay." She took a deep, shaky breath. "It's nice to see you. How's your mom?"

"She's good. She's at the bakery right now." Alessandra gestured downhill. "You should stop by. You know she'll hook you up with some free pastries and coffee."

"Oh, I couldn't," Mrs. Caldwell said, waving a thin hand, but she looked touched. Hannah wondered if the woman might burst into tears.

"Uh, yeah you could!" Alessandra said with a smile. "Please do. If I tell her I bumped into you and you don't stop in, she'll nag me about it all night."

The woman smiled reluctantly, but kindly. "All right, you twisted my arm. It really was good to see you, hon."

She squeezed Alessandra's forearm, gave Hannah a quick nod, and kept walking.

"What was that all about?" Hannah asked in a low voice, reaching up to tuck her hair behind her ears. "She looked like she was about to cry."

"That was Mrs. Caldwell. She owns the make-your-own-fro-yo place in town." Alessandra watched the woman pause to feed a parking meter. "I'm friends with her daughter, Claudia. Well, we used to be friends, I guess." Distractedly, Alessandra pulled out her phone and checked for messages, then shoved it back in her pocket.

"Used to be?"

Alessandra shook her head as if she was coming out of a trance. "She . . . uh . . . she kind of disappeared a couple months ago."

"What?" Hannah blurted. "What do you mean, disappeared?"

"It was this past May, right before Memorial Day," Alessandra said, frowning. "Claudia went to bed one night and when her family woke up the next day, she was gone." Alessandra started walking again, turning sideways to let a couple of joggers pass. "There was no note, no sign that anything was wrong. I mean, she had no reason to run away. Her family was great, she had friends. It's totally bizarre."

Even though the sun was strong, Hannah felt a chill. She hugged her arms. "What about the police?"

"Oh, they searched. There were posters and flyers and dogs and everything, but nothing ever turned up," Alessandra said. "I'm kind of hoping she ran away to follow some band or something and she'll just turn up one day, but honestly? I don't think so. I think something happened to her."

A hot, painful ball formed in Hannah's chest and her grip on her own arms tightened. Something had happened to the girl? But what? How could someone just disappear without a trace?

"Did they ever have a suspect or anything?" Hannah asked quietly. "I'm sorry, is that rude to ask?"

"No." Alessandra shook her head. "It's the standard question. They did have one person in mind, but it turned out he had an alibi."

"Who was it?" Hannah asked.

"Hey, guys! Catch up!" Jacob's voice interrupted.

Up ahead, Katie had emerged from the sporting goods store carrying a shopping bag that sagged with the weight of whatever was inside. Beside her, Jacob waved to them. Colin was right on Katie's heels, still looking down at his phone.

"What's up?" Hannah shouted back.

"Everyone's at Slices!" Jacob shouted. "Let's go! Free pizza!"

"Sweet!" Alessandra exclaimed, clapping her hands together.

She hurried up the street, the conversation about Claudia clearly forgotten or put aside, and Hannah followed slowly. She looked back over her shoulder. To her surprise, Claudia's mother was still standing there, by the parking meter. And she was gazing curiously back at Hannah.

Slices was a cozy pizza place, all red and green and chrome, with a tile floor up front near the counter and a dining room with slightly more formal decor at the back. The moment they were through the door, Alessandra and Colin made a beeline for the back room, leaving Jacob, Hannah, and Katie by the counter.

Hannah watched as Colin and Alessandra joined two other kids their age—a girl and a guy—who were waiting at a table with pitchers of water and soda. The girl immediately huddled close with Colin and Alessandra, the three of them talking in low voices and laughing. The guy at the table sat off to the side, slumped back and scrolling on his phone. He looked up every once in a while to scowl at the other three, and for some reason, Hannah got the sense that he was particularly scowling at Colin.

"Hey! Raj!" Jacob greeted the guy behind the counter. Raj slapped Jacob's hand, then leaned in for a one-shouldered bro hug. "This is Raj," Jacob told Katie and Hannah. "He's the guy that keeps me in free pizza every summer."

"Ladies," Raj said with a nod and a toothy grin. He had a scrawny build, dark skin, and black hair that stuck out every which way from beneath his Slices baseball cap. There was a birthmark above his upper lip that made it look like he was trying to grow a mustache. "Let me guess," he said, eyeing the girls unabashedly. "You're the best friend, Hannah." He pointed at Hannah and she nodded with a smile. "And you're the *lovely* Katie."

Katie preened as Hannah's heart sank. Jacob had told Raj that Katie was *lovely*? Argh!

"I guess our reputations precede us," Katie said, smiling smugly at Hannah. It was all Hannah could do not to stick out her tongue in return.

"So . . . I say we get one meat lover's, one veggie lover's, and one just extra pepperoni," Jacob said, drumming his hands on the red marble counter. Raj jotted down a few notes on a sauce-stained notepad, then looked up at Jacob expectantly.

"And what're you gonna get for your friends?" he joked.

Jacob reached over the counter and yanked down on the brim of Raj's baseball cap. Then Jacob laughed and glanced over at Hannah, as if expecting her to give him an award for his awesome pranking. Instead, she simply looked away. She just wasn't in the mood right now.

"Guys! Get some diet soda!" Alessandra called from the table.

"A pitcher of Diet Coke," Jacob told Raj. "You good?" he asked Katie.

"I'll definitely eat the extra pepperoni," Katie said, glancing up from her phone. She'd been busy posting half a dozen selfies on Instagram—pictures of herself posing in front of the old jukebox near the counter; standing in front of the Slices sign outside as she pretended to eat the huge slice; pointing at the endless list of toppings with her mouth and eyes wide open like it was the coolest thing ever.

Ugh.

"I'll put the order right in for ya," Raj said, straightening his cap. Then, as Katie turned away to pocket her phone, he mouthed to Jacob, *"You were right! She's hot!"*

Hannah swallowed hard. She wished she hadn't seen that. She used a fingertip to draw a circle in a pile of salt someone had left behind on the counter, trying to pretend like she didn't care about Jacob, or Katie, or anyone.

"Hang on," Colin said. "Did anyone ask Hannah what she wants?"

Hannah flinched. She hadn't even noticed that Colin had gotten up from the table and was now standing behind her at the counter.

Jacob and Katie paused.

"What? No. I'm fine," Hannah said, flushed.

"Aren't you hungry?" Colin asked, leaning his hands into the edge of the counter so that his shoulder muscles visibly flexed.

"I guess." Hannah shrugged. She hated that everyone was looking at her now, but it was also sort of cool, Colin pointing out that exactly no one had thought to ask if she wanted the meat lover's or the veggie lover's or the extra pepperoni. She'd just assumed she'd pick the pepperoni off, not wanting to make trouble. But now . . .

"I'll have a plain slice," she said.

Katie rolled her eyes. "Shocker."

"And one plain slice for the lady," Colin told Raj, then shot Hannah a brief but genuine smile.

"Thanks," she said.

"Anytime," he replied.

They all headed back to the table. Hannah sat at the far end, not wanting to negotiate a spot next to Jacob. She gulped down a cupful of water, then refilled it, making sure she got plenty of ice. The hot, dry air outside had left her parched.

"Hey, guys," Alessandra said to Katie and Hannah. "Meet my friends Prandya Sai and Nick Freeman. Prandya and Nick, meet Katie Chen and Hannah Webster. They're staying at Jacob's for the weekend."

"Hey," Nick said, not looking up from his phone.

Katie shot Hannah a look like *rude*, but Hannah was getting a shy vibe off Nick, rather than a rude one. He had sandy, shaggy hair and a blotchy redness was slowly creeping up the pale skin of his cheeks. Even though she was sure he was about her age, he was one of those guys who just looked young, like he belonged on stage playing one of the Lost Boys in *Peter Pan*. He barely flicked his eyes up as Katie sat down next to him.

"Nice to meet you," Hannah said, feeling empathetic. Maybe he didn't like meeting new people, either.

His eyelids flickered again, but this time, his gaze froze. He stared at Hannah as if he'd never seen a girl before.

"Do I have something on my face?" Hannah asked, reaching up to rub under her nose.

"No! Uh . . . no. Sorry," Nick said. "Hi."

Then he grabbed the container of Parmesan cheese and gripped it in both hands atop the table.

Okaaay, Hannah thought.

"Prandya is Raj's sister," Jacob said, sitting down across from Alessandra. Prandya nodded and smiled. She had dark skin like Raj, and her black hair was cut into a bob. She wore a white shirtdress that looked like silk. "They have a house on the lake, too."

"Yeah, but their family's, like, filthy rich so it's five times the size of Jacob's," Alessandra joked, causing Raj to almost drop one of the pizzas as he brought it over to the table.

"Dude. I can't believe you just said that," Raj chided her, tossing the metal pizza tray on the table with a clang before retreating back to the front counter.

"What? It's true! They can see it with their own eyes when we get back to the lake," Alessandra replied, grinning at Hannah.

"Anyway," Prandya said, reaching for a slice of pizza. "We should all take out the Jet Skis one day while you're here. We have four of them and two are two-seaters, so we almost have enough seats to all go together."

"That's okay. Katie doesn't swim," Hannah heard herself say.

"Hannah!" Katie snapped.

"What? Sorry. Do you want to go out on a Jet Ski?" she asked her stepsister.

"I don't know." Katie was clearly embarrassed and beyond annoyed. "Forget it."

"Awkward!" Alessandra sang, and Colin chuckled under his breath.

At that moment, Raj came over with the other two pies and placed them down more carefully. Steam rose up off the toppings and no one even bothered to try to touch them. A minute later, Raj returned with Hannah's slice and the pitcher of Diet Coke.

"Did I get everything? Cuz if I didn't you're just gonna have to deal. I'm sick of waiting on you fools," he joked.

Jacob and his friends all balled up napkins and tossed them at

Raj as he ducked and laughed his way back to his post. Then everybody dove into the food and the conversation devolved into shouts about burning their mouths, commentary on messy cheese, and moaning over how good the sauce was.

"Here, try this," Colin said, passing a container of red pepper flakes to Hannah. "It's completely transformative."

"Transformative?" Nick said, his mouth full. "What are you, studying for the SATs?"

Hannah paused. Nick's comment wasn't teasing. It was legit sarcastic. Like, *mean* sarcastic. Colin, however, clearly wasn't bothered. He casually lifted a shoulder.

"I'm not going to apologize for having a big vocabulary." He looked at Hannah and smiled. "Some people appreciate intelligence."

He held Hannah's gaze until she blushed. Jacob kicked Colin lightly under the table and Colin kicked him back. Hannah pretended not to notice and shook some pepper onto her slice. She took a big bite. Colin was right. It totally transformed the taste.

"Because when have you ever apologized for anything?" Nick muttered under his breath, grabbing his own slice of pepperoni.

Alessandra shot Nick a scathing look, then turned a big smile on Hannah.

"I bet you're, like, the smarty-pants of your grade, right, Hannah?" Alessandra said.

Katie groaned and got up from the table. Hannah chose to ignore her.

"Why do you think that?" Hannah asked.

"Oh, please. You're obviously one of those straight-A students.

You can just tell," Colin said. "Not that there's anything wrong with that."

Hannah grinned. Somehow, she didn't mind him teasing her about this. "I'm not about to apologize for my four-point-oh."

"Oh!" Alessandra shouted, placing her fist over her full mouth.

"I like this girl," Prandya said, leaning into the table.

Alessandra smiled. "Me too."

Hannah took another bite of pizza, feeling happy and comfortable for maybe the second time since she'd arrived. She glanced around for Jacob and realized he was no longer at the table, either. Hannah placed her pizza down on her plate and lifted out of her chair an inch, scanning the restaurant.

Then she spotted them. Jacob and Katie were standing together in front of the old-school Pac-Man game across the dining room. Her stomach shrank.

Katie giggled at something Jacob said and shoved him playfully. Jacob got behind her and put his arms around her so that they were both holding the joystick controller and her back was leaning into his chest. It was the closest pose she'd ever seen them in—the closest pose she'd ever seen Jacob in with anyone—and it made her lose her appetite entirely.

"Hey."

Hannah startled. Colin was leaning over next to her. She tried to turn to face him, but could hardly shift without bumping faces with him.

"Wanna get out of here?" he asked. His expression was thoughtful, and Hannah knew he must have picked up on her simmering frustration toward Jacob and Katie. "There's something I want to show you."

"Yeah," Hannah said without giving herself a chance to over-think it. "Let's go."

Colin got to his feet. Hannah stood up quickly, waving to the others. As she turned to head for the door, she got the oddest chill, as if someone was watching her. She glanced back at the table.

There was Nick, sitting straight up in his chair for the first time all afternoon, his eyes like hard marbles as he glared in her direction.

EIGHT

"Where're we going?"

Colin had just ducked down an alleyway between two build-ings. Only now, cut off from the hustle and bustle of the street, did Hannah realize she was following a stranger around in a strange place.

The bright sunshine was blocked by the high walls of the buildings that formed the alley, and it was weirdly cool and dark—getting darker the farther they walked. Hannah glanced over her shoulder, recalling the look on Nick's face as she'd walked out of Slices. A stray thought about turning and running left behind a prickle of sweat across her brow. But if she did that, Colin would think she was out of her mind.

He's Jacob's friend, remember? And he's been nothing but nice to you since the second you arrived. The thought made her feel a bit better, and she took a deep, calming breath. *Forget about Nick. There's clearly something odd about that guy.*

"We're going . . . right here."

Colin paused outside a door marked EMPLOYEES ONLY and shot her a winning smile.

"Employees of what?" she asked.

"You'll see," he replied.

Hannah shivered and wiped her palms on the back of her shorts. "You . . . work here?"

She glanced up for some indication of what the business was, but all she saw was a brick wall, a fire escape, and a few large garbage pails. Out on the street, a child screamed and then started to cry.

"Didn't say that."

Still grinning, Colin reached past her, brushing her arm with his, and pulled the door open. It was even darker inside than it was outside, but something about Colin's easy demeanor calmed Hannah's nerves. At least enough to shoot him a narrow-eyed look and step inside.

Air-conditioning made the hair on her arms stand up and she found herself following Colin down a long, narrow hallway. At the end was another door, and as soon as he opened it, soft light poured in along with the smack-you-in-the-nostrils scent of buttered popcorn.

"A movie theater?"

Colin lifted his finger to his lips to shush her and tilted his head. They slipped out the door and rushed across a short stretch of velvety carpeting to another door also marked EMPLOYEES ONLY. Colin raised his eyebrows and opened this door, too. They ascended a set of black stairs and Colin pushed open a final door at the top.

It was noticeably warmer inside, with a metallic tang in the air, and it took Hannah's eyes a second to adjust to what she was seeing—a small glass window, a bright light, a large, humming machine giving off its own heat. Colin led her around the machine to a larger window and Hannah could see the theater down below, the movie being projected onto the big screen. Colin flipped a switch, and the sound of the film surrounded them—two men discussing whether someone else was a spy.

"This is so cool," Hannah whispered.

"It's called a projection room."

Colin unfolded two chairs from the wall behind him and brought them over. He gestured for Hannah to sit. She did, and then Colin took a seat next to her. Their legs brushed and Hannah felt warm. She wasn't sure if he'd done it on purpose, but she didn't want him to think that *she* had, so she squirmed sideways a little.

"I love watching movies from up here," Colin said, not seeming to notice she'd moved. His voice was just above a whisper, which gave it a throaty quality and made her feel all goose-pimply—in a good way. "It's so much better than listening to the running commentary from the idiots around you."

"Yeah, I hate that," Hannah whispered back. "Or when people start typing on their phones."

"Totally." Colin's face brightened. "Just the glow from their screens is so annoying in a dark theater."

"Also, up here no one's going to kick your seat."

"Or throw up on you."

Hannah snorted a laugh. "That didn't happen."

"Swear on my life." Colin crossed his heart and held up one palm. "When I was eight, I went to see whatever Disney thing was out that summer and some kid ate too many gummy bears, then puked on the back of my neck. I was traumatized for months."

Hannah laughed loudly, then covered her mouth. "That's gross."

"I know! I'm the one it happened to," Colin said, laughing as well. He had a nice laugh, low and unassuming.

They fell into a companionable silence and watched a few minutes of the film. The spy in question turned out to be a kickass woman with a penchant for disguise, which made it slightly more interesting. For a while, Hannah enjoyed the dark of the theater, the movie flickering onscreen. She even forgot about the thing she'd seen in the lake this morning, and that Jacob was out there somewhere flirting with Katie.

"Thanks for bringing me here," she said quietly.

Colin turned to look at her, and she could feel his gaze warm on the side of her face. "Any time."

Hannah took a breath and glanced at him. His eyes were intense. "I do have a question, though."

"What's that?" he asked. Was it just her, or had he shifted a smidgen closer to her? He smelled of pine trees and soap and something else—something fresh and minty.

"Should we really be up here?" she asked. "I mean, what if we get caught?" Even though Hannah knew she was being a buzzkill, she couldn't seem to stop herself. It was just automatic.

Colin didn't move. Didn't break eye contact. "We won't get caught." He moved in even a little closer to her. She could see the outline of his lips in the dark.

Hannah swallowed nervously.

"You say that, but—"

At that moment, the door behind them opened. Hannah yelped and scrambled to her feet, as if she could escape, but the only way out was by the door through which a woman was now stepping. She had auburn hair pulled back in a tight bun, wore black from head to toe, and had a stern look about her—pointed chin, pointed nose, dark eyeliner.

"What's this?" the woman asked, her eyes sharp.

Colin stood up slowly next to Hannah, who was about to have a heart attack. Could she get arrested for this? Was ignoring EMPLOYEES ONLY signs punishable by law?

And then Colin spoke. "Hey, Mom," he said. "This is Hannah."

"Do you kids want some popcorn?"

Hannah's heart still pounded every which way as she and Colin trailed his mother back down the stairs and into the movie theater lobby. It was wide and brightly lit and deserted, aside from the one girl reading a copy of *Entertainment Weekly* and popping her gum behind the concessions counter. There were three screens in the theater, and each was playing a different movie at the moment, so all the customers were safely tucked away inside.

"Always," Colin said, smiling at Hannah.

"Sure. Thank you," Hannah added. She felt hot all over from being caught and she hoped Colin's mom didn't think they were kissing up there or something. Even though, well, if she'd come in a few minutes later . . .

But no. She couldn't go around thinking every guy she knew was going to kiss her. She suddenly remembered Alessandra asking if Theo was her boyfriend and she blushed all over again. When had she become so boy crazy? This wasn't her. She needed to get a grip.

"So, your mom works here?" Hannah whispered to Colin as his mom slipped behind the concessions counter.

"She's the manager," he said. "I work here sometimes for extra cash, too. My grandfather actually owns the place. He's lived here forever."

"That's cool," Hannah said. "So why didn't we just walk through the front door?"

Colin's face turned adorably pink. "I thought I'd look cooler if you thought I was actually breaking into the place. Is that lame?"

Hannah laughed. "Actually, it's kind of sweet."

Colin grinned and they crossed the rest of the way to the counter.

"Sorry about sneaking in," Hannah said to Colin's mother. "Please don't blame Colin. He was just trying to get me out of an . . . annoying situation."

Colin's mom grabbed a couple of popcorn bags and started to fill them. She shot Hannah a friendly smile that instantly softened her looks. "Don't worry about it. Colin's up there all the time." She handed Hannah a full bag of popcorn and looked sideways at her son. "Although I do believe I've told him a few dozen times he's not to bring any friends up there."

"She was having a bad day," Colin said with a shrug as his mom handed him his own full bag. "I was trying to cheer her up."

"Well, next time cheer her up with a free seat *inside* the theater," she said, eliciting a short laugh from the concessions worker, who didn't even look up from her magazine. Colin's mother ran both hands over her skull, smoothing down her already perfectly smooth hair, then sighed. "Colin, can I talk to you privately for a moment?"

"Sure." He put his bag of popcorn on the counter and slipped past Hannah. "I'll be back in two seconds," he assured her. Then he followed his mother into a room marked MANAGER'S OFFICE.

Hannah ate a few pieces of popcorn before realizing she wasn't hungry. She put her bag down, too, and looked at the concessions worker, feeling awkward. Clearly the other girl wasn't up for making conversation.

Hannah moseyed over to the nearest theater and glanced through the small, square window in the door to see a colorful cartoon playing on the oversize screen. Her phone buzzed in her bag. It had been so long since it had made a peep, she actually jumped.

The girl behind the counter glanced at her and Hannah blushed, embarrassed. She tugged her phone out and checked the screen. It was a text from her dad.

Hey kiddo! Haven't heard from you in a while. How's it going?

Hannah's palms began to sweat. This was it. This was her chance. There was no one around to stop her. She glanced over her shoulder again.

"Colin's pretty cool, huh?" the girl behind the counter said.

Hannah blushed even harder. Was she that obvious?

"I guess," she said, not wanting to share her actual feelings and thoughts with a stranger.

"He doesn't bring just anyone by here, you know," the girl said, closing her magazine. "Only the ones he really likes."

Hannah let out a laugh, wondering how many "ones" he'd "really liked" in the past.

She looked down at her phone again and bit her lip. She started to type before she could change her mind.

Sorry. Been busy. We're in town right now and all good.

She waited while her dad wrote back.

Katie OK?

Hannah gritted her teeth.

She's fine

You and Katie OK? ☺

Fine

OK let me know if you need anything

I will! Love you!

Love you too.

Trying not to feel guilty, Hannah stuffed the phone back in her bag and glanced around for something to occupy her while she waited for Colin. The concessions girl had now thankfully returned to her magazine. Hannah spotted a bulletin board on the wall, covered in flyers and ads and photographs. She walked over for a better look.

The overlapping flyers advertised everything from cat-sitting to private harp lessons. Dreardon Lake sure was an interesting town. Then Hannah noticed a pair of eyes staring out at her, and did a double take. It was a photograph, printed in black and white on light blue paper. The other flyers covered up everything but the eyes, which gave Hannah the eerie sensation that someone was staring out at her from the other side of the wall.

And even more freaky, the eyes . . . they could have been her own.

Same shape, same size, and if the photo were in color, she was certain the shade would be similar, too.

Hannah swallowed hard. Gathering up her nerve, she reached for the flyer blocking the bottom half of the girl's face. Her fingers were quaking.

"Whatcha doing?"

Hannah jumped and spun around. Alessandra was right behind her, along with Katie and Jacob.

"Nothing! Nothing, why?" Hannah's heart was like a bouncy ball inside her chest.

"I knew you guys would be here," Alessandra said. "Colin can't stay away from this place for more than a couple of hours at a time. It's why he thinks all movie versions are better than novel versions. He sees every movie ever."

Just then, Colin came out of the office with his mom and sauntered over. His mother cast one last glance over her shoulder at Hannah before disappearing around the corner. Colin's mom didn't look happy, but Colin was all smiles.

"Cool, you're all here," he said, rubbing his hands together. "Let's go back to the lake."

Dear Future Me,

I just read my last entry and OMG I can't believe I was being so morbid! Especially because right now at this very moment, I am the happiest I have ever been!!! I think I just had my first official date! Well, I guess it wasn't officially official because he didn't ask me and I didn't ask him, we just sort of bumped into each other at the Spring Festival, but then we spent the whole rest of the night together and it felt like a date and at the end he actually kissed me! Me! I swear I was starting to think I was never going to be kissed. I mean, how pathetic is it to get to fifteen years old without anything other than a couple of stupid, dry kisses at lame school dances? But here I am, telling you, I've finally been kissed for real.

And yes, I'm talking about N. As if you didn't know that. You're me. Just older. And if you don't remember who your first real kiss came from then I don't know you at all. Wait. Maybe you're MARRIED to N! Oh my God, I'm dying laughing right now. What if you're, like, THIRTY and you're reading this and you're MARRIED to N? You must be dying laughing, too.

Except no. I can't marry the first person I kiss. That would just be wrong. But MAYBE.

I'm getting off topic. So I bumped into N at the Ping-Pong game—the one no one ever wins because it's rigged—and he offered to buy me a lemonade. And A was really cool about me ditching her for a boy, because she knows how much I like him and besides, P and

some other people were there, too. So I went off with N and we had
the BEST time. We did bumper cars and he never even tried to
bump my car—just went after the little kids that were being
annoying. And we went on the swings and the Drop Zone. And then
he asked me if I wanted to go on the Ferris wheel and I said sure and
I just sort of KNEW, you know? You don't just go on a Ferris wheel
at Spring Festival alone with a guy and not expect to get kissed. But
then we went through the whole ride and even stopped at the top
where we could see the whole town and the stars and everything and
he DIDN'T KISS ME! I was so disappointed I actually almost said
something. But then afterward we went in the fun house and the first
dark room we walked into he pulled me to him and the next thing I
knew we were kissing. All these kids were running and screaming
around us like we weren't even there and I honestly felt like we
weren't even there because I felt like I was outside my body, floating,
just being perfectly happy somewhere.

And then he walked me home. Like a total gentleman. It was the
perfect night.

NINE

"You bought baseballs?"

Hannah stared at the ground, where Katie had just dumped the contents of her shopping bag from town. Hannah had been wondering what was in there, and now that she knew, she was still confused. Yes, Katie played varsity softball—was the starting first-base player for their high school, in fact, having bumped Missy Faulkner from her spot her senior year, which had not gone over well. But that didn't explain why there were now thirty scuffed—apparently used—baseballs rolling around at Hannah's feet.

"Why do they look so sad?" Hannah added, nudging a scratched one with her toe.

"Apparently, Greta at Sports Stuff pays this group of kids to go to all the ball fields after games and collect the forgotten balls," Jacob explained. He finished tethering his skiff to the dock, and walked over to join Colin where he stood on the grass. "Greta resells them for a dollar each. My dad says it's a total racket. Brilliant, but a total racket."

"So why did you *buy* them?" Hannah asked her stepsister. On the boat ride back from town, she'd almost felt a little bit sorry for Katie, who'd once again looked terrified crossing the lake. Hannah, who was still on edge, could empathize. Fortunately, they had made it back to Jacob's dock without incident.

"These guys don't believe I can hit an outside-the-park home run," Katie replied, tilting her head toward Jacob and Colin, who were now standing with their arms crossed, as if in challenge. She reached up to gather her long black hair into a high ponytail, holding the hair band between her teeth until she needed it. "So I'm gonna prove them wrong." She punctuated her declaration by snapping the hair band into place.

"Found it!" Alessandra called out, emerging from the house and tromping toward them. She swung an old-school wooden bat like a baton. "I'm so excited to watch you shut these guys up, Katie."

Alessandra handed the bat to Katie, who held it over her head with both hands and started to stretch out, bending backward so far her shirt rode up to expose her belly button ring. Jacob smacked Colin's chest with the back of his hand and Colin smirked appreciatively. Hannah wanted to vomit. Why couldn't guys ever stop acting like guys for five seconds in a row?

Oblivious to their ogling—or perhaps not—Katie continued her limbering routine, reaching to one side, then the other, and stretching her legs.

Maybe Hannah didn't feel so sorry for her after all.

While Katie stretched, Colin strolled over to Hannah and bumped her lightly with his shoulder. Which, of course, made her blush.

"What do you think, Webster?" he asked under his breath. His using her last name as a nickname sent a pleasant little thrill right through her. She glanced past him at Jacob to see if he was watching them. He was. "Can she do it?"

"If I told you what I know, wouldn't that be cheating?" Hannah whispered back. Her ears felt warm. She was flirting. With a hot guy. In front of Jacob. She thought back to how close she and Colin had been sitting, up in the projection room.

"I'll make it worth your while," he replied, and her blush deepened. Because what the heck did he mean by *that*?

"Oh, she can do it," Hannah answered truthfully. She didn't want to be petty by downplaying Katie's skill, and she was actually kind of proud of her stepsister's athletic prowess. If there was anything Hannah could appreciate in another person, it was commitment to a sport. And it *had* been pretty sweet when Katie's three-run homer in the seventh had wiped the grins off the Lakewood High fans' faces during the semifinal game back in May. "I've seen her hit a softball at least three hundred and fifty yards."

Colin grinned, which made Hannah's heart do a backflip.

"Ten bucks says she can hit it past the third buoy," he called out, turning toward Jacob and whipping a bill from his back pocket.

Jacob stared out at the lake toward Mystery Island, squinting against the bright sun. The third buoy had to be at least two hundred fifty yards offshore.

"I'll take that action," Jacob said. "She's good, but she's not that good."

Hannah tried not to smile. She was both gratified Jacob was betting against Katie and giddy over the fact that he was so going to lose. His school had played Oak View twice this season. Hadn't he heard what Katie could do? Hadn't Katie told him herself in the midst of all their secretive little text conversations?

"How many chances do we give her?" Colin asked.

"I say five," Jacob relied. "If she does it in five, you win. If not, I win."

"You're gonna regret that, Faber," Katie said, and winked at Jacob over her shoulder.

"Why'd you get baseballs instead of softballs?" Hannah asked Katie, leaning toward her so the boys couldn't hear.

Katie grinned at her. "Because baseballs are lighter."

Hannah grinned right back. Katie moved a couple of steps away so she could execute a few practice swings. The *whoosh* the bat made as it cut through the air made even the boys take notice.

Alessandra clapped her hands once. "So you need somebody to pitch to you, or . . . ?"

"No. That's fine. I got this," Katie replied. "Hannah, if you could just hand me a ball?"

Hannah bent and grabbed one of the dirtier baseballs. She gave it to Katie, then stepped back.

"Prepare to lose," Jacob teased Colin.

"Nah. I have a good feeling about this," Colin replied, crossing his arms over his broad chest and shooting Hannah another smile.

Katie tossed the ball so far into the air, Hannah lost it in the sun. Katie got into her batter's stance, swung, and *crack!* The ball went sailing out over the lake, but plopped into the water a good few yards before the third buoy.

"Ha! Told ya!" Jacob crowed.

"I'm just warming up," Katie chided, swinging her ponytail jauntily.

"Warm up fast," Colin said under his breath. "I got a tenner on this thing."

"Don't worry," Katie said with a wink. She was literally the only person Hannah knew who could pull off a wink without looking like a dork. "I got this." Then she turned to look over her shoulder. "Hannah?"

Hannah handed her another ball. Katie tossed it straight up again and swung. This time the ball was a line drive. It skidded across the surface of the water for a foot or two before being swallowed up just before the third buoy.

Hannah tensed up, suddenly struck by the eerie thought that *something* could have pulled the ball down.

Stop it, Hannah told herself firmly.

"How far out did it go?" she asked Jacob, shaking off her fear.

"Two hundred and fifty yards. About halfway between us and the island," Jacob said smugly.

Katie sighed, scowled, then held out her hand to Hannah. Hannah slapped a baseball into it silently. Her own adrenaline was up, which meant Katie's had to be sky-high. She wondered whether it would make Katie hit the ball farther, or throw her off her game.

Katie tossed the ball. It came down. Katie swung—and missed. The bat made an awful whipping sound as it caught nothing but air.

"Oh!" Jacob shouted, and both the boys laughed. Even Alessandra snickered.

"Whose side are you on?" Hannah said through her teeth.

"Sorry. Sorry." Alessandra waved it off and straightened her face. "You got this, Katie."

Hannah bent and picked up a fresh ball. This one looked fairly new. No visible marks anywhere. Katie took it, tossed it a couple of times, then threw it high.

Please hit it this time. Please hit it this time, Hannah prayed.

Crack!

The ball rocketed over the water in a high arc. It looked like something Big Papi would have hit at the Home Run Derby on All-Star Weekend. Everyone scurried to the edge of the lake. Hannah watched the ball cut through the sky and waited for the splash. It was definitely coming down beyond the buoy—the question was how far. She watched the water. And watched. And watched.

Out of nowhere, a shiver skittered down her spine, and she glanced around quickly, but there was nothing. Nothing near the house, nothing in the woods, nothing in the water.

Nothing. Not even a ball coming down from the sky to make a splash.

"Where'd it go?" Jacob asked. And then half a dozen birds took flight from the charred end of the island, squawking as their black bodies darted across the bright blue sky.

"Guys." Colin turned to them, his brown eyes bright. "I think it hit the island."

Jacob's face screwed up. "No. Freaking. Way."

Five minutes later, Jacob, Hannah, and Katie were back on the skiff, put-putting toward Mystery Island. Colin and Alessandra had stayed behind, claiming laziness. But Katie had finally overcome her terror of the water so that she could see for herself if she'd broken her own distance record. Hannah had felt a zing of pride for her stepsister as she'd watched her strap on her life jacket and decide to come along. If that ball was on the island, she wanted to help Katie gloat over it. Apparently, girl power trumped all else.

The closer they got to the island, the more Hannah found that she couldn't tear her eyes away from the blackened tree trunks and cracked branches. Some of the rocks were discolored, too, burnt until they looked like charcoal, or streaked with gray-and-white ash. She noticed the yellow-white insides of some shattered trees near the periphery of the destroyed section, jagged and pointing toward the sky like an accusation. It might have been her imagination, but Hannah could swear she smelled the scent of smoking wood. How could anyone do this to such a beautiful place?

"There's no way it's out here. We just missed the splash," Jacob said as he circled the shoreline, sticking to the healthy, verdant side of the island, looking for a safe spot to run the boat ashore.

"Please. All five of us? No way," Katie replied, fingernails digging into the straps of her life jacket.

"She's right," Hannah said. "You're gonna owe Colin ten bucks, guaranteed."

"And have to kiss my feet the rest of the time we're here," Katie added.

Jacob ignored them and maneuvered the boat into a little inlet, near where the living vegetation gave way to the dead. He dropped the small anchor and hopped out. The water came up to his knees. Hannah followed, the hems of her cargo shorts trailing through the water, and helped Jacob tug the boat a little bit closer to shore.

She couldn't believe she was really here—on the creepy island that had been haunting her since she arrived on Dreardon Lake.

Hannah and Jacob both helped Katie out of the skiff as she held her sandals aloft with one hand. She quickly ran up to dry land, then pushed her feet back into the shoes with a relieved breath.

"Mystery Island," Jacob said quietly.

"Freaky," Hannah replied, glancing around. She could see a skinny path cutting inward through the lush area.

"Have you ever been out here before, Jacob?" Katie asked, wrinkling her nose as she studied the charred trees.

"A couple times." Jacob shrugged. "There's really not much to see."

"Except a lone baseball, waiting somewhere to mock you with its very existence," Katie joked.

And all those burnt trees, Hannah thought, giving a little shiver.

Jacob rolled his eyes to the sky. "Let's go. If it's here, it's back this way."

He walked up into the underbrush and hooked a right. Hannah and Katie followed, shoving aside branches and trampling grasses and weeds. Every now and then, a stiff breeze would blow through, and Hannah could hear the decaying trees on the south side of the island groan and crack as if in pain.

They were moving uphill slightly, and the farther they walked, the less recognizable the path was. Then suddenly, they came to a bit of a clearing. Jacob tromped right across it, but Hannah paused. Right at her feet, there were strange trenches in the muddy earth, like something had been dragged across it recently. Here and there, the trenches disappeared—probably thanks to the recent rain filling them in, but there were definitely two long, thin tracks.

"What do you guys think this is?" Hannah asked.

Katie turned back and her brow furrowed. "Huh. I don't know."

"What?" Jacob was so far ahead he had to jog over to see. He stood next to Hannah, hands on hips. "That's weird."

"It looks like they end over there." Hannah began to follow the tracks.

"Hannah. Come on. You're going the wrong way," Katie chided. "The ball definitely fell closer to the burnt trees."

But Hannah's curiosity was piqued. Maybe it was all the mysteries she'd been reading lately. Maybe she was determined to get past her childish fear of the island, of the lake. But something was telling her to investigate. "You guys go ahead. I'll catch up in a second."

"Whatever, dude!" Jacob replied, and he and Katie headed off toward the south side of the island. It wasn't until they were out of sight that Hannah realized she'd just sent the guy she liked off alone with the girl who liked *him*. But she decided not to stress this time. It wasn't as if she could keep the two of them apart forever.

She looked back down at the trails and her fingertips prickled. Her neck went slick with sweat and once again, she felt like she was being watched, and not by her friends—by someone else. Some*thing* else? When she got to the edge of the clearing, she saw that the grasses on the other side were flattened in two long trails, but after a few feet, the trails ended. She swallowed hard, her eyes scanning ahead. Had someone created the trails? Who had been out there recently and what had they been doing?

And then, a shape caught her eye. There was something there—a dark lump on the ground.

"You guys."

No one answered her. They were too far away at this point to hear. Hannah stepped forward—one foot, then another. Her throat was dry. She reached out a hand and pushed aside a curtain of leaves. There, at her feet, was a small mountain of rocks. It was about a foot high and clearly man-made, carefully assembled with a wide base tapering to a point at the top. Beneath the rocks the earth looked dark, and there were more of those skinny trail marks.

"What in the world—"

"Hannah! Come on!" Jacob's voice sounded far off.

"I'm coming!" she shouted back.

Slowly, Hannah started to turn, and then noticed a flash of color in the brush. A flash of blue.

She took a couple of steps forward. It was the corner of a blue metal box, sticking out from under a sort of shelf made out of rock. Someone had clearly shoved the box in there to hide it, but hadn't covered it up very well.

The wind tickled the back of her head and the moaning of the trees intensified. Holding her breath, and feeling distinctly as if she was doing something she was not supposed to be doing, Hannah gripped the cold box between her hands and pulled it out. It was a bit wider and taller than a shoe box, and had a latch, but no lock. Turning her face away slightly, as if the thing might explode, Hannah undid the latch and flipped the box open. The hinge squealed, but the top swung harmlessly to the side.

"What the?" Hannah whispered.

Inside the box was a collection of random items—a blue hooded sweatshirt with a streak of mud on the sleeve, a University of Michigan iPhone case, a couple of hair ties, a set of keys with a glittery heart key chain, and—Hannah saw when she pushed the sweatshirt aside—a leather-bound journal. It was a small book—a little bit larger than Hannah's hand—and had clearly been used often.

Fingers trembling, Hannah opened the book to the first page. It was crinkled around the edges from water that had dried, but the wetness hadn't disturbed the words.

Dear Future Me, it read across the top of the page.

"Hannah!" Katie's voice shouted.

Startled, Hannah shoved the journal into the pocket of her cargo shorts and snapped it shut. Then she shoved everything else into the box and pushed it back into its hiding place, making sure it was entirely concealed this time. As she clambered to her feet, she wondered why she'd done any of it—taken the book, re-hidden the other things, or tried to hide them even better. But she had. And then Jacob and Katie were emerging from the woods and there was nothing she could do to fix it.

TEN

"You are never going to live this down!" Katie crowed, sitting on the front bench and holding up the baseball with her free hand. The other hand was, as always, clutching the boat's side.

"I know." Jacob rolled his eyes, but smiled. "You are a home-run goddess."

"I think he should just call me that from now on, don't you?" Katie grinned at Hannah, who forced a smile back. She was happy Katie had found the ball and Colin had won his bet and girl power had ruled the day, but she was still a little bit freaked out by what she'd found on the island. Why would someone leave a dirty hoodie and some random hair ties and all that other stuff out there? And why protect it all from the elements in a metal lockbox? The journal she could see wanting to keep intact, but what was so important about the rest of it?

The journal. It felt as if it was burning a hole through the fabric of her cargo shorts and leaving a mark on her thigh. Why had she taken it? Those were someone's private thoughts. She had no right to read them. Hannah had never kept a diary of her own, but if she did, she was sure she wouldn't want anyone else getting ahold of it. What if the book's owner came back to the island and found the diary missing? She—Hannah was sure that the small, loopy handwriting pegged the writer as a girl—was going to be so upset.

Hannah glanced over her shoulder at the eerie two-faced island, wishing she could think of a reason to get Jacob to turn back. From this angle, she could only really see the green, northern end, and she realized suddenly that Jacob wasn't heading for home.

"Where're we going?" she asked.

"I thought I'd take you guys around the north side so you could see Prandya and Raj's house," Jacob told her.

"And also so you could avoid Colin and Alessandra for longer?" Katie teased.

Jacob half frowned, half smirked. "That, too."

"I must have hit that ball at least seven hundred yards," Katie said.

"Try five hundred," Hannah replied automatically.

"What?" Katie snapped.

"Five hundred. If the buoy is at two-fifty and that's halfway between the shore and the island, that's five hundred. The southern part of the island is actually wider, so it was probably even shorter than that."

Katie rolled her eyes and scoffed. "Okay, four-point-oh. We all get it. You're smarter than me."

"Um, what are you talking about?" Hannah asked.

"It's not like I got the equation wrong, okay?" Katie said. "I was just exaggerating. Or am I not allowed to do that around you?"

"Ladies, ladies, please tell me we're not getting involved in a math-based fight right now," Jacob said. "It's summer, for the love of Pete!"

"Whatever." Katie tossed the ball to Jacob, who caught it one-handed. Then she reached up, undid the clasps on her life jacket, and shook it off her shoulders. She leaned back on her hands, letting her hair cascade between her shoulder blades. It was a decidedly casual pose, but Hannah could see that Katie's elbows were trembling, probably from a combination of nervousness and anger.

"Katie? What're you doing?" Jacob asked, placing the ball at his feet and keeping his other hand on the rudder.

"That thing was suffocating me," Katie replied, tossing her head so her hair rearranged itself into even more perfect waves. The boat turned slightly and Katie flailed to grip the side, then blushed and let go again when she realized she wasn't going over. "And besides, the sun is finally out for real and I'm not going back to school next week with weird tan lines."

"Katie," Hannah said in a warning tone.

"*Hannah*," Katie shot back. "You're not my mother. Don't tell me what to do."

"Okay. Fine." Hannah raised her hands. "Your funeral."

Katie glowered at Hannah until Hannah finally looked away.

"Whoa. Is that Prandya and Raj's house?" Hannah asked in shock.

Off to her right, a huge, modern structure rose out of the trees. It was all glass along the lake-facing side and gray shingle everywhere else, with a rooftop walk that probably offered an amazing sunset view. An elaborate set of stairs led from a huge deck down to a wide dock, where cushy-looking chaises were lined up facing the water. A second dock had at least six slips for boats, three of which were full, and Hannah could also see the Jet Skis tied off, bobbing in the water.

"That's it," Jacob said ruefully, and slapped at a bug on his arm. "I'd hate them if it wasn't for Raj and all the free pizza."

Katie laughed at his joke, but it sounded strained. "Prandya was pretty cool, too, though. Great style," she added. "How long have you known them?"

"Since we were little," Jacob said. "Our families always hang out together when we're up here. Their dad's, like, the ultimate outdoorsman. He owns that catalog. You know, Edward Ollis? They sell camping gear and fly-fishing equipment that only, like, Hollywood actors can afford."

"I bet they've had some serious parties out at that house," Hannah said, studying the cool-looking deck.

Katie laughed wryly. "Do you even know what a serious party looks like?"

Hannah's skin went hot and she shot a glare at her stepsister. "What's the matter with you?" she asked.

"Dude, chill," Katie said. "It's just a fact."

"Don't tell me to chill." Hannah could feel the last of her patience disappearing. "So what if I'm not a huge party animal and like to do well in school? Does that really make me so uncool?" she demanded. "There's nothing wrong with being smart, Katie. And it's not like I don't have fun."

Katie barked a laugh. She sat up and turned all the way around on her seat so she was finally facing Hannah. The boat rocked with her movement, but for once she didn't even seem to notice.

"Please," she said, planting her feet squarely on the metal bottom of the boat with a thud. "When was the last time you had fun? And going out for ice cream with your little swim team pals doesn't count."

"First of all, that *is* fun!" Hannah said, leaning forward. "But you wouldn't know that because you never bothered to come along, and secondly, *this trip* would've been fun if you hadn't glommed your way onto it uninvited!"

"I *was* invited!" Katie snapped. "Jacob was just too big of a wuss to tell you!"

Hannah turned to glare at Jacob.

"Okay, let's not drag the innocent bystander into the sisterly squabble," Jacob said, raising the hand that wasn't busy steering the boat.

"We're *not* sisters!" Hannah and Katie both shouted at the same time.

Well, at least we agree on something, Hannah thought, her scowl deepening.

"Ooookay," Jacob said.

"And news flash, Hannah. It wasn't even Jacob that wanted to invite you," Katie continued. "It was Colin."

Dead. Silence. Hannah's chest heaved as she attempted to catch her breath. She turned and looked at Jacob, whose guilty expression said it all.

"Excuse me?" Hannah said finally.

"He . . . he saw your picture on my phone," Jacob said. "The selfie we took at the wedding. It's my wallpaper," he added gamely, as if that was going to make her feel better.

"And?" Hannah prompted.

"And he thought you were cute and suggested I invite you up for a few days. That's all." Jacob shrugged with his hands, removing them briefly from the boat's rudder.

Hannah's eyes prickled. "So this whole weekend was a setup? You were setting me up with Colin?"

"No! No! Not exactly," Jacob said, and shot Katie an annoyed look. Somehow this just irked Hannah more. It reminded her that these two now had secrets. From her. "I wanted you to come, I just . . . didn't think of it myself at first!" He swallowed audibly. "Colin gave me the idea, that's all." He glanced nervously at Katie. "I wanted both of you to come."

Hannah pressed the heels of her hands into her eye sockets until she saw spots. Colin thought she was cute. Colin told Jacob to invite her there. And she'd accepted.

"Does he think I know about this? Did he think I *came* here as, like, a *date* for him?" she demanded.

"No. Not at all. I just—"

"So what if he did?" Katie cut in. "Would that be *so* horrible? A cute guy thinking you two had a shot? Or is romance part of your fun allergy?"

"Oh, shut up, Katie."

"Shut up?" Katie screeched. "Shut up? What are we, five?"

"Ladies, please!" Jacob tried again. "Look around you! It's a beautiful day, we're out on the lake, and we have a whole day and night without parents to look forward to. Why don't we just—"

Suddenly the engine sputtered, and then died. Silence.

Jacob's face fell.

Katie's forehead crinkled. "Um, what just happened?"

"I don't know." Jacob turned around and yanked the rip cord on the engine. There was a violent whirring, but then nothing. He pulled again, then again, but the engine refused to turn over.

"Is it jammed?" Hannah asked. She knew from the few boating trips she and her dad had taken that sometimes vegetation in lakes and ponds could get sucked into the engine and stall it. The reeds would get wrapped up around the propeller and jam the mechanism.

"I don't think so," Jacob said, popping the engine up out of the water on its hinge so he could inspect it. "How could it be? We're in the middle of the lake and this is the deepest part. There's nothing growing out here."

"The deepest part?" Katie asked tremulously. She grabbed up her life jacket and began to fumble with the straps.

Hannah looked over the side of the boat at the water. Even in the heat of midafternoon, she felt a sudden chill and all the tiny hairs on her arms stood up. Something wasn't right. The water looked dark. Too dark. Almost like ink or oil. At first, she thought a cloud must have blocked the sun, so she was looking at its shadow, but no. When she glanced back over her shoulder there wasn't a single cloud in the sky, and suddenly the sun felt very hot on the back of her neck.

Her heart thunked. That thing she'd seen in the lake that morning . . . had it been near here? As if that even mattered. It was a lake. It could be anywhere by now. Part of her wanted to tell Jacob and Katie about it: *Hey, guys . . . remember that lake monster Colin mentioned yesterday? Well, I think I saw it . . .*

But something held her back. Maybe the fact that she didn't want it to be real, and saying it aloud would make it real.

"You guys. Does the water look . . . weird to you?" she asked instead.

Katie clucked her tongue. "Hannah—"

Jacob looked up from the motor and glanced around. "No. She's right. It almost looks . . . thick."

Katie leaned over for a better look. At that moment, something bumped the underside of the boat. Katie yelped. She had her arms in the life jacket now, but hadn't had a chance to click the three buckles.

"What was that?" Hannah asked.

"I don't know." Jacob was pale.

"Jacob," Katie said calmly, though her knuckles were white as she gripped the seat at her sides. "Could you please get us out of here?"

"Uh-huh." Jacob shoved the motor back into place with a splash and yanked on the rip cord, then yanked again.

Nothing. Jacob's house looked so far away, suddenly, and they were drifting farther out, rather than closer. Hannah scanned the shoreline for Colin or Alessandra, but they must have gone inside. The house was perfectly still. She turned to look at Prandya's house, but the decks were all empty—not a soul in sight.

Someone, Hannah thought. *Someone do something.*

Another bump.

Then came a long, shoulder-curling *scraaaaaape* along the bottom of the skiff. It was like someone had taken a pirate's hook and dragged it across the metal. Or maybe it had been a claw. A long, sharp, blood-hungry claw . . .

Jacob cursed under his breath.

"Omigod. Omigod, you guys," Katie said, curling her knees up toward her chest.

Hannah's teeth clenched. "Jacob . . ."

"It's probably just a lake trout or something," he said, his voice tense. Sweat beads trickled down his temples. "They can get pretty big."

Suddenly the bow of the boat lifted up so high that when it came down again, it made a splash. This time, Hannah screamed, and Katie started crying, fumbling for the stays on her life jacket. Jacob reached for the cord but then the boat tilted sideways again and the cord slipped from his grasp. Hannah gripped the sides of the boat for dear life as Katie let out a screech and was thrown overboard.

ELEVEN

"She can't swim!" Hannah shouted, her voice cracking painfully. "She can't swim!"

Her fingers dug into the sides of the boat, her nails screeching on the metal as they clawed, sending teeth-jarring tremors up her arms. There was no way a lake trout was strong enough to lift the entire front end of the skiff with three people in it, nor tip it far enough for someone to tumble out. Something else was out there. That *thing*. And whatever it was, Katie was now in the water with it, her life jacket floating uselessly on the surface of the lake.

Why didn't I tell anyone what I saw? Hannah thought desperately, her brain whirling with terror and regret. *Why didn't I say anything?*

Hannah looked over her shoulder at Jacob, but he seemed frozen with fear. She ripped off her life jacket, yanked off her shorts, and dove into the lake in her bathing suit and T-shirt. Her muscles seized up the second they hit the cold water. So much colder than it had felt this morning. Was it because the lake was deeper out here, or was something really wrong with the water? She thought of how viscous and dark it had looked just moments ago and then shoved that thought away. If she dwelled on that, she'd have a panic attack, and that wasn't going to help anyone.

Holding her breath in her lungs, Hannah dove deep at the spot where Katie had gone under. There was another splash as Jacob finally shook himself out of his catatonic state and followed her down. Under the surface, Hannah opened her eyes, searching the murk for a flash of Katie's white tank top. Her eyes stung. She saw nothing. Even when she put her hand directly in front of her face, she could barely make out the blurry shape. She reached all four limbs out, stretching them until her joints locked, hoping to feel her toes or fingers brush Katie's arm or face or hair—and at the same time praying they wouldn't brush anything else.

The skull, she thought. *The hand* . . .

Her fingers caught on some reedy vegetation, and her toes slipped over something soft—more plants, she hoped—but there was nothing solid. She swam farther out, staying down, pushing her lungs to their breaking point. When they began to burn and beg for air, she shoved herself to the surface.

Her chest screamed as she sucked in a full breath and let the oxygen revive her. Hannah could hold her breath longer than anyone she'd ever met—two full minutes at last test. Her friends on the swim team had taken bets on how long she could last and no one had even come close. Hannah could remember sitting at the bottom of the room-temperature lap pool at her school, her legs crossed yoga style as she counted out all the Mississippis in her head, completely calm and cool and collected. This was nothing like that.

She dog-paddled for a few seconds to catch her breath. By her estimation, she'd probably been under for at least a minute and a half just now, and there was no sign of Katie. The lake around her was still. Disoriented, Hannah flailed in a circle until she spotted the boat.

It looked terrifyingly empty, bobbing on the surface. The sun reflected off the back of the skiff, and she had to squint her eyes shut. She heard something splash up out of the water and screamed.

"It's just me!" Jacob shouted, gasping for air.

Hannah wrenched one eye open, reaching her hand up to clear water and sunlight from the other. Jacob was treading water a good twenty yards away.

"Anything?" she shouted.

With nostrils flared, he shook his head, droplets of water arcing off his soaked hair.

Hannah started to swim toward him, and something caught at her ankle. She let out a mewl and kicked at it. After a brief struggle, she was free. More lake plants. Apparently Jacob had been wrong about there not being vegetation this far out.

"I'm going down again!" he shouted, and before she could reply, he was gone.

Hannah dove down, too, but she couldn't see Jacob or Katie or anything else for that matter. When she resurfaced, she spotted someone pacing on the shoreline in front of Jacob's house— Colin, she was pretty sure—but he was so far away, he wouldn't have understood her if she tried to shout. She flailed her arms instead, hoping he would figure out something was wrong and call for help.

What was he doing over there? Was he talking on his phone? How could he be if there was no service? When Colin didn't stop walking back and forth, Hannah gave up trying.

Where the hell was Jacob? She'd already been above water for at least thirty seconds, and he'd been under since before that. Where *was* he? Had something gone wrong? Was he caught in the weeds?

Katie, where are you? Tears suddenly filled Hannah's eyes and a sob caught in her throat, making it harder to tread water. Her stepsister had been under for a couple of minutes now. She'd probably sucked in water on her way down, inexperienced as she was with swimming and survival tactics. If her lungs had filled, she would have sunk like a stone. What if she was at the bottom of the lake? What if she'd drowned, right beneath Hannah's toes?

The sob escaped and Hannah swam as hard as she could toward the boat. She needed to hang on to something or she was going to go down, too. She was a few yards from the skiff when Jacob broke the surface right next to it, scaring the living daylights out of Hannah. She let out a yelp when she saw that Jacob had one arm around Katie's upper torso. Katie flailed her arms and coughed, spitting up lake water and some sort of brown goop, but she was alive. She was breathing.

"Katie!" Hannah shouted in relief.

"You're okay," Jacob said to Katie, using his free arm to crawl toward the boat. "You're okay now, Katie, you need to calm down."

"Something grabbed me!" Katie sputtered. "Something's down there, Jacob. Get me out of this water. *We have to get out of here!*"

Jacob turned in a slow circle, found Hannah, and shot her a *help me* look. Hannah swam over to them. Her lungs and throat burned and her legs were beginning to feel the strain of so much treading under so much duress, but she managed to keep her head and shoulders above water.

"Katie, take a deep breath," she said as calmly as she could. Her own breath was of the panting variety, thanks to all the terror. "Jacob can't get you back to the boat if you're flailing, and if you don't stop, you're both going to drown."

It was as if Katie didn't even hear her. She just kept throwing out her arms and kicking her legs, pushing herself and Jacob farther from the skiff. Hannah grabbed Katie's wrist as it came close to whacking her across the face.

"Katie Marie Chen! Stop it now!" she shouted.

Katie instantly went still. She blinked, surprised, and then started to cry, going completely limp. But at least she wasn't freaking out anymore, and it was a lot easier to drag dead weight through the water. Jacob shot Hannah a grateful, exhausted look, took a deep breath, and paddled for the boat one-handed. Hannah swam ahead and grabbed the hull to tug it closer to him and give him less distance to cross. Finally, they got to the skiff's side and placed Katie's hands over the edge, so that they gripped the rim. Then Jacob crawled into the boat to counterbalance it and pulled on Katie's arms, while Hannah did her best to push her stepsister up from behind. After what felt like a lifetime of struggling, Katie and Jacob tumbled back onto the bare metal floor of the skiff. Then Jacob reached over to help Hannah up as well. She was grateful. At this point, her arms and legs were like jelly. Swimming for her life was a lot different from swimming to beat her own best time.

On the bench in the center of the boat, Katie and Jacob gripped each other.

"Why'd you take off your stupid life jacket?" Jacob demanded, reaching up to hold both sides of Katie's face in his hands.

"I'm sorry! I'm really sorry," Katie replied, heaving with sobs.

Hannah looked away. It was an oddly intimate moment and now was not a time to wallow in jealousy. Katie was alive. That was all that mattered.

"It's fine. Everyone's fine," Jacob said. He stumbled to the rear of the boat and took his position by the motor again. "Let's just get back to the dock."

"There's something out there," Katie said, sniffling. She touched the side of her hand to her nose. "Something grabbed me."

Hannah and Katie locked eyes. "So you felt it, too?" Hannah said.

Katie nodded, a movement so small it was almost imperceptible. "It felt like a hand . . . it grabbed my ankle and pulled me down. I swear. Someone . . . some . . . *thing* was trying to drown me."

"It was just the weeds," Jacob said stiffly. "One of them probably wrapped around your ankle and you got tangled up. That's all. There was way more vegetation out there than I thought there'd be."

"It wasn't a *weed*," Katie protested. "I felt it . . . I felt its flesh."

Hannah shuddered.

The three of them glanced around the lake, which was now silent. Was something circling beneath the boat right now? Were they about to be tipped again?

Jacob tried the rip cord. The motor whirred for half a second— a pathetic, high-pitched sound—and then stopped.

"That's it. We're rowing out of here," Jacob said, getting up and plopping down on the middle bench next to Hannah. "Katie, sit at the front. Hannah, grab that oar."

Hannah scooted over a bit to give them more room to maneuver, her bare thighs sticking painfully to the bench. Jacob lifted the oar out of the inside of the boat and turned it, locking it into its bracket on his side of the boat. Hannah did the same on her side.

"You ready?" Jacob asked, looking her fiercely in the eye. He was scared, and trying very hard not to show it.

Hannah nodded. "Ready."

They placed the paddles in the water.

"And, pull!" Jacob said.

They started to row, and Hannah instantly felt the relief of doing something active—something to help. The boat moved slowly at first, but as she and Jacob got into a rhythm, it started to fly over the water, the breeze hitting the cold droplets on her neck and cooling her adrenaline. Her eyes focused on the spot where the boat had been at the moment Katie had gone over, searching for anything out of the ordinary, but there was nothing, so she lifted her gaze. Instead, she watched the far shoreline grow more and more distant, and, with every yank of the oar, felt a little bit freer of the terror.

Whatever was out there, they were escaping it now. Katie was fine. It hadn't won.

"We're almost there," Katie called.

Hannah glanced over her shoulder. She could see both Colin and Alessandra at the shoreline now. Alessandra wore a bathing suit and her hair was wet from swimming. Colin shaded his eyes with one hand. Hannah was surprised at the sudden desperation she felt at the sight of him, and she rowed even faster. It didn't matter what Katie had told her. All that mattered right then was how she felt in this moment of total panic. And in this moment, all she wanted to do was get back to the shore, explain to Colin everything that had happened, and let him tell her everything was going to be all right.

Half an hour later, after the story had been rehashed twenty times and Alessandra and Jacob had insisted that the whole lake monster thing was just a myth, while Colin sat mostly quiet and eyed Hannah concernedly, Hannah and Katie went upstairs to shower and change. The second they got to their room, Katie closed the door behind them and grabbed Hannah's arm.

"I don't care what they say. There's totally something out there," she whispered.

"I know!" Hannah whispered back.

They sat down next to each other on the springy mattress and Hannah drew one leg up to turn sideways. Katie did the same, so that they were mirror images of each other. Katie's hair had half dried into knotted clumps on her shoulders, and her eyeliner was smeared down her face but she didn't reach for a mirror or her phone to check her reflection or fix anything—which told Hannah that she was legitimately freaked out.

"It felt like a cold, hard hand," Katie said, and shuddered. "And it was strong. Is that what you felt?"

"Sort of," Hannah replied. "It felt like a hand, but it felt soft—almost . . . rubbery?" Katie made a grossed-out face. "I didn't feel anything hard until I kicked out, and then my foot hit a rock or something," Hannah finished.

"Or maybe a skull," Katie replied.

Hannah let out a nervous laugh. "I thought that, too. But . . . come on . . . what are we saying here? There are skeletons in the lake? Zombies?"

"I have no idea, but I know I felt something," Katie said, glancing over her shoulder at the wide stretch of water outside the window. "And I know the whole idea of a lake monster sounds certifiable, but aren't those sorts of rumors usually based on some kind of fact? Like, someone must have seen *something* at some point."

Hannah hesitated half a second, chewing on her lip. "I wasn't going to tell you this, but . . ."

Katie's face was pale, but her eyes were bright with interest when she refocused on Hannah. "Tell me what?"

Hannah stood up and walked to the window, pushing the curtain aside slightly to look out. The lake looked beautiful just then, the afternoon sunlight glinting off the ripples in the deeper water— nothing but cerulean blue as far as the eye could see.

"I saw something out there this morning," Hannah said quietly. "After my swim, when you guys were down by the dock and I was up here alone."

"What do you mean *something*?" Katie asked. "What was it?"

"I don't know. It was . . . I think it was some kind of animal, but it wasn't like any animal I'd ever seen before." She shivered at the memory and turned her back on the lake, hugging her suddenly goose-bump-covered arms. "It was all gray and grotesque and malformed."

"Oh my God!" Katie whispered, standing as well and hugging her elbows tightly. She looked younger suddenly, like a little girl who had been playing in her mother's makeup case. "Do you think it was the monster? Do you think that was what tipped the boat?"

"I honestly have no idea. But it was definitely big enough," Hannah said, lifting her shoulders tight near her ears. "It sounds insane, I know, and I thought I imagined it. Like maybe all that stuff Colin and Alessandra told us was just messing with my brain, or that maybe it was a trick of the light. But now . . ."

Katie walked up next to her and they both gazed out at the water. Hannah could feel an electric charge running between them, and realized it felt kind of nice to agree with Katie on something. To be in it together for once. Even though *it* was something impossible and fairly terrifying. Couldn't they have bonded over the last season of *The Bachelor* or something?

"Okay, there's no way," Katie said finally, throwing up her hands. "I mean, a lake monster? Come on. We're losing our minds here."

Hannah laughed uncomfortably. "You're right. You're so right. We're just imagining things."

"Exactly. I probably only thought I felt something because you thought you felt something," Katie said.

Hannah nodded. "I mean, Jacob and his family have been coming here for years and no one has ever mentioned a legendary lake monster before. It has to be a joke . . . right?"

"Exactly! So there's nothing out there. It's just your average, run-of-the-mill lake," Katie said. "Right?"

Hannah nodded once, resolutely. "Right."

"Those guys just made up the whole lake monster thing to mess with us."

"Sure," Hannah said.

"So let's not bring this up again." Katie grabbed a towel and some clothes, holding them in a ball against her chest. "We don't want them to think they got to us—that we're believing their crazy story, right?"

Hannah nodded, and they held each other's gaze in a silent promise. Then Katie walked out, headed for the bathroom and what Hannah assumed would be a long, hot, mind-erasing shower. As soon as Katie was gone, Hannah grabbed the blind and pulled it down over the window, casting the room in relative darkness.

"Right."

"You guys! Nick and Raj are here!" Jacob called up the stairs just as Katie walked back into the room fully clothed, with a towel wrapped around her hair.

Hannah's heart sank. She'd been hoping to take some time for herself to read and calm her nerves. But now, more socializing. Fan. Tas. Tic.

"Cool! We'll be right down," Katie called out.

"Actually, I think I'm gonna take a shower, too," Hannah said, grabbing a towel and some clothes.

"Okay. I'm gonna go downstairs and tell Nick and Raj about my epic home run." Katie grinned and tossed her wet towel on the chair, turning to the window to start combing through her hair. "Just come down when you're done."

Wow. That shower really was mind-erasing, Hannah thought. Apparently, the trauma of a near-death experience was easy to shake off.

Hannah sighed. Laughter wafted into the house from the front yard and Hannah could hear a motor revving—probably a Jet Ski or small boat. Maybe if she took a long enough shower, everyone would forget about her, and she could hide out with her book until Nick and Raj went home.

She walked to the bathroom, which was full of steam, and turned the water back on. She unbuttoned her shorts and they fell to the floor with a *thwap*, heavier than they should have been. It wasn't until that moment that she remembered the diary. She crouched down and fished it out of her shorts pocket, glancing over her shoulder as if someone was about to walk in on her. With a flick of her wrist, she locked the door.

Using a washcloth, Hannah cleared a section of the mirror of condensation and looked herself in the eye. Was she really going to do this? She swallowed hard and turned away. Yes, in fact, she was. Just a couple of pages. Just to see what sort of person would hide their diary in a lockbox on an island in the middle of a lake.

She sat down on top of the toilet seat, opened the diary, and began to read.

Dear Future Me,

N and I have gone out on three real dates now. Three! He asked me to Slices and then I asked him to the Star Wars *movie marathon at the theater* and tonight we went water-skiing on the lake. True, P and R came with us to water-ski. But it still ended up being the best time ever.

You remember that high drop-off on the northwest side of Dreardon Lake? Well, after we went water-skiing, N got P to drop us off at the bottom of the hill alone together so we could hike up there and explore. He said he's been there a few times and he really likes it because it's so peaceful and you can see all the stars. He called it his "special place" and he was so sweet about the fact that he was sharing it with me, like it was a big deal to him. We walked along the cliffs as far as we could go—there's one point that's too rocky and there are all these trees, so we had to double back. And then we sat out on the rocky outcropping and looked at the sky. And then, well, he kissed me. Again. It was amazing.

On the way back down, he showed me this little clearing where he'd left a fire pit behind from a night he came camping out there all by himself. He got a little misty-eyed when he talked about getting out of his house to be alone and it made me wonder if maybe there's something going on there. Maybe with his parents or something? I don't know. I didn't want to ask because it felt too personal or *too forward or something. But maybe one day he'll tell me on his own.*

I feel really close to him now—closer than I've ever felt to any other guy. Is that cheesy to say? I don't care. I hope he takes me out to his special place again. Maybe one night we could camp out there together, just the two of us, and he'll tell me everything about him. I want to know it all.

TWELVE

Hannah ended up reading more than a couple of pages—a lot more. She probably would have stayed up there all night, reading the entire diary, if Jacob hadn't called her down for dinner. Reluctantly, she stashed the book away in her bag, took a quick shower, and came downstairs, her thoughts swirling.

The story about the girl committing suicide in the lake had been super disturbing to read. As if Hannah needed to be *more* creeped out by the water just outside the front door.

One thing was clear, though—whoever had written the journal lived in town. And Hannah had a feeling that the girl was friends with Alessandra and Prandya. It was the description of the surprise slumber party that had started her thinking about it—the details about the sick house owned by "P." There was no way that was a coincidence. And if P was Prandya, then there was a good chance that the writer's friend A was Alessandra. It wasn't foolproof, but Hannah had a feeling she was right.

She considered asking Alessandra about it, but then Hannah would have to admit she'd stolen the journal—and that she'd read it—which was not going to happen. She'd just have to figure out a way to get the book back out to the island before the writer realized it was gone.

But clearly, that wasn't going to happen tonight—not with all these people around.

For dinner, Jacob and Colin had put together a pretty decent meal of grilled chicken and vegetables, which would be chased by a dessert of s'mores roasted over the outdoor fire pit. Hannah scarfed down the meal, starving from the long and full day. The conversation around the dinner table was upbeat and shallow. Raj started telling stories about the worst teachers he'd ever had, and others joined in to share, as if it was a competition.

Hannah thought about chiming in, but whenever she looked up, she caught Nick staring at her, which made it hard to focus. Plus, Nick and Colin definitely didn't like each other. Every time one of them spoke, the other one either laughed mockingly or said something derisive. The tension was thick enough that it felt like a heavy blanket set to suffocate them all. At least, that was how it felt to Hannah. No one else seemed to notice.

"You guys ready for dessert?" Jacob asked, pushing back from the table.

"So ready," Colin replied.

And Nick rolled his eyes.

Hannah stifled a yawn as she stood up. She was exhausted and kind of just wanted to crawl into bed, but s'mores also sounded pretty good.

Colin and Alessandra gathered the chocolate, marshmallows, and graham crackers from the kitchen while Jacob, Katie, and Raj went outside to find some sticks to use as skewers. Hannah took a blanket off the couch and slowly followed the others, trying to ignore the fact that Nick was hovering behind her.

The night air out on the lake was cool. Hannah wrapped the worn, red blanket around her shoulders, craving not just warmth but comfort.

"You cold?" Nick asked as he trailed her outside. "You can borrow my hoodie."

He made as if to take off his black sweatshirt and Hannah held up a hand. "No. That's okay. I like the blanket. Thanks, though," she added, when his face sort of fell.

Nick jogged down the steps ahead of her, head down as if in a sulk. Hannah stepped onto the grass. The light of the half-moon shone on the water's surface and stars sprinkled the night sky. All the beauty of it was lost on Hannah, though. The breadth of the lake confronted her, and she physically itched to escape it all.

I should steal Jacob's phone, call my dad, and tell him to come get me, she thought. *I just want to go home.*

But down the hill the others were laughing and tearing open bags of marshmallows while Alessandra got the fire going. Hannah blew out a sigh and reluctantly joined them, pulling over one of the wood benches Jacob's dad had apparently fashioned out of fallen tree trunks. They weren't super comfortable—or super level—but it was all part of the ambiance.

"I'll just have a marshmallow," Katie volunteered as Jacob started to push the marshmallows onto skinny sticks. "I'm not really a big fan of chocolate."

"Okay, weirdo," Jacob teased her, knocking her knee with his own. "One toasted marshmallow coming up."

"I like mine burnt," Raj said, pulling up another bench, and Nick sat down next to him.

"The key to a good s'more is getting the hot marshmallow onto the chocolate right away," Colin instructed, laying graham crackers out on a plastic plate and then carefully positioning chocolate bars on top of them. "It's all about the melt."

"Who're you, Bobby Flay?" Nick snapped.

"I agree," Hannah said, shooting Colin a smile as she gamely tried to join in on the fun. "There's nothing worse than hard chocolate inside a s'more."

Nick grumbled something under his breath and pulled out his phone, facing away from the fire. Hannah and Katie exchanged a look. *What's up with this guy?*

Soon, they all had their skewers and Alessandra managed to get the fire roaring. They sat around the fire pit in a circle, Hannah between Katie and Colin, and let their marshmallows get nice and toasty. As soon as Hannah withdrew hers from the fire, Colin was ready with the graham crackers and chocolate. She mushed her sandwich together and then took a big bite.

Perfection.

Okay, so maybe she didn't need to go home just yet.

"So have you guys told Katie and Hannah about the ghost?" Raj asked, licking some melted chocolate off his fingers.

Jacob and Colin both groaned, and Nick looked up with interest.

"Can we not?" Alessandra said.

"What?" Raj was all wide-eyed innocence. "Isn't that what you do around a campfire? Tell ghost stories? We're just lucky enough to have stories that are actually true."

"What do you mean, *true*?" Hannah asked, glancing at Katie, who looked like she was bracing herself for some really bad news. "Have you ever seen a ghost up here?"

"I haven't *seen* any," Raj said. "But I mean, with all the drownings, this lake has to have some serious ghost stuff happening."

The drownings. All *the drownings.* Hannah's throat was dry.

Unbidden, the creepy diary entry about the girl who had drowned herself sprang to mind.

"Um, who drowned?" Katie asked. Her eyes were enormous. Hannah knew she had to be remembering her own close call earlier that day.

"Okay, I just want to go on record as saying I did *not* want to talk about this." Jacob grabbed another three marshmallows, stabbed through them with his skewer, and scowled as he roasted them. His curls danced in the glow from the fire.

Hannah glanced toward the lake. She saw something bubble up, but then the bubbles popped. Just one of the amphibians coming up for air, she was sure.

"Back in the early two thousands, there were a bunch of random drownings up here," Alessandra said, leaning close to the fire to toast her marshmallow. "All these people, some of them even really experienced swimmers, drowned in the lake for no apparent reason. It was almost like . . . a pattern. A trend."

"A drowning *trend*?" Hannah said.

"Yeah," Jacob said, his eyes flashing. "It's why my dad got this house for so cheap. No one wanted to buy on Drowning Lake."

Hannah's dinner hardened in her stomach and she immediately regretted the s'more. "*Drowning Lake?* That's an awful nickname."

"I know. It wasn't something *I* came up with," Jacob said. "It's just something people say."

Hannah's skin crawled. She glanced up from the fire and saw Nick glaring right at her, and she quickly looked away. No wonder this whole place gave her the creeps. There was actually a dark history here. She thought of Alessandra's friend Claudia—the one who'd gone missing without a trace.

"How many people . . . died?" Katie asked in a whisper.

"How many drownings?" Raj took a big bite out of another s'more as if they were discussing the latest series to binge watch, rather than a bunch of people dying horrible deaths, possibly yards from where they now sat. "I don't know exactly."

"Fourteen," Colin said flatly. "At least, that's what I heard."

"Fourteen?" Hannah repeated incredulously. She was starting to sweat, and not from the fire.

"Yeah. This one distance swimmer from Pennsylvania—she, like, swam the English Channel or something—even drove out here to prove the lake wasn't cursed, and she drowned during her second lap around the island," Alessandra explained, wide-eyed. "How freaky is that?"

Hannah really didn't understand how they could be so casual about this. They were talking about real people who had drowned just yards from where they now sat, merrily making s'mores. And Alessandra's own friend had disappeared not that long ago. What if that girl Claudia had fallen victim to this . . . curse? *Was* the lake actually cursed? Hannah shuddered just thinking about it. It all crowded in her head: Alessandra's friend, the diary, the girl she had read about who had drowned herself . . .

And then, like a bolt of lightning to the chest, it hit her. *The diary.* In the diary, if A was Alessandra and P was Prandya, could the girl writing it . . . could *Dear Future Me* be . . . Claudia?

Hannah's heart raced and she felt light-headed. The fire seemed to flare hotter against her face, and when she breathed in the ash she felt like she might faint.

Colin cleared his throat. "Anyway, supposedly those fourteen souls haunt the lake, looking for new souls to join them."

There was a long silence, interrupted only by the crackling of the fire. Hannah felt the fingers closing around her ankle as she raced Jacob. She saw that gray, wrinkled . . . *thing* rising out of the lake from her window. Felt the *bump* under the boat and heard the *scrape*. Saw Katie go flying and heard her scream.

It was too much. It was just too much.

Katie was staring her down, but Hannah refused to look at her. She couldn't.

Could it have been the fourteen ghosts out there, trying to drown us? Throwing Katie into the lake?

Did she even believe in ghosts? Hannah wasn't sure. She'd never had to think about it before now.

She tried to take another deep breath and coughed.

"Are you okay?" Colin asked, patting her on the back.

Hannah put her head between her legs and took a few deep, bolstering breaths, trying to get ahold of herself. Finally, when she felt able to sit up straight again, she looked right at Jacob.

"Why haven't you ever told me this?" she demanded.

"Because!" He rounded his shoulders, clearly prepared to go on the defensive. "First of all, no one told me these stories until last summer. It's not like my dad sat me down to tell me why the cost of real estate around here was so low. But last year I overheard something at a party and asked my dad about it so then he had to tell me."

"So you could have told me *then*," Hannah said.

"Yeah, but why? Why freak you out?" Jacob asked. "I mean, I've been coming up here for years and I swear, nothing weird has ever happened before."

"Until today," Hannah muttered under her breath.

Jacob's marshmallows caught fire and he pulled them out quickly, blowing the flames out. "Okay, fine. What happened on the lake today was weird, but all this haunting stuff? It's just stories. No one here actually believes in ghosts, right?"

He looked around the group beseechingly. They were all quiet as they glanced at one another, gauging the general mood.

"No. Of course not," Katie said at last, and gave a dismissive laugh. "That's ridiculous."

"Totally," Colin said, and shot Hannah a reassuring look.

From somewhere in the distance, there came a high-pitched shriek that raised all the hairs on the back of Hannah's neck. Everyone froze as the screech went on and on and then finally, pathetically, died away. There was half a second of silence, and then they all laughed. Everyone except Nick. He stared into the distance as if he could see something the rest of them couldn't.

"Probably just a screech owl," Colin said.

Hannah nodded, but she couldn't relax. She had an awful feeling that she was going to be hearing that sound in her dreams.

THIRTEEN

"Are you sure that wasn't human?" Hannah asked a few minutes later. The conversation had continued, but Hannah hadn't said a word. She could still feel the scream down the back of her neck as if it was a tangible thing.

"Honestly, Hannah. It was an owl," Jacob said, shifting in his seat and glancing up at the dark night sky. "Or some other kind of bird."

"A bird with excellent dramatic timing," Alessandra said wryly, looking over her shoulder at the trees.

"It's really fine," Colin said, reaching around to give Hannah's shoulder a squeeze. Nick stared at Colin's arm as if he was trying to incinerate it with his heat vision.

"I'm going inside."

Hannah stood and handed her skewer off to Katie so quickly that Katie fumbled it into the dirt, ruining the marshmallow. Hannah didn't care. She stepped over the bench, clinging to the blanket around her shoulders. Now that she'd started thinking that the journal's author might be Claudia, she was dying to read more. Maybe there was some clue as to what had happened to her—where she had gone.

"Come on, Hannah. Don't get scared off," Jacob chided.

Hannah paused before turning around. "I'm not scared. It's

just . . . somebody's gotta do the dishes and I know it's not gonna be you."

Jacob nodded. "Fair point."

"I'll help," Alessandra said, dusting her hands off on the back of her jeans. "It's too cold out here anyway."

Hannah waited for Alessandra to catch up to her and they walked inside together. After clearing the table, they stood at the sink, Hannah washing and Alessandra drying. The silence was companionable, but Hannah was bursting with questions she wasn't sure how to ask. She scrubbed a platter with a brush, her arms halfway submerged in sudsy warm water, enjoying the mundane normalcy of the chore. All the time, though, she was aware of the lake outside the window as if it were a living, breathing thing.

"What's your friend's name again? The one who disappeared?" Hannah asked finally, even though she remembered quite well.

"Claudia?" Alessandra said, wiping the water from a small plate. "What about her?"

Hannah scrubbed at a stubborn barbecue-sauce stain, her skin aflame with nerves. "Did they look for her here by the lake?"

"They looked *everywhere*," Alessandra said. "Why?"

"Just . . . when you live near a place called Drowning Lake . . ."

Alessandra let out a short laugh. "You think she drowned out there? No way. Claudia hated swimming. She never would have gone out there on her own—especially not at night. She was afraid of her own shadow."

She turned to put the plate away and sighed as she gazed out the window. Hannah couldn't imagine what it would be like, always wondering what had happened to someone she cared about. Wondering if they'd been hurt, if they'd been scared, if they were . . .

"But they did trawl the lake looking for her, just in case," Alessandra added, closing the cabinet door. "Her mom was a mess that week."

Hannah shivered, remembering the story from the diary— how they'd found that girl . . . what were the words the writer had used? *Bloated and veiny.* Should she tell Alessandra about the journal? Or wait until she knew for sure that it was Claudia's?

Hannah let out a long, shaky breath. "God. I can't even imagine."

"They didn't find anything except a whole lot of old trash, though. So don't worry," Alessandra added, forcing a small smile. "If anyone's haunting that lake out there, it's not her."

"Got it." But maybe it was the girl from the journal. Or one of the other fourteen people who had lost their lives out there. Hannah handed the wet platter to Alessandra, then reached into the sink to pull out the stopper. It made a loud sucking sound as it began to drain.

"You know what's weird, though?" Alessandra said, tilting her head to one side as she worked the dish towel over the large plate. "You kind of look like her. I said that to Jacob the first time I saw your picture on his phone."

Hannah's heart tripped. "Like who? Claudia?"

"Yeah." Alessandra frowned. "Same hair color, similar eyes . . . You're even just about her height. Although, like I said, she hated swimming. Claudia was more of a runner."

"Huh." Hannah's mind turned over this information. Similar eyes. She thought back to earlier that afternoon. The flyer in the movie theater that was almost entirely covered by other ads and business cards. "Did they . . . put up flyers and stuff when she went missing?"

"Are you kidding? The entire town was wallpapered with them. It was like everywhere you went, there was Claudia staring out at you. Which was totally weird, since she wasn't actually anywhere." Alessandra bent to put the platter on a low shelf. "I'm kind of glad they're mostly gone now. But every once in a while, I see one, all faded on a telephone pole or something, and it just gives me the chills."

"Yeah. That must be weird." Hannah found herself staring past Alessandra at the dark lake waters outside.

"Why do you ask?"

"Oh, I think I might have seen one today, that's all. At the movie theater."

"Yeah, you probably did." Alessandra took a deep breath and blew it out. "My mom says all we can do is hope and pray that she's out there somewhere, living the life she wants to live, and that one day she'll come home and tell us all about it."

"I like that," Hannah said as the last of the suds got slurped down the drain. "I hope that, too."

Alessandra put a plate into an upper cabinet, then closed the door.

"Remember earlier . . . you said they had a suspect or something?" Hannah pushed on, her heart pounding. "Was it anyone you knew?"

A slight flush lit Alessandra's cheeks. "Oh, yeah. It was Nick."

Hannah gripped the edge of the cold sink. "Nick? That Nick?" She gestured at the window.

"Yeah, they were kind of dating," Alessandra said. "It was a whole big thing. But like I said, he had an alibi."

Wait. Hannah felt like an idiot for not realizing it earlier. Nick. N. The diary's author was dating a guy she called "N."

It was Claudia's diary. It had to be.

"Alessandra, I—"

"You guys!" Katie burst into the kitchen, her eyes shining with excitement. "Get your butts out here! We're gonna play Truth or Dare!"

"Oh, I'm totally in!" Alessandra balled up her towel and tossed it on the counter and was gone before Hannah could utter another word.

Hannah grabbed her mystery novel from the living room and took it out onto the porch. She cuddled up on one of the rocking chairs with her blanket and placed her phone next to her on the arm of the chair—somehow, she felt better with it close by. Alessandra was back at the fire with the others, but Hannah felt like she needed a little time to herself with all the information and theories swirling through her mind. She was sure Jacob or Katie would think she was weird for not rejoining the group, but she didn't care. The last thing she wanted to play now was Truth or Dare.

Under the dim porch light, Hannah pretended to read, her mind a rush of possibilities. If it was in fact Claudia's diary that she'd found, what was it doing buried in a box at the lake? Had Claudia hidden it there before she disappeared? If so, why? Or had someone stolen the journal and stashed it in that box so that the police couldn't find it? Was Hannah, even now, harboring evidence? Could she get arrested for this?

Every now and then, someone down by the fire would laugh or shout or exclaim at something, but she was able to tune them out. After a while, though, she found herself looking toward the lake. It was as if her eyes were drawn there by some magnetic force. What was she hoping to see out there? A girl's ghost? The lake monster? Did she *want* to spot it again so she'd know she wasn't crazy? Or was she hoping to not see anything?

"Hey."

Hannah flinched. She hadn't heard Colin approach, but there he was, his hands in the front pockets of his jeans.

"Want to go for a walk?" he asked. "There's a path around the lake and the stars are really pretty tonight."

Hannah's pulse thrummed in her wrists like feathery moth wings beating at her skin. She laid her book aside. "Um . . . sure."

Hannah stood up, letting the blanket fall back onto the chair. She grabbed her phone to shove it into her back pocket. Colin smiled as she followed him down the stairs and toward the water, moving away from the others at the fire.

"Where're you guys going?" Jacob called after them.

"For a walk!" Colin shouted back.

"Alone?" someone replied.

Jacob? Probably. It hadn't exactly sounded like him, but who else would have asked? And she kind of liked the idea of Jacob being jealous.

As soon as they were out of the reach of the firelight, it was all but pitch black, the only light coming from the half-moon and the smattering of stars.

"I hope you know where you're going," Hannah said, keeping her eyes on the white strip around the soles of Colin's sneakers.

"There's a little beach not too far from here," he said. "It's good for stargazing."

"Oh. Cool."

Hannah's palms were suddenly wet, as she remembered what Katie had told her earlier about the setup. Had Colin really thought she was cute? The whole stargazing plan sounded fairly romantic. And now his mom wasn't around to walk in on them.

She followed after him in silence, trying to sort out how she felt about all this. Did she want to kiss Colin? Did she want to turn back? Apparently not, because her legs kept right on walking, keeping pace with his. She could hear her own breathing and wondered if he could, too. The thought made her cheeks burn, so she focused instead on the chirping crickets and the rocks crunching beneath her feet.

"You okay back there? You got quiet."

Hannah bit her lip to keep from smiling too broadly. "I'm fine. Just enjoying nature."

Enjoying nature? You're such a dork! Katie's voice said in her mind.

"Good. It's just past that big evergreen up there." Colin gestured ahead and Hannah looked back over her shoulder. They'd come around a bend and she couldn't see the fire anymore. She couldn't even see the house. She could, however, see the lake, which stretched out to her left for what seemed like miles. In the distance, lights on some other house flickered, but it all seemed very far away.

This was good, though, going for a hike along the lakeshore. The more she acted normal around the water, the more normal it would feel—the more she would be able to shrug off everything that had happened as paranoia. It was all a figment of her imagination. That's what she told herself.

Colin jogged ahead a few paces and Hannah followed him onto a short stretch of sandy dirt. He paused, tipping his chin up to look at the sky. "Amazing, right?"

Hannah looked up, too, and instantly lost her breath. The sky was blanketed in stars. It seemed as if there were so many more than there had been just a few minutes ago. On all the camping trips she'd taken in her life, she was sure she had never seen this many at one time before.

"Wow," she murmured.

"Hard to believe anything bad could have ever happened up here, isn't it?" Colin said, stepping closer to her and never taking his eyes off the sky.

Images of the monster and of Katie splashing into the water and of a girl who looked like Hannah stashing a diary in a lockbox flitted quickly through Hannah's mind. But Hannah shooed them away.

"Yes, it is."

Colin reached out and took her hand, cupping it at first and then—when she didn't pull away—lacing his fingers through hers. Her whole arm was on fire. "This okay?" he asked quietly.

Hannah didn't trust herself to speak, so she just nodded. She could feel the warmth coming off Colin's body.

Then her phone vibrated in her pocket. Hannah used her free hand to pull the phone out and found new texts from both Theo and her father. Theo's read:

Current Situation?

Hannah deleted it, feeling slightly guilty. She wasn't about to snap a picture of moonlit Colin and send it to him. The one from her dad read:

How's everything? What did Jim make you guys for dinner?

A rock formed in Hannah's chest.

"What's the matter?" Colin asked, studying her face.

"It's my dad," she said. "I still haven't told him that Jim and Frida aren't here."

"Ah." He nodded.

Reluctantly, Hannah tugged her fingers from Colin's and texted back.

We had grilled chicken. Then s'mores. ☺ Miss you!

The reply was instantaneous.

Miss you too!

Hannah sighed and shoved her phone away. And now she wasn't sure what to do with her hands. Should she hold Colin's hand again? Could she even remotely be that forward? One glance into his brown eyes and she had her answer. No. No, she could not.

"I just feel bad that he doesn't know we're alone out here," Hannah continued. "Is it a lie if you're just not telling?" she asked, even though she already knew the answer.

"It depends."

"On what?" she asked.

"On how good a person you are." It was obvious Colin was trying not to smile, and she knew why. He'd said "good," but what he'd meant was "goody-goody."

"I know, you think I'm a dork." Her face was on fire.

"No! I don't. I think it's cute." He reached out and tugged on her sleeve.

"Cute. Great," she groused. "So I'm like a five-year-old."

She turned as if to walk back to the house, and Colin gently grabbed her wrist. Hannah's heart went into a tailspin and for half a second she actually felt dizzy.

"No. I didn't mean cute like baby cute. I mean . . ." He glanced out at the lake, at a loss for words, which somehow made him more attractive. "It's nice, you know? You own who you are. You're not like everyone else faking it all the time, trying to act cool." He paused and looked her in the eye. "You're cool just the way you are."

Hannah pressed her lips together. She wasn't sure how he could think that he knew her so well after barely twenty-four hours in each other's presence, but it was a nice thing to say anyway.

"Thanks," she said.

Colin's smile lit up his whole face. "You're welcome."

He slipped his hand into hers again and for a moment they simply stood there, smiling goofily at each other.

"I guess we should be getting back," Colin said, looking past her in the general direction of the house. "Thanks for coming out here with me. I was too scared to come alone."

"Okay, *now* you're mocking me," Hannah said with a laugh.

He raised his free hand. "Me? Never."

Hannah followed him off the beach, chuckling under her breath. As they came around the big evergreen, there was a loud splash nearby and she flinched. She saw ripples in the water, very close to the shore—close to where she was walking. Up ahead, Colin was whistling as he walked, oblivious to everything else. Hannah held her breath and ran to catch up to him, telling herself it was all in her head.

When they came around the bend, Nick was hurrying toward them, blotchy and out of breath. He stopped so abruptly he skidded forward on the gravel and almost hit the ground.

"What're you doing here?" Colin asked.

Nick caught his balance and glanced from him to Hannah. "Nothing. You're back."

"Way to state the obvious, dude," Colin said. Then he slapped Nick on the back and tugged Hannah forward. Hannah could have sworn Nick muttered a curse under his breath as he saw their entwined fingers pass him by.

Nick. *N.*

That was it. Hannah had to know more about Claudia and Nick's relationship. She was going to read the rest of that journal the second she had the chance.

Dear Future Me,

Tonight was really weird. N texted me asking me to meet him at our special place. It was after midnight and he knows I'm not supposed to leave the house, but of course I did. I snuck out the window and climbed down the dogwood tree and then jogged to the docks (2.5 miles in 20 mins, thank you very much), and got our kayak out of the boathouse and ROWED all the way over there. But when I got there he would barely even look at me. I've never seen him act like that before. It was like I wasn't even there. And HE asked ME to come! For the longest time he just sat there drawing lines in the sand with a sharpened stick. I sat next to him and tried to get him to talk, but he basically ignored me. I got so angry I was shaking. I mean, does he have any idea how long I would have been grounded for if I'd gotten caught sneaking out? My dad would kill me! No, he'd kill N and then he'd kill me. Whatever. There'd be a lot of bloodshed.

And then I noticed he was writing a word in the sand. Not drawing lines—writing a word. And you know what that word was? MIRANDA. I'm not even kidding. He was sitting there writing some other girl's name in the sand right in front of me? What kind of crap is that???

Anyway, I got so mad I finally stood up to go and that's when he finally said something. He said, "Don't go." And I said, "Really? Why not?" And he said, "Because I have something to tell you." Well. Here's what he told me.

He told me that his family moved here last year because he got thrown out of school. And he got thrown out of school because he stopped going to class. And he stopped going to class because he had this girlfriend named Miranda who died in a car crash.

Yeah. I just about died. Sorry. I guess that's the wrong thing to say. But I did. Anyway, tonight was the two-year anniversary of her death and that's why he was sort of freaking out. He said it was just a freak accident—another driver ran a stop sign they claimed to not have seen and that person walked away fine, but Miranda's neck was broken. He said they went on a date the night before and they had the best time and she was all smiling and saying she loved him and stuff (I know—LOVED!) and then the next night, she was dead. I can't even imagine what that must be like. I mean, what if I woke up tomorrow and N was just gone? Forever?

Oh, God. Why is so much of my life about death lately? I had no idea what to say to him. I just felt so bad. So I put my arm around him and he put his arm around me and we just sat there like that for a really long time. By the time we left to go home I was almost too tired to row the kayak, but I couldn't leave it there. N had his Jet Ski and he put-putted along beside me and then drove me home. But even then I couldn't fall asleep. I was too wired and full of his story. And then I was so exhausted this morning I passed out in math class.

What do I do to make him feel better? I mean, seriously. What do I do?

FOURTEEN

Hannah was only half asleep, phrases and words from the journal scrolling through her mind, when something yanked her awake.

She blinked a few times, trying to figure out where she was. It was still nighttime. Her eyes focused in on the cut-glass doorknob of the closet and she remembered. She was at the lake house. In Jacob's parents' room.

But what had woken her up? She lay very still, listening, breathing quietly. Nothing. Then she realized she was cold. She flipped over. The other half of the bed was empty, the blankets undisturbed. Katie was still downstairs.

Hannah thought back to the rest of the evening. Raj and Nick had left after all the s'mores had been eaten, and Hannah had felt a zillion times better once they were gone—Nick's constant staring had made her super self-conscious.

Then she, Jacob, Katie, Alessandra, and Colin had come inside and played Apples to Apples at the dining table. Hannah kept losing because nobody agreed with her matches except for, occasionally, Colin. She'd finally gotten completely fed up when she'd matched "tool" to "computer" and Jacob, who had been the judge, had gone with Katie's match—"orange." His reasoning? That oranges were like apples and Apple was a computer company.

That was when Hannah knew for sure that this was not her weekend. She'd faked a massive yawn and headed upstairs. She'd gotten into bed and read a little bit more of the journal until her eyes got too tired to stay open. Now, she rolled over and checked her phone. It was 12:45 a.m. Which meant Hannah had come upstairs almost two hours ago. Where the heck was Katie?

Slowly, Hannah sat up. Dead. Silence. There was no TV on. No videos playing on phones. No voices. She put her feet down on the cool wood floor and stepped up to the window. The lake outside was flat, black, motionless. Then, in the distance, something moved. Hannah leaned forward, holding her breath. Something was moving across the lake swiftly, soundlessly. A shadow. But then she blinked, and it was gone.

Bang!

Hannah whirled around with a gasp. She instinctively grabbed the baseball bat Katie had used earlier and moved forward on her tiptoes. Her door let out a long, low creak as she opened it and she winced, but nothing happened. No monsters lunged at her from the darkness. Nothing swooped out of the rafters to attack. The hallway was still, but there was a sliver of light coming from a half-open door across the way. The door to Jacob's room.

Hannah heard a giggle. Katie's giggle. She lowered the bat.

No freaking way. Katie was in Jacob's room. Hannah glanced over her shoulder, knowing she should just go back to bed. That she should pretend she hadn't heard anything—didn't know anything. Whatever was going on in there, she didn't want to see it . . . right? But she couldn't seem to make herself turn around. Instead, she walked over to Jacob's room and, ever so slowly, ever so silently, pushed open the already ajar door.

They were sitting on Jacob's bed, facing each other. Katie's legs were crooked over Jacob's and he was playing with her fingers, looking into her admiring eyes. It was so intimate, so innocent, it made Hannah want to cry. They were so wrapped up in each other, they didn't even notice her standing there.

And then someone screamed outside. And this time, it was no bird.

Hannah gasped. Jacob and Katie both looked up and found her watching them, in her pajamas, with a bat in her hands.

"What was that?" Jacob was the first to recover.

"That one was definitely a person," Katie said.

Gripping the bat even tighter, Hannah turned and ran for the stairs, the two lovebirds right on her heels.

The scream had come from Prandya, courtesy of Colin and Alessandra. They were all in the lake, splashing and messing around, and Prandya was screaming as Colin and Alessandra turned their attacks on her.

"I don't understand. Two seconds ago there was no one out here," Hannah said, leaning the bat against the outside wall on the porch.

"Well, they're out here now," Katie replied. She smiled but sounded frustrated. Hannah was sure her stepsister was annoyed at having her private moment with Jacob interrupted.

"What's that saying? If you can't beat 'em . . ." Jacob stripped off his shirt, sprinted down the dock, and cannonballed into the water, which made Alessandra and Prandya shriek some more. Hannah noticed that the fire in the fire pit was raging again and that a black kayak was tied up to the end of the dock. Prandya's, she was sure. That was probably what Hannah had seen out the window a few minutes earlier—Prandya's stealth approach across the lake. And the *bang* must have been Prandya's kayak bumping into the dock.

She had to admit to herself, she felt marginally better having a reasonable explanation for that shadow.

Katie, social being that she was, sauntered down to the end of the dock and sat, dangling her feet in the water and immediately joining the jovial conversation. Jacob splashed her and she laughed, then kicked water back at him. Hannah watched, feeling awkward and unnoticed—maybe even unwanted.

She had thought that she and Colin had . . . connected earlier. She hadn't imagined that starry walk to the beach. But maybe it hadn't meant anything to him.

Jacob and Colin started pushing each other under the water in that super mature way guys had of trying to exert their prowess. Prandya and Alessandra shook their heads and Alessandra swam farther out, toward the third buoy, while Prandya went the other way and pulled herself up next to Katie on the dock. Prandya whispered something to Katie and Katie let out a loud laugh.

Hannah frowned. It was so easy for Katie. She never even questioned her inclusion in any group. If there was fun to be had, she joined it. The idea that she might not be welcome never even occurred to her—which made sense, because Hannah had never witnessed a situation in which Katie was *not* welcome.

"Dude! Hannah! Are you just gonna stand there?" Jacob shouted over to her.

Hannah flinched. It wasn't exactly an open-armed invitation, but it was something.

"I'm going to go get my bathing suit," she replied.

And that was exactly what she was going to do. She was going to get her suit on and join them, darn it. She was going to prove to Jacob and Katie that it didn't bother her that they were hanging out together in the middle of the night—even though it did. She was going to prove to Colin and Alessandra and Prandya that she could be spontaneous and fun—even though it went completely against her nature.

She was just about to turn and go inside when something near the far buoy caught her eye.

The moon's reflection shone silvery white against the surface of the water. But something about the reflection was changing. It looked like the water was moving, which didn't make sense. There was no wind at all. Hannah squinted, and then her heart slammed against her rib cage so hard it almost left a painful dent.

The silvery-white celestial reflection was turning . . . red.

Hannah automatically glanced up at the moon, as if the hunk of rock itself was changing color, but it wasn't. Of course it wasn't. There the moon hung, innocent and bright as ever. Which meant it was the water that was changing. The water of "Drowning Lake" was turning red.

And the red was . . . *growing*. It blossomed out from the buoy in all directions, undulating and flowing, reaching its eerie tendrils out.

Hannah screamed and ran toward the water.

"Get out of the lake!"

"What?" Alessandra asked, shoving sopping curls out of her face. She was pretty far from the others now, and closer to the strange red stain than anyone else.

"Get out of the lake!" Hannah screeched. "There's something out there! Jacob, look!"

Katie and Prandya scrambled to their feet on the dock. "Oh

my God," Prandya said quietly. Colin and Jacob glanced around, submerged in the water from their shoulders down.

Colin saw the red liquid and his eyes widened. "What the—? What *is* that?"

He turned and began to swim toward the dock.

"Swim!" Hannah screamed at Jacob and Alessandra. "You guys! Come in!"

Alessandra turned around, searching the lake, and didn't seem to see anything, and Hannah wondered if maybe it wasn't visible from her angle somehow. Colin, meanwhile, got to the dock first, reaching his strong arms up to hoist himself out, and then Prandya and Katie bent down to help Jacob up out of the lake. Alessandra just stayed where she was, treading water as if everything was fine.

What if the red stain reached her? What would happen if it touched Alessandra's skin?

Hannah ran toward her, splashing into the shallows, gesturing for her to swim in.

"Alessandra! What're you doing? Come on!"

"What are you screaming about?" Alessandra asked. "There's nothing here!"

The others ran down the dock toward Hannah, their footsteps pounding the old wood boards that creaked and sighed under their weight.

"You don't see it?" Hannah screeched, gasping for air. "The water around you! It's all red! It looks like—"

She paused, unable to say it, wishing Alessandra would just listen to her.

"Like what?" Alessandra said, starting, at least, to move toward shore.

Like blood, Hannah thought.

And then Alessandra stopped swimming. Even from a hundred yards away, Hannah could see the fear cross her face. She'd swum right into the undulating red water.

"What was—"

Suddenly, Alessandra jerked. Her head whipped back.

"Hey! What!" she yelled.

"Ali?" Colin shouted. "What's wrong?"

Terror contorted Alessandra's face. "Omigod! What the—"

Her arm flew up, then splashed, and then she screamed as her whole body went under.

Something out on the island screeched.

"Alessandra!" Prandya screamed.

Katie grabbed Hannah, her fingernails digging into Hannah's flesh. Hannah's heart pounded in her throat. She wanted to run into the lake and help Alessandra, but she couldn't make herself move. The red stain had grown, polluting the water for several feet all around the spot where Alessandra had gone down.

"Alessandra!" Colin shouted, running into the water. "Ali!"

"Colin, no! Don't go out there!" Katie yelled.

Colin looked back at her, wild-eyed. "What do you expect me to do? She's drowning!"

"You guys?" Jacob's fingers clutched his head on either side. "*What just happened?*"

Suddenly, Alessandra's face came up, a look of horror twisting her features. Blood ran from her nose and smeared over her lips.

"Help!" she cried. "Help! Me!"

Colin didn't hesitate this time. He dove into the water as Katie and Prandya screamed. Hannah was still frozen in shock.

Alessandra went under again. Silence. Bubbles surfaced. There was a beat. Two. Three. In the distance, something let out a low, mournful howl. Then more red bloomed in the spot where Alessandra had disappeared.

Horror gripping her heart, Hannah grabbed Katie by the hand and ran for the house.

FIFTEEN

This wasn't happening. It wasn't happening. Hannah's feet pounded. Her heart bruised itself trying to hammer through her rib cage. Katie was in hysterics, sobbing and choking and gasping for air as they stumbled up the porch steps.

Help! Help! Me!

What had happened to Alessandra? Where was she? What was in that water?

Katie tripped on the top step and doubled over, her knees hitting the porch floor, and Hannah's foot caught on her arm, sending them both sprawling. Hannah's throat was dry and her pulse throbbed in her ears, so hard she wouldn't have been surprised if her eardrums had started bleeding. She reached for the door handle, but the world spun around her as she sat up, and she couldn't see straight. She pressed the heels of her hands to her forehead and tried to focus, but she couldn't stop seeing it—the terror on Alessandra's face, the unnatural angle of her arm as she went under, the bubbles coming up, up, up. And then the blood.

Her jaw and cheek thrummed with pain. Jacob and Prandya raced toward them, Prandya crying so hard snot ran down her face.

And then, behind them, Colin emerged from the lake. He looked so pale his skin shone like wax.

"Colin!" Hannah shouted.

"Where is she?" Prandya cried. "You didn't find her?"

Colin moved slowly at first, as if stunned, and then started jogging toward them.

"What happened? Did you see anything?" Jacob demanded.

Colin fell to his butt on the bottom step and wiped water from his face with both hands. He was shaking all over, his teeth chattering noisily. Everyone stared at him, but Hannah stared at the water. It looked perfectly normal now. Undisturbed. It was as if Alessandra had never been there.

"There was nothing," Colin said finally. "I saw nothing."

"What happened to her?" Prandya demanded. *"What happened to Ali?"*

"I don't know!" Colin snapped, his eyes flashing with anger and terror. "She's just . . . gone."

Hannah struggled for breath. She couldn't pull in air. It was like she'd forgotten how.

"Breathe, Hannah. Just breathe." Colin got up, tromped up the stairs, and knelt next to her. "Breathe."

Hannah gazed into his eyes and concentrated on her lungs. She took in a breath. Then another. She tried to reach out for Katie, but she misjudged the distance and caught air.

Focus, she thought. *Come on, Hannah, focus.*

"I'm okay," she told Colin. "I'm okay now."

He released her and she brought her knees up and hugged them. She breathed in through her nose and out through her mouth, like after a big race.

"Good. Just keep breathing," Colin said, his hand on her back. "You're okay. You're okay." He sounded like he was trying to convince himself rather than her.

"No, dude, she's not okay," Jacob spat. "There's some kind of . . . some kind of . . . *thing* in that lake! And it just attacked Alessandra."

They all fell silent as his words hung in the air.

"What was it?" Prandya demanded. "What's out there? Where's Ali? Do you think she swam off somewhere and can't get back to us? Or is she—"

She clearly couldn't bring herself to finish that sentence.

"I have no idea," Colin said throatily.

"We have to call the police," Prandya said, pushing herself up, her eyes wide as if she'd just come to. "Where's my phone? Where's my—"

"I'll get mine." Jacob shoved open the door and barreled into the house. He was back ten seconds later, looking stricken. "The power's out."

"What?" Katie said. "How?"

"I don't know, but without the booster we can't call . . . or text." He threw his phone down hard and it bounced on the ground.

"What the hell is going on?" Colin said.

Hannah had to say something. It was too late now, clearly, but she still had to say it.

"You guys, I saw something out in the—"

"Hannah!" Katie snapped.

"In the lake," Hannah continued, ignoring Katie. She didn't know what the point was of keeping the secret anymore. In fact, right now, she couldn't fathom why she'd kept it in the first place. "I saw some kind of . . . monster."

Colin's jaw stiffened. "Tell us exactly what you saw."

Hannah stood up because she had to move—had to do something to work out her adrenaline. "It was big and gray and, I don't know . . . monster-like," she blurted. "It almost looked like a whale or . . . or a seal, but deformed. It rose out of the water and sort of hovered there for a second before it dove back under."

"Why didn't you say anything?" Jacob demanded. He retrieved his phone and clutched it as Hannah began to pace the porch.

"Because! I didn't think you guys would believe me. No one else saw it but me, and I'm the one who wanted to leave, right? So I figured you guys would think I made it up," she rambled.

Hannah paused with her back to them. It had started to rain lightly. When she looked up, the moon was obscured by clouds.

"I wouldn't think that," Jacob countered.

"Oh, come on, Jacob," Hannah shot back. "Yesterday if I'd said the words *lake monster* you would've laughed in my face!"

That was when the tears started falling. Alessandra was gone— probably dead—and it was her fault. Hannah began to convulse, tears running down her face. She couldn't get control of herself as the guilt and the fear and the anger overwhelmed her. From the corner of her eye, she saw Colin make a move toward her to comfort her, but she turned away and suddenly found herself locked in Jacob's arms instead.

"It's okay," Jacob said into her hair, running his hand over the back of her head. "It's okay, Hannah. It's going to be okay."

"We have to do something. If we can't call the police, we have to get to them somehow." The words fell out of Hannah's mouth before she even realized she was thinking them. She clutched Jacob's shoulders and held on for dear life as she pictured Alessandra sinking beneath the surface over and over and over again—saw the blood pool up. Alessandra's blood.

"We can't," Katie spat. There was venom in her voice, even though it was still thick with tears. "The only way to get there is to go out on the water, and there's no way I'm doing that now, are you?"

A sudden wind howled through the trees and the branches overhead cracked and squealed. Hannah began to shiver violently and Jacob held her even tighter. Colin slowly looked around, then back down toward the water. The skiff and Prandya's kayak bobbed on the now choppy surface.

"I want to go home," Prandya said quietly.

"Let's do that. We'll go to Prandya's house," Jacob said.

Thunder rumbled in the distance and Hannah's stomach clenched. "But that also involves going out on the water."

"Or if Prandya stays here, maybe her parents will come looking for her?" Katie suggested.

Prandya shook her head. Her eyes had an eerie, vacant look. "They're not home. They had a charity event in Dearborn. And Raj is staying at Nick's for the night. No one'll miss me."

Hannah's throat itched. No one was coming to help them. No one even knew anything was wrong.

And for all they knew, Alessandra was dead.

SIXTEEN

Eventually, the rain got so bad that they had to go inside the house. But no one slept. All night long, the storm raged, and all night long Hannah and Katie tossed and turned in bed next to each other. Hannah knew her stepsister was awake, and felt totally awkward lying there in the dark not speaking, but she had no idea what to say. All she could see in her mind's eye was Alessandra being yanked under the water, and she definitely didn't want to talk about it.

Hannah rolled from her right side to her left for the millionth time and Katie let out a loud sigh.

"What?" Hannah said.

"What, what?" Katie replied.

"You sighed."

"So?" Katie said. "You've been sighing all night."

Hannah gritted her teeth. "I'm sorry. I just . . ." She took two short breaths and closed her eyes. "What do you think it is?"

There was a long beat of silence. "What do I think what is?"

"The thing in the lake. The thing that . . ." She couldn't say *killed*. She just couldn't. "Attacked Alessandra?"

Katie groaned and sat up straight, punching her pillow behind her to fluff it up. Hannah could barely see Katie's outline in the darkness as she stared straight ahead.

"I don't know," Katie said. "You're the brains of this operation. And you also apparently *saw* it. Where do you think it came from?"

"Maybe it's some sort of fish?" Hannah suggested. "Something, like, deformed by years of swimming in polluted waters?"

"This lake can't be that polluted," Katie asked. "At least it doesn't seem like it is. Especially compared to some other lakes in the world."

"True," Hannah said. "I bet Jacob thinks it's an alien."

Katie snorted a laugh. "He does love his alien invasion movies."

It stung a bit, Katie having this insider knowledge of Jacob, but Hannah let it go. "Maybe some extraterrestrial ship visited the planet eons ago and left behind one of its own to troll Dreardon Lake for all eternity," Hannah said, surprised by her ability to strike a light tone.

"Or maybe it's a poltergeist," Katie joked. "Some freaky manifestation of negative energy left behind after all those drownings in the lake."

They both fell silent. Hannah shivered. Because somehow, that actually seemed plausible. How could that much sorrow and despair and death *not* have an effect on a place?

Outside, thunder crashed. The storm had only picked up since they'd come up to bed. Rain pelted the windowpane and wind lashed the house so violently, Hannah could swear she felt the structure sway beneath her. The wind whistled through the eaves, making a painful, howling sound that stopped her blood cold.

"Is it ever going to end?" Katie asked, glancing toward the window.

"It's like a cruel joke," Hannah said. "What time is it?"

"After two," Katie said, checking her phone. She yawned. "I wish I could sleep."

A flash of lightning and a crack of thunder punctuated her words.

Hannah grabbed her book off the bedside table and flicked on her phone's flashlight. Maybe if she could just lose herself in the story . . .

"Oh, come on!" Katie said with a groan. "No way. If you want to read, go down to the kitchen."

"Fine," Hannah said.

She flung the covers off, nearly vibrating with anger and fear and exhaustion, then tripped on the lip of the throw rug, jamming her knee against the corner of the dresser. She cursed under her breath and fumbled for her book, which she'd dropped in the process. When her fingers found it, she grasped the spine and stood up straight again, coming face-to-face with the rain-drenched window. Another flash of lightning lit up the lake and Hannah gasped.

"What now?"

"It's out there."

Hannah took a staggered step backward. In the moment of light, she'd seen the monster, hulking and deformed and menacing, reaching out of the lake.

"What? You saw it again?" Katie scrambled out of bed and over to the window.

Hannah struggled to catch her breath. "Oh my God, Katie. What about Alessandra? What if she's still out there and—"

"I don't see anything." Katie leaned bravely toward the window, squinting out at the night.

"Of course you don't see anything now. It's pitch black."

The two of them stood at the window, waiting for another flash of lightning. Hannah's mouth was dry and she wished fervently to be anywhere else.

Home. I just want to go home.

Lightning flashed, accompanied by a crash of thunder so loud Hannah stumbled back from the window. Katie stared, pressing her fingers to the glass.

"Did you see it?" Hannah asked. "Did you see it?"

Katie turned around slowly and looked Hannah in the eye. "Stop trying to freak me out," she said. "There's nothing there."

Katie flopped back into bed and pulled the covers over her head. Hannah's free hand curled into a fist and she clenched her teeth to keep from screaming in frustration. The monster was taunting her. That was the only explanation. But she wasn't going to let it scare her anymore. First thing in the morning, she was getting into that boat—alone if she had to—and going to the police.

She could only hope to make it across the lake alive.

Dear Future Me,

The Summer People are starting to arrive. That's what the locals call them: "The Summer People." They say it with a little bit more sarcasm in their voices than they use when they say "The Winter Lodgers" or "The Foliage Folk." It's almost as if "The Summer People" are some evil race of zombies coming to pillage the town and eat our souls.

But they're not. They're really not. I can vouch for them because I've already met one of them and he is no zombie.

Okay, before you freak out, no, I haven't broken up with N. But he's been so moody lately. Ever since that night when he told me about Miranda, it's like I never know which N I'm going to get. The N I first met who was all sweet and attentive and into me, or the N who refuses to look me in the eye and scowls all the time and actually grunts when I ask if he wants me to bring over cookies or cupcakes. Who grunts at the choice between homemade cookies or cupcakes? I care about him—I do—but I just don't know if I can do this anymore. And I was thinking that well before S.B. came into my life. (S.B. = Summer Boy!!!)

Unlike N, S.B. walked right up to me the second we met and introduced himself. He said he's going to be here for a few months and he wants to meet some people and I look like the kind of people he wants to meet. I mean, come on! Who says stuff like that? I was about to go on my break, so I gave him a little tour of the town, and it felt kind of nice, you know? Being the person who knew stuff for once. He doesn't know that I haven't even lived here a year yet, and he kept asking me all these questions about the town and I actually knew the answers. And the whole time we were together I didn't once think about Drowning Lake or Miranda or even about N. I just had fun.

I mean, school hasn't officially let out for us yet, but it's almost summer, and that's what summer's supposed to be for, right? Fun?

SEVENTEEN

The next morning, when Hannah opened her eyes and saw gray light, she was completely disoriented. She couldn't believe she'd dozed off long enough for the night to end without her noticing. She got out of bed and the journal fell on the floor. Right. The diary. She'd retrieved it from her bag last night after Katie had fallen asleep, and had managed to read some of it before passing out herself.

Hannah shoved the diary back into her cross-body bag and went to the window. It was still pouring down rain outside, and there was so much fog clinging to the lake she couldn't even see as far as Mystery Island.

"Katie, wake up," Hannah said, reaching out to shake her step-sister's shoulder.

Katie awoke with a start and her eyes went wide. "What? What's wrong? Is Alessandra okay?"

"I don't know." Hannah swallowed thickly. "It's morning."

"Is the power back?" Katie swung her legs off the bed and tried the light switch. Nothing.

"I wonder if anyone else is up," Hannah said. She walked into the hallway and slammed right into Jacob's chest. The scream was halfway out of her mouth before she even realized it was him.

"Shhhh! You'll wake up Prandya!"

Hannah smacked Jacob's shoulder as hard as she could. Since when did anyone wake up before her?

"Ow! What did *I* do?" he complained.

The master bedroom door flew open just as Jacob's door creaked open, too. Katie and Colin looked out at them from either side of the hall, Colin wide-eyed and alert, Katie annoyed.

"What's with the yelling?" Colin grumbled.

"What's going on?" Katie added.

"We haven't heard from Alessandra, have we?" Hannah asked, looking from Colin to Jacob. The boys shook their heads mournfully.

"We have to go to the police," Hannah said firmly.

"Um, yeah . . . about that," Jacob said.

"Jacob! I know it's risky going out on the lake after what happened, but we can't just sit here," Hannah said, her adrenaline pumping.

"I understand." Jacob used the towel in his hands to rub at his wet hair. Apparently he'd already gotten cleaned up, and it occurred to Hannah that he might not have slept at all. "It's just, I can't take you. The boat's gone."

"What?" Hannah and Katie blurted in unison.

"It's gone," Jacob said flatly. "And so is Prandya's kayak. They must have come untethered in the storm last night and floated off."

Hannah and Katie exchanged a panicked look. Then Hannah shoved Jacob aside and ran down the stairs. Prandya was still asleep on the couch as Hannah slammed through the front door, then the screen door, and careened outside, where the rain was crashing down. Sure enough, the dock was empty. Heart pounding, Hannah jogged down to the very last wood plank, letting the rain soak her straight through. She searched the water. There was debris everywhere—pieces of driftwood, a couple of broken chunks of white Styrofoam, a random beach ball. The coastline was dotted with more junk. The storm had definitely left its mark. And Jacob's little metal skiff was nowhere. Because of the weather, there were no boats on the lake at all—no jet-skiers, no fishermen—nothing.

And no sign whatsoever of Alessandra.

"This is *not* happening," Hannah whispered under her breath, tears prickling at her eyes.

What if the boats didn't just float off in the storm? What if the lake monster untethered them? Hannah thought. *Or sank them. Or got rid of them some other way.*

She turned around to find all four of them were out there now—Katie, Jacob, Colin, and Prandya—watching her from the dry safety of the front porch.

"That's it. Give me your phone." Hannah stormed up the hill and held out her hand to Jacob. "I'm calling my father."

She no longer cared about looking like a loser, a wet blanket, a goody-goody. This was an actual emergency.

"It won't do you any good," Jacob said. "The power's still out."

Hannah groaned so loudly and emphatically it ended in a growl. She'd spaced on the power. Her heart began to pound beneath every inch of her skin. There was no way out. Nothing she could do.

"Oh my God," Hannah blurted, her stomach turning. "Oh my God."

Prandya edged down the steps. "Hannah, calm down."

"Don't tell me to calm down!" Hannah shouted, backing away from the girl. "You're not my friend! You don't get to tell me to calm down!"

"Hannah, you're freaking out," Jacob said. He kept his distance, as if she were a strange animal he wasn't sure how to approach. Something about the look on his face broke her heart. It was as if he didn't even know her, even though he was the person she'd known longer than almost anyone else on earth. He was supposed to be her best friend, but at that moment, he looked exasperated with her, like he wanted to just tell her to shut up. Or worse—like he wanted to walk away.

And Katie looked scared. Pale and wide-eyed and scared. Which somehow made Hannah feel even worse.

"Of course I'm freaking out!" Hannah shouted. "We're trapped! We're trapped here and there's something in the water. Alessandra is . . . she's . . . And now someone . . . or some*thing* has taken our boats."

Hannah's teeth chattered and she shivered in her drenched clothes. Colin grabbed a towel off the pile on the porch swing and shoved between Katie and Jacob to jog down the steps to her. She flinched away from him at first, but then he threw the towel around her shoulders and started rubbing her arms up and down as he pulled her back up onto the porch.

"Okay," he said, his voice low and calming. "Okay. It's okay, I've got you."

Hannah looked away from him toward the lake, until he reached up with one hand and turned her chin so she had to face him—had to look him in the eye.

"It's okay, Hannah. We're all here with you. No one's going anywhere . . . obviously," he said, and then chuckled drily. "Jacob's dad is going to be home in the morning, right? All we have to do is make it through the next twenty-four hours."

Hannah took in a shaky breath, then another, then a third that was far less shaky.

"Look me in the eye," Colin said.

Hannah did. She locked eyes with Colin and breathed. His eyes were such a warm brown. And there were green flecks in them that she hadn't noticed before. Something about the way he looked at her, looked *into* her, was riveting. The longer she stared, the faster her pulse raced, but in a good way this time. He was looking at her as if there was no other person, no other thing, in the entire world. He was looking at her like he wanted to kiss her.

Do it, she thought. *Kiss me.*

It came out of nowhere, and it was so inappropriate in that moment, she laughed out loud.

Colin smiled and hugged her to him. He looked back at the others. "I think she's gonna be okay."

Hannah didn't add what the rest of them were all surely thinking: that they couldn't say the same for Alessandra.

Dear Future Me,

OMG OMG OMG OMG I can't believe what just happened. I'm sorry this writing is so horrible I just can't I can't I can't.

Okay, I took some deep breaths and now I can sort of hold this pencil and write. I can't believe what just happened. N caught me with S.B. Like CAUGHT me caught me. As in me and S.B. were making out in the park and N and his friends just sort of walked right up to us. I didn't even realize they were there for, like, a good few seconds. I mean I noticed something shift in the light, but I was so into the kiss with S.B. that it wasn't until R cleared his throat that I even looked up. And OMG the look on N's face. It was horrible. I feel gutted just thinking about it. He looked like I'd reached into his chest and just ripped out his heart. Which I guess I kind of did.

The second I saw that look on his face, I knew. I'm in love with him. I'm totally in love with N. And there I was, sucking face with some Summer Person in the middle of our town. I think I sort of shoved S.B. away and jumped up. I honestly don't really remember. The whole thing is a blur. But N told me off right in front of S.B. and all his friends and then he turned and stormed away. I didn't even think about it—I just went after him. He was so angry and hurt he was actually crying. He told me S.B. was a jerk—I didn't even know N knew him—but I told him it didn't mean anything and that I was so so so so sorry, but he didn't even seem to hear me. He just told me he never wanted to talk to me again and that was it. He walked off and I yelled after him and he didn't even turn around or stop or pause or anything.

I think he really hates me and my heart is totally breaking. How could I have cheated on him? What was I thinking? He was hurting and sad and deep and sweet and I just stomped all over him for the first cute guy who showed up for the summer?

I'm a horrible person, Future Me. Are you still a horrible person? I really hope not. I really hope that, somehow, things get better.

PS When I got back to the park bench, N's friends were all gone and so was S.B. I had to walk home alone in the dark and the whole time I felt like someone was following me—watching me. Probably just my paranoia, right? I'm being haunted by my guilty conscience? God, I just wish this night had never happened. I wish stupid S.B. had never come to this stupid town. I wish I could wake up from this nightmare.

EIGHTEEN

Hannah's eyes stung. They were dry from spending the last hour staring out the window at the lake. She kept telling herself to move. That this was unhealthy. That this was insane. But she couldn't seem to make herself turn away. That monster was out there. It had murdered Alessandra, and she was the only one who had seen it. She was going to get a picture of the thing if it was the last thing her slowly dying cell phone ever did.

In her lap, she held the diary—she'd come to think of it as Claudia's diary. She'd read one more entry in between her lake-watching vigil, and it hadn't helped her feel any better.

Maybe Dad will just show up, Hannah thought. Maybe he would think it was weird that Hannah hadn't texted him all day long and come up to see if something was wrong. And once her dad was here, everything would be all right. They could go to the police. They could try to find Alessandra.

But then, Hannah hadn't been in touch with her dad all that much since she'd arrived at Jacob's—for obvious reasons. So the chances of his driving all the way here were minimal. He thought his friends were here taking care of his daughter and stepdaughter. Why would he think anything could be wrong?

Hannah sighed and pressed her forehead to the cool windowpane.

The only positive in all of this was that Nick and Raj had left before they'd gotten stranded here as well. Hannah wasn't sure she could handle being stuck at the house with Nick. Especially now that she'd read Claudia's entry about him getting into that fight with "Summer Boy."

There was a knock on the door, and Hannah blinked. She reluctantly looked away from the lake and quickly crammed the diary back into her bag.

"Yes?" she called.

The door creaked open. Katie stuck her head inside, her black hair swinging into view first, just before her face. "Hannah? Can I come in?"

Hannah shrugged. "Sure. It's your room, too."

Katie silently stepped inside and closed the door. "Can we . . . talk?"

"Sure," Hannah said again.

Katie climbed onto the bed and scooted over, leaving room for Hannah to join her. Hannah didn't move from the window.

"I have a question," Katie began, running her fingers through her hair over and over again. "Last night . . . before everything happened . . . what did you see? I mean, when you were outside Jacob's room."

Hannah's jaw clenched as she remembered the private moment she'd caught between Katie and Jacob. "Nothing."

Silence. The way Katie was looking at Hannah got right under Hannah's skin.

"Okay, fine. I saw you guys, like, holding hands or whatever," Hannah blurted. She finally turned away from the lake, and her vision clouded over with purple splotches in the shape of the water, with a blank spot for Mystery Island in the middle. Her brain felt muddled—hazy. But the anger was pulsing through loud and clear. "You could have any guy you want back home," she said, her arms clutching her elbows. "Why do you have to steal mine?"

"First of all, I can*not* have any guy I want back home," Katie replied. "Did you see me with a date to the spring formal? Um, no! There's a reason me and my friends went as a group. And secondly, Jacob is *not* yours! Just because you knew him first—"

"Knew him since birth," Hannah interjected.

"Doesn't mean you guys are, like, destined to be together," Katie finished. "I mean, doesn't he get a say in anything?"

There was a long moment of silence as the two of them faced off. Hannah couldn't believe they were even talking about this, what with them being trapped and Alessandra being, most likely, dead. Did any of this even matter? But if the pounding of her heart was any indication, it did.

"Come on, Hannah. You and Jacob have had sixteen years together and nothing has happened between the two of you," Katie said, pushing herself off the bed to stand across from Hannah. "What does that tell you?"

Katie's tone was so condescending it made Hannah want to tear out the girl's vocal cords. But then the urge suddenly died, burning out as quickly as it had flamed up. Because what Katie was saying was true. How pathetic could Hannah be, pining after the same guy her *entire life*? Jacob had had half a dozen girlfriends and Hannah had gone out with exactly one guy on exactly one date. In all that time, if Jacob had been interested in her, he could have said something—*would* have said something. It wasn't like he was remotely shy.

"I really like him, Hannah," Katie said quietly—pleadingly, almost. "And I think he likes me. We'd like to, you know, try dating. If we happen to get out of here alive." She let out a wry, flat laugh. "But neither one of us wants to hurt your feelings or make you . . . uncomfortable."

You already have, Hannah thought. But her heart wasn't in it. Not anymore. Maybe she was exhausted after not sleeping all night. Or maybe she was just sick of being the girl who said *no* to everything. Outside, the rain kicked up again, lashing the window. Hannah wondered if, in an alternate universe, the sun was shining and she and Jacob were out there right now, water-skiing or swimming or sunning themselves on the dock. For a moment, she felt nostalgic for something that had never even happened. And then she brushed the thought away. It was time to deal with reality.

"It's okay," she said finally. "I mean, if you both like each other . . . it's not like there's anything I can do about it." She took a deep breath. "You have my . . . blessing? I guess," she said, then shrugged. "If that's what you came in here for."

It was going to suck, watching Katie and Jacob flirt. And hold hands. And . . . ugh . . . *kiss.* But the good news was, Jacob went through girls at a clip of about four a school year. If he and Katie had already gotten started, they were probably halfway to finished. Not that Hannah would be saying that out loud. It did, however, give her a slightly lighter feeling that she felt like holding on to—a little hope.

Not that she thought that she and Jacob would ever be together now. She couldn't date him after Katie, because *ew.* But at least she had hope that she wouldn't have to watch them together forever.

That was assuming, as Katie had said, that they even got out of there alive.

"Thank you," Katie said. She kicked the toe of her sandal against the floor a couple of times, filling the awkward silence. "Besides," she said, her expression changing as she smiled, "you know Colin has a thing for you. And he is *totally* hot."

Hannah blushed. "No."

"He's not totally hot?" Katie teased.

"No! I mean, yes. He is. But he doesn't have a thing for me. Just because he thought I was cute on Jacob's phone doesn't mean he likes me."

"Oh, please. You're so full of it," Katie replied. "I didn't see him asking me to go for a private stroll to check out the stars."

Hannah knocked her fists together a few times just to have something to do with herself. "That *was* kind of nice. But how are we even talking about this? Alessandra is—"

Loud voices suddenly rose up from downstairs, cutting Hannah off.

"Forget it, Jacob! I'm going!" Prandya shouted.

Hannah and Katie exchanged an alarmed look and ran for the stairs. Colin, Jacob, and Prandya were all in the living room, and Prandya was shoving granola bars into the pockets of her hoodie.

"What's going on?" Hannah asked as she reached the bottom step.

"I'm hiking home," Prandya said, trembling.

Hannah's heart gave a flutter. "Hiking? Is that even possible? I thought you couldn't get anywhere without a boat."

"You *can't*," Jacob said. "That's what I've been trying to tell her."

"I can do it," Prandya said.

"How are you gonna get down the other side of the cliff?" Colin asked.

"You know who my father is. I've been certified in three different types of rock climbing," Prandya said. "I'll be fine."

She started for the door and Jacob grabbed her arm. "Prandya, it's pouring out. There could be rock slides . . . mudslides. What if you get hurt?"

Fear flashed through Prandya's eyes before she lifted her chin. "I'll be fine. If I stay here one more second I'm going to lose my mind." She pulled her hood over her head and glanced around at them. "I'll call the police when I get there. We have an emergency radio if our power is out. This will all be over soon."

And with that she turned and walked out the door. Colin followed, letting the door close behind them, and Hannah could hear them talking in low, tense tones. After thirty seconds, he came back in, his face red and blotchy.

"Is she gonna be okay?" Katie asked quietly.

Colin lifted his shoulders. "There was no talking her out of it."

"Someone should go with her," Jacob said.

But nobody moved. Hannah knew they were all thinking the same thing. The only place they were safe was inside the house.

"What if we try the hill behind the house?" Hannah suggested later that afternoon. It had been hours since Prandya had left and there was no sign of her or the police. Or of Alessandra. The rain had stopped, but there were still no boaters out on the lake, and Hannah had never felt so isolated.

"Try it for what?" Jacob asked. He and Katie were out on the porch, playing catch with one of the battered baseballs. Hannah was attempting to read her mystery novel on the couch inside, the window open so they could all talk. Colin was preparing some food in the kitchen, and Hannah could hear the sound of a knife thunking against the cutting board at a steady rhythm as he made the salad. They hadn't eaten all day.

Since there was still no electricity, the plan for dinner was to roast hot dogs out at the fire pit. Hannah did not like that idea. The fire pit was so close to the water, and she'd spent most of the day pretending the water wasn't there, trying as hard as she could to concentrate on her novel and not think about Alessandra. She felt dread, though, knowing that nightfall was coming. Then reading wouldn't even be a possibility for passing the time.

"For a signal," Hannah said.

She tugged her phone out of her back pocket and checked the screen. She had about half her battery life left, but the words NO SIGNAL still stared back at her. The longer she went without talking to her dad, the more uncomfortable she felt. Her legs kept bouncing underneath her and she'd shifted her position about a million times in the last hour, the couch letting out an annoying *creak* every time she did so.

The thunking stopped and Colin appeared in the doorway to the kitchen, holding a rather large serrated knife.

"It's not worth it," he said.

"He's right. There's no signal anywhere on this side of the lake," Jacob told Hannah, throwing the ball so hard the *thwack* reverberated from Katie's glove. She pulled her hand out of it and shook out her fingers. Jacob winced. "Sorry."

"I've had worse," Katie shot back.

"Whatever. I'm gonna try," Hannah said, pushing herself up off the couch. She grabbed her phone and walked outside. The afternoon air was thick and warm and she reached back to gather her hair off her neck and into a loose bun. "I'm going crazy sitting here anyway. I have to get some exercise."

And it's not like I can go for a swim, she added silently, with one glance at the water. For the millionth time, she saw Alessandra go under—heard her calling for help.

"I'll be back," she said as she walked around the side of the house.

"Good luck!" Jacob sang after her facetiously. "You're gonna need it!"

"God, leave her alone," Katie said under her breath, which made Hannah smile.

It was out of the ordinary, Katie having her back, and it felt kind of nice. Hannah sort of hoped her stepsister would throw a wild pitch and knock Jacob's block off just for good measure—or maybe just bruise something. For the last couple of hours, everything Jacob did irritated Hannah, and she was starting to wonder if he'd always been this annoying or if spending an entire day with him without any electricity, and with that underlying current of fear, had brought out the worst in the both of them.

Swiping at mosquitoes and gnats, Hannah followed a skinny dirt path alongside the house. The world seemed to be turning grayer and grayer around her as the sun went down somewhere behind all those clouds. She tried to avoid stepping in any muddy puddles in her flip-flops.

Up ahead, the path veered right, away from the house, and disappeared into the thick tree line. Hannah paused, something niggling at the back of her neck. Slowly, she turned around. From this slightly higher vantage point, she could just make out Prandya's house in the distance, off to the north of Mystery Island. The windows were all lit up like a church on Christmas Eve and she could swear she heard a stray peal of jazz music carry across the water.

Hannah's heart punched a hole in her chest. She'd thought Prandya's parents were away and Raj was in town. If Prandya had managed to get home, then where were the police? And why did they have power, but Jacob's house didn't?

She looked down at her phone again. 48% battery power now. NO SIGNAL.

Hannah turned back toward the house. It wasn't like she knew anything about electricity or how it got to homes or what made it work or fail, but it seemed weird that the very next house—even as far away as it was—had no problems.

When she reached the back corner of the house, Hannah noticed the black power lines snaking into a silver tube that ran down the rear wall. The silver tube ended at a big metal box, the door of which was dented and yawning open.

"That doesn't seem right," Hannah said under her breath.

She had taken one step toward the box when a figure stepped out of the shadows right in front of her.

NINETEEN

Hannah was still screaming when she realized it was Colin smiling back at her.

"Calm down!" he said, putting his comforting hands on her shoulders. "Man, you've got good lungs."

"You scared me!" Hannah's hand was on her heart, still clutching her phone as she tried to catch her breath. The power lines were all but forgotten.

Her hair was falling into her eyes, and Colin reached up to brush a strand of it back. Hannah couldn't tell for absolute certain because of the rapidly encroaching dusk, but she was pretty sure he was blushing.

They both heard footsteps and glanced back to find Katie and Jacob racing toward them. "Are you okay?" Katie asked Hannah.

"We're fine," Colin answered for her. "Apparently I'm terrifying."

Katie rolled her eyes. "Don't scream like that! You're going to give me a heart attack!"

Shaking her head, Katie turned to walk back to the house, and Jacob slowly followed, but not before casting an unreadable look back over his shoulder at Hannah and Colin. Was it forlorn? Angry? Jealous? Impossible to tell in the waning light.

"Were you . . . following me?" Hannah asked Colin once the others were gone.

A cool breeze tickled the back of her neck, then disappeared, allowing the thick warmth of the evening to surround her again.

"Yeah, I guess I was. But not because I . . . well, not like that." Colin shuffled back a step. "It's getting dark. I thought it'd be safer if someone went with you. Even though Jacob is right—you're never gonna find a signal."

Interesting that Colin had been concerned enough for her well-being that he'd come after her, and Jacob had not, of course. Playing catch with his new girlfriend was clearly far more important.

"Well, I have to try," Hannah said, holding up her phone. "Although it is pretty creepy out there."

Somewhere in the distance, someone shrieked. A girl. It was impossible to tell whether she was happy or scared. Was it Alessandra? Or . . .

Hannah glanced across the lake toward Prandya's house again. Now that it was darker, the lights glowed even brighter. It was almost as if they were mocking her.

Nah nah nah nah nah nah! We have Wi-Fi! We have cell service! We have air-conditioning!

Colin's brow knit and he turned to follow her gaze.

"If Prandya's home, why hasn't she called the police?" Hannah asked.

"Maybe it's not her. Maybe her parents came home early." He turned Hannah's phone toward him so he could see the time. "Honestly, on foot, she probably wouldn't be back there yet."

"Okay, don't you think it's weird that they have power and we don't?" Hannah asked.

"Are you kidding? Her family's rolling in money," Colin said with a scoff. "They probably have one of those generators that powers the whole house. Or an in with the power company."

Hannah nodded, but she still didn't like it. She glanced uphill along the trail.

"If we're gonna go, we should probably go now," she said.

"Yeah. Let's see how far we can get before it's so dark we can't see our hands in front of our faces."

Colin nudged her jokingly with his elbow and started up the path. Hannah glanced back one more time at the lights in the distance before ducking into the trees after him. She held her phone out in front of her, both for the comfort of the screen's light and to keep an eye on the signal. Colin trudged ahead, showing her where to skirt around rocks and holding aside low tree branches so she didn't get smacked in the face. It wasn't long before she was sweating, tiny droplets coursing from her temples and down her cheeks. At a leveling of the trail, Colin stopped abruptly and Hannah walked right into him.

"Oof, sorry," she said, dropping her phone.

It bounced a couple of times and tumbled off the trail into the wet underbrush.

"Dang," Colin said.

"I got it," she replied. Her heart began to thrum when she realized exactly how dark it had gotten. The world around her was a deep purple and every tree branch and leaf cast a menacing shadow. Hannah bent down and felt for her phone and suddenly, her toe tipped over a ledge and she was falling. Falling into pitch-black weeds.

"Colin!"

He grabbed her arm at the last second, wrenching her shoulder, but yanking her upright. The momentum pulled her to him and they were chest to chest, his arms around her waist, her fingers digging into his biceps. She could feel his warm breath on her face, though she could barely see his features in the dark.

"Are you okay?" His voice was low.

"Fine," she said. "Thanks . . . thank you. I'm so embarrassed."

Colin brushed her cheek with the back of his fingers. "Don't be," he said.

And then his lips were on hers. She had no idea how he'd even found them in the dark, but he had. The pressure of his own lips was sweet, soft, insistent.

It was her first kiss and it was exhilarating, scary, but exciting. It was, in a word, perfect.

After a moment or ten years, Colin pulled away, but not so far that he let go of her waist.

"I'm sure this is going to sound totally cheesy," Colin said at a whisper. "But I feel like I've been looking for you my whole life."

Hannah didn't know how to respond. It *was* cheesy. But also incredibly romantic.

"That's the nicest thing anyone's ever said to me," she said honestly.

She saw the flash of his smile in the darkness, before he leaned in and kissed her once more.

Dear Future Me,

I'm freaking out. When I came home today, this journal wasn't where I left it. I mean, it was where I left it—where I always leave it—between my mattress and my box spring—but it was facedown. I never leave it facedown. For some reason it feels unlucky to leave it that way. I don't know why. I know. I'm weird. But I always leave it with the cover up.

Did my mom find it and read it? Maybe she came in here to straighten up and found it? But who am I kidding? She never straightens up my room, and all my clothes are on the floor exactly where I left them. So who the heck was in my room?

The other weird thing is, I keep feeling like someone is watching me. At first I thought maybe it was N because maybe he was trying to figure out a way to talk to me. But clearly that's wishful thinking. As far as I can tell, he hasn't even looked at me since we broke up.

But there are all these little things, like I'll hear a footstep crunch behind me, but when I look no one is there. Or I'll see a shadow and in the next second it disappears. I'm kind of scared, to be honest. Is it possible that someone's been following me and that same person snuck in here and read my journal?

Oh, God. The thought of that made me shiver just sitting here. But what am I supposed to do? Go to the police and tell them I see shadows? That my diary was turned over in its hiding spot?

Ugh. I just need school to be over and then I'm going to spend the entire summer on the beach wallowing in my jerkdom. Also, I need a new hiding place for this journal.

Dear Future Me,

OMG, I'm so happy! N wants to see me! He left me a note in my locker today—the last day of school (woo-hoo!)—and he wants me to meet him tonight at our special place. I don't know why he didn't just text me or come over or just TALK to me in class. I mean, he ignored me all day long just like he's been doing ever since that stupid thing with S.B. But whatever. It doesn't matter. I can't wait to talk to him. I'll apologize all night if I have to. I love him so much. I just want to spend the whole summer with him.

I hope he's ready to get back together. Please don't let me have ruined everything.

TWENTY

"Does anyone know what time it is?" Hannah asked, leaning forward in her Adirondack chair next to the fire. She didn't have her phone on her. She'd managed to rescue it from where it fell, but now she had left it inside the house. It was stashed inside her bag, along with the journal—the journal she'd finally finished reading.

And she kind of wished she hadn't. Because if that *was* Claudia's journal, and she really had written in it for the very last time right before going out to meet N, aka Nick, who'd left her a note . . .

Then Nick—Jacob and Colin's friend Nick—could be a murderer.

"It's just after eight," Colin said, checking his phone.

Less than sixteen hours, Hannah thought. *In less than sixteen hours, Jacob's parents will be home and this nightmare will be over.* In actuality, she had no idea what time Jacob's parents planned on returning, but putting a number on it somehow made her feel better. She leaned back in her chair and blew out a sigh.

Jacob had found some old plastic furniture in the shed, hosed it off, and dragged it out so they could sit by the fire pit and not spend the whole time shifting on the uncomfortable benches. The electricity was still not working, so the firelight was the only real light they had. Hannah had made sure that her chair was positioned so that her back was to the lake.

Colin reached over to hand her a napkin, and when their hands brushed her entire body reacted. Even with all the questions and worries crowding her head, she couldn't help smiling, and he grinned back.

Part of her couldn't believe they had actually kissed. She couldn't believe it for any number of reasons, but the biggest of those was the fact that last night, they'd basically watched a girl die. Every time she thought about the kiss, she felt a heady sense of euphoria, followed by a sinking, swirling, acidic guilt.

So before she even broke eye contact with Colin, her face fell. And then so did his.

"The hot dogs are good," Colin said, looking across the fire at Jacob. "Where'd you get them?"

"They're just regular hot dogs. They taste better because I'm a total grilling genius," Jacob joked half-heartedly.

"Or it's because we went for a hike first, and worked up an appetite," Colin suggested, shooting Hannah an almost hopeful look.

"Or it's because you're so giddy from this whole flirty thing you two have got going on that anything would taste good," Katie said, popping the last bite of her hot dog into her mouth.

Hannah shot Katie a look of death, then glanced away, her face ten times hotter than the fire.

"Okay, that's gross. Let's talk about something else." There was an edge in Jacob's voice that brought Hannah up short. What was he, jealous now? What a joke. She stared at his profile and saw his jaw working. If they had been alone at that moment, she would have flicked his earlobe as hard as she could. Instead, she pulled her hoodie closer around her and stared at the fire.

"Where do you think Prandya is?" Katie said, glancing out at the lake. There was no more rain, but the clouds were still thick.

"Honestly? She might not even have gotten home yet," Jacob said.

"Then who turned all their lights on?" Hannah asked.

Jacob shrugged. "It's gotta be her parents, right? They came back early?"

Hannah shifted in her chair. Something wasn't right. It just didn't make sense that Prandya's house was alive and kicking while Jacob's cottage was dead as a doornail. Jacob reached over and rubbed her back.

"Don't worry, Champ. It's gonna be okay," he said.

Hannah turned and looked into his eyes and felt herself relax. It was just Jacob. Just her best friend. He wasn't the enemy. When she turned to face forward again, Colin was staring at her, his expression tight.

Hannah's heart thunked. Was *he* jealous? How sweet. And since when was *she* such a heartbreaker?

"I have an idea," Colin said, brightening suddenly. "What if we go up to Killer Point and try to signal them from there?"

Hannah's chest tightened. *Killer Point?*

"Signal them? How?" Jacob asked, leaning back again.

"We could light a fire or something," Colin said. "Prandya's parents can see the cliff from their place. If they notice a fire up there, they'll call it in."

There was a long moment of silence, filled only by the crackling of the flames in the pit. Katie watched Hannah expectantly.

"What?" Hannah said.

"Aren't you going to ask?" Katie said.

Hannah scowled. "Ask what?" she demanded, even though she knew exactly what Katie was thinking.

Katie sighed. "Okay, fine. I'll ask. What's Killer Point?"

"It's just a drop-off with a really unfortunate nickname," Colin said, spearing another hot dog on a skewer and holding it over the fire. "People used to cliff dive off of it, apparently."

"Used to?" Hannah asked.

"It's kinda high," Jacob said. "There were some accidents, so people stopped going."

Colin pulled out the hot dog and checked it. "I don't know. I went hiking up there with my family a couple weeks ago and the cliff's not *that* high. They say it's not the height that'll kill you, it's the rocks down below. You've gotta know exactly where to jump or you'll break your skull."

Hannah cringed.

"And your legs and your arms and your ribs . . ." Jacob muttered, sucking some mustard off his thumb.

"Stop it," Katie ordered.

"But we're not talking about jumping off it. We're just talking about trying to get rescued, right?" Hannah said, feeling a little zing of hope.

Katie glanced warily at Hannah, like she'd been counting on Hannah to shoot down the plan.

"What? This could work," Hannah said.

"I don't know," Katie replied. "I think we should just stay here and wait for Jacob's parents."

"I can't," Hannah said. Now that there was a plan on the table, her whole body felt jittery. Katie and Jacob exchanged surprised looks. "I can't just sit here anymore. If there's a chance we could get help tonight, I say we try it."

"When did it get so cold?" Hannah asked, shivering as she clutched her hoodie tight around her torso. Jacob and Colin were walking on either side of her, close enough that their mutual body heat should have been keeping her warm, but it wasn't working. Katie trudged behind them, head down, scowl on. "I swear the weather out here has commitment issues."

"Where *are* we?" Jacob asked, gazing into the sameness of the trees all around them.

"This is the north side of the lake," Colin replied, hands stuffed in the pockets of his sweatshirt. "My grandfather says they haven't built any houses up here because it's basically solid rock."

"You know, it's not too late to turn around," Katie muttered. "I still can't believe you agreed to this, Hannah."

Hannah paused, and everyone else did, too. Colin, Jacob, and Katie all looked at her expectantly, as if truly interested in what she was about to say. For the first time in the past two days, Hannah actually didn't feel invisible. She had the sense that if she told them she wanted to go back, they would, and if she told them she wanted to keep going, they would. Since when did she wield this kind of power? For half a second, it felt exciting, and then her stomach clenched. She didn't want to be responsible for everyone.

"I still think it's worth a shot," Hannah said, glancing at the duffel bag Colin was carrying. They'd packed it with a few logs, a fire-starter nugget, and a box of matches.

Katie shivered. "Fine. If you guys think it'll work." She looked around at the trees crowding the path. "But if we burn down the forest, it's your fault."

"We're not gonna burn down the forest," Jacob said.

"But if something goes wrong, we can't even call the police," Katie said. "Anybody think about that?"

Jacob and Hannah locked eyes and his lips twitched. A laugh bubbled up in Hannah's throat and she doubled over. It was one of those laughs fueled both by humor and nervousness, and it took over her whole body. Jacob cracked up, too, and Katie looked at them like they were crazy. But Hannah couldn't stop. She laughed so hard she had to wipe at her eyes with the sleeves of her sweatshirt.

"What's so funny?" Katie asked finally.

Hannah leaned one hand on Colin's strong shoulder as if for balance. "Nothing, it's just—"

"It's like you switched personalities," Jacob supplied. Having already gotten control of himself, he pointed back and forth from Hannah to Katie. "And it's totally freaking me out."

"Sorry. Sorry. I'm not laughing *at* you, I swear. It's just . . . funny," Hannah said.

"Yeah, well. Someone's gotta be the levelheaded one around here," Katie snapped.

And that just made Hannah laugh harder. Finally, Katie let out a frustrated groan and trudged ahead up the path. Colin adjusted his grip on the duffel bag strap and followed, leaving Hannah and Jacob behind. Alone. For the first time since they stood on the dock yesterday morning. That seemed like a lifetime ago.

"Dude," Jacob said as Hannah's laughter turned into high-pitched gales. "Are you okay?"

"No." Hannah shook her head, hugging herself around her waist. "I think I might be delirious."

Jacob narrowed his eyes at her. "H, come on."

"Sorry. I'm sorry." She took a deep breath and blew it out. Her abs were sore from laughing. She looked at Jacob again, and saw that his expression had turned somber. "Everything okay? I mean, aside from the obvious."

"You're not upset, are you?" he asked. "About me and Katie?"

Hannah pondered this for a second. A day ago she would have killed to be alone with Jacob. And she would have felt heartbroken about him choosing Katie over her. It did sting, but not half as badly as she would have imagined. Was it because of Colin? Because of one—well, two—stolen kisses in the woods? Was she really that fickle?

She didn't have it in her to figure that out right now. All she knew was how she felt, right in this moment.

"No. I'm really not," she said, briefly rubbing at her tired eyes.

"Is it because you're obsessed with Colin?"

Hannah snorted, glad that the dark hid her blush. "I'm not *obsessed* with him. But okay, I don't know why I'm not upset. I'm just not. If you guys are happy, then I'm happy."

"But you are obsessed with Colin," he said flatly. "Just so we're clear."

Hannah sighed. "Jacob, you've been texting Katie behind my back for months. You're not allowed to be jealous of me and Colin."

Jacob's knee bounced as he pushed his hands deeper into the pockets of his hoodie and looked away. After a long pause he finally said, "Well, if you guys are happy, then I'm happy."

"Thank you."

Jacob chewed on his lip. "You're my best friend, you know?"

Hannah's heart felt full. "I know."

Together they turned and started to follow the path the others had taken. Jacob bumped her arm with his and she bumped him right back. Before long they hit a sharp incline and Hannah's quads began to burn.

"Up here!" Colin called out.

Hannah and Jacob exchanged resigned glances, then slowly followed. As soon as Hannah stepped out onto the flat rock surface of the cliff, her stomach flip-flopped. The cliff loomed so high over the lake she could see the tops of some of the trees on the other side, which made her dizzy.

Colin and Katie stood right at the edge, and it was all she could do to keep from begging them to come back. There was a reason she'd never taken to diving, even though she spent so much time in the pool and hanging out with the diving team. And that reason was, she hated heights. Hated planes, hated Ferris wheels—she even hated looking out the fifth-story windows at her high school.

"See? It isn't so bad." Colin leaned over the edge and Katie turned her back on him, shuddering.

"You going for it, man?" Jacob joked.

"I will if you will," Colin challenged.

There was a charge in the air that Hannah didn't like. "We didn't come up here to jump," she reminded them. Sure enough, she could see the glowing lights of Prandya's house down below.

"So?" Colin lifted one shoulder and dropped the duffel on the ground. He seemed puffed up suddenly, as if his chest had widened. He looked Jacob in the eye. "No one said we can't."

Jacob walked up to the edge and peered over.

"Think you can handle it, Faber?" Colin said.

Hannah's heart fluttered uncomfortably.

"Guys. Come on," Katie said. "Let's just light the fire and get the heck out of here."

"She's right, man. Let's just do this." Jacob bent at the waist to reach for the duffel bag.

"Why? You scared?"

Everyone froze. Hannah's mouth went clammy as the wind whistled through the trees. Slowly, Jacob stood up straight. He and Colin stared each other down.

"What's your problem all of a sudden?" Jacob asked.

Colin stepped around the duffel bag to go toe-to-toe with Jacob. "I don't have a problem. Do you have a problem?" he asked, perfectly calm.

Hannah and Katie locked eyes. What the heck was happening here?

"My problem is that you suddenly seem to have a problem," Jacob said, his eyes aflame. "What is it? You jealous?"

"Jealous?" Colin spat, bumping Jacob slightly with his chest. Jacob backed up a step—backed up closer to the edge. "Of what?"

Katie took in a sharp breath. "You guys—"

"Of me and Hannah? Because we had five seconds to ourselves back there?" Jacob threw out a hand. "She's my best friend, dude. You knew that going in."

He bumped Colin right back, but Colin didn't move. Hannah's pulse thrummed like crazy.

"Check yourself, Faber," Colin said, bumping Jacob again. A few pebbles bounced off the rocky shelf.

"Jacob!" Hannah shouted.

"No. You know what? I'm sick of your attitude, Barnes," Jacob said, giving Colin's shoulder a shove. "Back off or I'm gonna—"

"No. You back off," Colin said, and he shoved Jacob clear off the cliff.

TWENTY-ONE

Hannah's scream nearly ripped her throat out.

"Jacob!" Katie screeched.

Down below, the splash was just starting to froth, and then it disappeared.

"Oh my God," Colin said, his hands to his head. "Oh my God, what did I do? What did I do?"

"You shoved him off a cliff, that's what you did!" Katie shouted, her eyes wild.

"I don't see him." Hannah stood as close to the cliff as she dared. "He hasn't come up, you guys. Where is he?" Her throat closed and tears began to course down her face.

It's not the height that'll kill you, it's the rocks down below, Colin had said earlier. *You've gotta know exactly where to jump or you'll break your skull.*

"We have to help him," Katie said frantically. "Hannah! We have to get down there!"

Hannah whirled on Colin. "Which way?" she barked.

Colin didn't even look at her. It was like he couldn't focus. Hannah grabbed his arms and squeezed.

"Colin! How do we get down there?" she said, giving him a shake.

Suddenly his eyes seemed to snap. "Follow me," he said. And he was off.

Katie ran after him and Hannah brought up the rear, shoving aside branches and crashing through the brush. Something nicked her face. Her lungs burned. But all she could think about was Jacob.

What if he had hit his head? Or broken his neck? Or what if he was totally fine, but that . . . thing—that thing that had attacked Alessandra—was now after him?

Hannah's toe jammed against something and she went airborne, then landed sprawled in the dirt, her face scraping against a jagged rock. Pain seared through her cheekbone and skull. When she sat up, the woods seemed to pulsate around her. Where was Colin? Where was Katie? She touched her cheek and winced. When she put her hand down to shove herself up, it scraped against something sharp and she saw that she was sitting next to a circle of rocks with a pile of old black ash at its center. Someone had set a fire in this clearing at some point. More than one fire, from the look of how much ash there was. Slowly, she dragged herself to her feet. She was facing an etching on a tree: N.F. + C.C. with a heart carved around it. The letters blurred as she stared at them.

N.F. + C.C. Nick Freeman + Claudia Caldwell. Was this the "special place" Claudia had talked about in her journal?

A branch snapped nearby.

"You guys!" Hannah shouted. "Where—"

She screamed when someone grabbed her arm.

"Shhhhh! It's just me!"

Blue eyes. Shaggy hair. Hannah blinked, disoriented. "Nick?"

Murderer. The word came to her out of the darkness. Hannah staggered back several steps. What was Nick doing here? How had he found them? He reached for her again—too fast for her to get away.

"Let go of me!" she shouted, ripping her arm out of his grasp.

Nick looked confused. "Hannah. Calm down. I have to talk to you."

This made no sense. How had he even gotten here? They were at least two miles from Jacob's house, in the middle of the freaking woods. Whatever was going on here, Hannah didn't like it.

"I don't have time for this," she said, starting along the path again. "Jacob fell into the water."

"I know. I saw." Nick grabbed her again and Hannah almost wailed in desperation. He yanked her elbow, forcing her to look at him. "I saw Colin *push* him."

Hannah paused. The last five minutes were a blur in her mind—a blur of panic and adrenaline and fear. "It was an accident," she said.

Nick shook his head. "I don't think it was. Hannah, I think he did it on purpose. And I think he killed my girlfriend, too."

"What?" Hannah breathed. "Nick, what are you talking about?"

"Colin. You can't trust him."

Hannah's heart gave an unpleasant squeeze. She opened her mouth to respond, but then came the sound of crunching gravel.

"There you are!"

Katie ran around a bend in the pathway, and Jacob was right behind her.

"Jacob!" Hannah cried, the relief so acute her knees went weak. "You're okay!"

She threw her arms around him, not caring that he was soaking wet.

"I'll live," he said ruefully. But he was pale as a sheet, and he was shivering.

"We have to get him inside," Colin was saying as he appeared. "I'm really—"

He stopped in his tracks when he saw Nick standing there.

"What are *you* doing here?" he demanded.

Nick glanced at Hannah, who clenched her jaw. "Just came to hang out," he said. "Where's Alessandra?"

"Someone should take Nick's Jet Ski back to town and go to the police," Hannah said as they rushed back into Jacob's house. There was a beach towel strewn across one of the chairs on the screened-in porch and she tossed it to Jacob. He wrapped the towel around himself, still shivering—more from fear, Hannah thought, than from anything else. They had told Nick the whole story about Alessandra and the attack on the way back to the house, and he seemed more freaked out than any of the rest of them.

"He should go," Colin said, lifting his chin in Nick's direction.

"I still don't think anyone should go out on that lake," Katie said.

"Personally, I think the person who just shoved someone off a cliff should be the one to face down the lake monster," Nick said as he glared at Colin.

"It was an accident." Colin's voice was a low rumble.

"Not from where I was standing," Nick said.

"And where *were* you standing, exactly?" Colin asked, advancing on Nick. "Anyone else here wondering what this guy was doing stalking us in the woods?"

"Back off, Colin," Nick said, shoving Colin's chest.

Colin reached back an arm and Hannah gasped as Jacob threw himself forward and grabbed Colin's fist before Colin could swing. "Everyone chill!" Jacob yelled. "We're not gonna fight right now!"

There was a long, tense moment in which no one moved or even breathed. Then Colin ripped his arm away and paced to the window. "You know what? Fine. I'll go."

"What?" Hannah said, reaching for his shoulder. "Colin, no—"

"It's fine." Colin looked at Hannah, took a deep breath, and steeled himself. His brown eyes were pained but determined as he reached up and quickly brushed his thumb down her cheek. "I'll go for help and be back before you know it." He looked over at Jacob and shook his head. "I really am sorry, man. I'm glad you're okay."

Jacob nodded silently. They all followed Colin back outside to Nick's Jet Ski. A thick fog clung to the lake now, and Hannah couldn't see more than a few feet into the distance. Nick tossed Colin the keys and Colin looked like he wanted to say something, but thought the better of it and turned away.

Hannah shivered. She couldn't believe Colin was leaving, and they were going to be stuck here with Nick. "Colin! Are you sure about this?"

"It's fine," he called back. "Just sit tight. This will all be over soon."

He strapped on a life jacket and climbed onto the Jet Ski. Jacob stood at the shoreline and helped Colin push off. Hannah heard the slurping of the water as the Jet Ski moved away from them, and she couldn't help thinking she should have kissed Colin good-bye. Or at least given him a hug for good luck. Something. Her throat tightened as he revved the engine. She kept her eyes on his broad back until the mist swallowed him whole.

TWENTY-TWO

"We need to talk," Nick said under his breath to Hannah the second Colin was gone.

Hannah glanced around for Jacob and Katie, but they were already walking into the house. She turned to follow them, hugging herself as tightly as possible. Every fiber of her being told her she wasn't safe around Nick. His own girlfriend hadn't trusted him, and now she was gone.

"No. We really don't," she said.

She jogged up the steps to the porch, yanked open the screen door, and hurried inside. Jacob and Katie were heading upstairs together. Her heart sliced down the middle. *Nice moment to get your alone time*, she thought.

"Yeah, we do." Nick closed the front door behind them and followed her to the center of the room. "Listen, a few months ago, my girlfriend, Claudia, disappeared."

"I know all about Claudia," Hannah interjected. Seeing Nick's confused look, she added, "Alessandra told me." Just saying Alessandra's name brought up bile in the back of her throat.

"What did she tell you?" Nick asked.

"That Claudia disappeared a couple months ago without a trace," Hannah said. "And that you were a suspect."

Nick reached up and rubbed his face with both hands. "That's just great. Is that all she told you?"

"Basically," Hannah said, choosing to ignore the fact that she knew about Nick's "alibi." Because she and Nick both knew he'd faked it somehow—that on the last night anyone had seen Claudia, she'd been planning to meet up with him. "But I happen to know a lot more than that."

"You're not making any sense. You never even met Claudia."

"Yeah, but I feel like I did," Hannah said quietly. She walked over to her bag on the sofa, where she'd stashed Claudia's journal. Suddenly all she wanted to do was see his face when he showed it to her. His reaction would reveal everything. Making sure not to turn her back on him, she yanked the book out and held it up. "Does this look familiar?"

Nick's jaw went slack. "You have Claudia's journal? How did you get that?"

Hannah hesitated. He didn't look guilty. Or scared. He looked . . . sad. Intrigued, maybe. His eyes seemed to droop as he gazed at her, waiting for an answer.

"I found it," she said.

"Where? How did you . . . ? Did her mother have it?" he asked. Then, before Hannah could answer: "Can I see it?"

He took a step toward her and she held the book back. "No. They're her private thoughts."

"So why do *you* get to read them?" he asked, a glower darkening his features. "You didn't even know her."

"Yeah, well, she was afraid of you, did you know that?" Hannah snapped. "So why should you get to read it?"

"She wasn't afraid of me," Nick said incredulously. "Does it say that?"

"Yeah, in fact, it does," Hannah said, hedging the truth. It didn't *really* say that—not explicitly. But it was clearly implied.

"Why?" Nick asked, his voice cracking. "Why would she be afraid of me?"

"I would have been, too, if I were her," Hannah told him, shoving the book back into her bag and clutching the whole thing in her arms. "The behavior she describes in there . . ." She paused as her heart choked off her air supply, then cleared her throat. "It's disturbing."

"Disturbing?" Nick spat, his face screwing up. "What's disturbing? Me getting angry when she cheated on me? If that's disturbing, then you better go out and arrest every guy who's ever had a two-faced girlfriend."

Hannah held her breath. "Wow. That's some way to talk about the girl you supposedly loved."

Nick turned away from her, toward the windows facing the lake, and pushed his hands up into his shaggy hair. Hannah cast a glance toward the stairs, wondering if she could make it up to Jacob and Katie in time if he suddenly whirled on her.

"Did you kill her?" she asked. Because she had to. She had to know.

Nick let out a short laugh. When he faced her again, there were tears in his eyes. "No. Are you kidding me? No."

"But you think Colin did," she snapped. "Why would Colin hurt Claudia?"

For a long moment, Nick just stared at her. Hannah could practically see the gears in his head turning as he decided what to say—what to reveal. Finally, he gave her a rueful smile.

"I can't believe I came out here because I was worried about you."

"About *me?*" Hannah asked, incredulous.

"Yeah, about you." Nick pressed his lips together. "Did anyone tell you how much you look like Claudia?"

Hannah said nothing, but Nick could see the truth in her eyes, apparently, because he smirked.

"After the other night, when it was obvious Colin was into you, I asked around a little and found out about his girlfriend back home," Nick said. "Did you know he had a girlfriend back home?"

Back home? What was he talking about?

"Her name was Vicki Palecki. Once you guys get the internet back in this place, look her up. It's an interesting read." He grabbed the blanket off the back of the couch and turned toward the door.

"Where're you going?" Hannah demanded.

"I'm gonna sleep on the porch," he said. "I think I feel more welcome with the lake monster than I do in here."

Then he walked out and slammed the door.

The rhythm of the floorboards' creak was mesmerizing. *Creak, creak, craaack . . . creak, creak, creak.* Hannah had been pacing the same five-foot tract for what felt like hours, and the repetition had become comforting in a way. She walked toward the screened-in porch—*creak, creak, craaack*—then she stopped, turned, and walked back toward the window—*creak, creak, creak.*

Outside, there was nothing but mist. It was so thick now that she couldn't even see the shoreline, let alone the lake. What if whatever was out there could *leave* the lake under cover like this? What if it was slithering across the rocky beach right now, pulling its bulbous, misshapen body toward the house, crunching bones between its jaws?

Alessandra . . . I'm so sorry. I'm so so sorry this happened to you.

And meanwhile, what had happened to Prandya? To Colin?

Creak, creak, craaaack. Creak, creak, creak.

Hannah pulled out her phone. There was only 5% battery left. Colin had been gone for two and a half hours and Nick had been on one of the porch rocking chairs for just as long.

Creak, creak, craaack. Creak, creak, creak.

Did Nick really think Colin had something to do with Claudia's disappearance? Or was he just trying to throw suspicion off himself? If that was the case, there was no reason for him to try to convince Hannah—for him to ride his Jet Ski all the way out here to talk to her. He had no idea she had Claudia's journal until she told him, which meant he had no idea she suspected him. So maybe he *had* come here to warn them away from Colin—to save them from the bad guy.

But that was insane. Colin wasn't the bad guy. Colin was amazing. He liked her. And she liked him. Until that whole shoving-Jacob-off-a-cliff thing, of course. But still. That had been an accident. She knew it had. He'd freaked out when Jacob had gone over the edge.

Hannah stared hard out the window, as if she could make Colin appear. She just wanted to see him again. She wanted to talk to him. But with every second he was gone, she was more and more certain he was never coming back.

Creak, creak, craaack. Creak, creak—

"Will you please stop it already?" Katie demanded. "You're driving me crazy."

Hannah flinched. Katie was sitting on the couch, staring at an *InStyle* magazine by the light of a flickering candle. Hannah would have accused her of being shallow at a time like this, but the magazine had been open to the same ad for hair gel for the past hour or so. It was pretty clear Katie wasn't actually reading it. She didn't even use hair gel.

"Sorry. But I can't sit still," Hannah said. "And it's not like I can pace outside with Nick out there."

"Yeah. He's a little weird, right?" Katie asked.

Hannah blew out a sigh. "Tell me about it."

"Colin should have been back by now," Jacob said. "Or Prandya should have sent the police. What is going on out there?"

He was standing at the front door, gazing out the window, chewing on his thumbnail. Hannah could see his jaw still working whenever he pulled his hand away and knew he was as tense as she was.

"Maybe he got lost in the fog," Katie suggested weakly.

"He would have gotten to town before the fog got this bad," Jacob said, his tone almost angry. "And the cops would be able to get here no matter what. They have equipment for this kind of weather."

They all fell silent. None of them wanted to say what they were thinking—that maybe the same monster that had attacked Alessandra had snatched Prandya and Colin, too. The thought made Hannah's throat close over.

"I'm going to bed," Jacob announced. He grabbed his dead phone off a side table and trudged upstairs into the darkness.

"Good night!" Katie called after him sarcastically.

His answer was to slam his bedroom door.

Trouble in paradise? Hannah thought, then hated herself. Who cared what was going on between Katie and Jacob at this point?

Alessandra was most certainly dead. Maybe Colin and Prandya, too. And now they were trapped with Nick lurking outside.

"We just have to get through tonight," Katie said to herself more than Hannah. "Jacob's parents will be back in the morning and this will all be over."

"Not for Alessandra," Hannah said flatly.

Katie looked at her as if she'd forgotten she was there. A surge of white-hot anger and frustration welled up inside of Hannah and she turned on her heel and opened the front door.

"What're you—"

Hannah stepped outside and closed the door behind her. The first thing she noticed was that she was entirely alone. Nick's chair was empty, the blanket left in a lump on the seat. The air was cool and the mist, oddly, swirled around the porch, but didn't penetrate higher than the first step. It surrounded the house on all sides so that she couldn't see the trees to the left and the right any better than she could see the water, which she knew for a fact was dead ahead.

She took a deep breath of the cool night air and shivered. It was so quiet, except for this constant, underlying sound, like a hissing. As soon as she became aware of it, Hannah reached back for the doorknob again, but then she realized where it was coming from.

The fog. The wetness was making a *shhhhhh* sound as it slipped over the grass and leaves.

"Nick?" Hannah called out quietly, then, somewhat louder, "Nick? Where are you?"

Nothing. Maybe he'd gone out to the woods to pee or something?

Steeling herself, Hannah stared in the direction of the lake.

Where are you, Colin? she thought. *Are you still out there?*

Far in the distance, Hannah saw the hint of a light. It undulated into view like a mirage—orangey yellow and seeming to move of its own accord. She stepped forward and narrowed her eyes, but then the light winked out.

What was that? It hadn't looked like a fog light or a flashlight. It had looked more like a flame. Suddenly, the mist shifted and she saw it again—yes, a flame—seeming to float in midair—and then it was gone.

Hannah gasped. Where was that coming from? In the fog it was impossible to tell whether the flame was three feet offshore or thirty. But why would there be a flame of any kind out there on a night like this? What was going on?

Then, to Hannah's left, came a sound. A crunch of leaves. She sensed something heavy moving nearby.

"Nick?" She clenched her teeth. "Nick, if that's you and you're messing with me, I swear to you—"

She choked in a breath and looked. The mist swirled, as if something—or someone—had disturbed it. Hannah's insides froze. She wanted to move forward to inspect it, but couldn't make herself go. Her feet were stuck to the floorboards. Her breath was short.

"Colin?" she whispered hopefully—fretfully. "Nick?"

Silence. An almost unnatural stillness.

What is happening? she thought wildly. *What is happening?*

She felt a presence as clearly as she could feel her own skin. Something was out there. Something was . . . watching her.

She stared into the mist. And stared. And stared. Defying whatever it was to show itself. To stop hiding. To get it over with already.

Then it happened again. Right in front of her, the mist swelled and withdrew—swelled and withdrew—as if it were breathing. As if the fog was a living thing in and of itself.

Hannah saw something move—a shadow, a form—of what she couldn't tell—and she ran inside, slamming the door behind her.

"What?" Katie said, sitting up. "What's wrong?"

Hannah gasped for breath, each inhale breaking over her panic. "Nothing," she said quickly. "I'm going to bed, too."

She ran upstairs as fast as she could, pulling the covers all the way up over her head as if that could protect her from the shadow in the mist, from the flame on the water. Her phone glowed inside the cave of blankets and she watched the time tick away on the screen until the battery finally died, and then she lay there in the dark, cold and alone, knowing she was never going to sleep again.

"It's going to be all right, Hannah. I promise."

Hannah clutched Colin's hand as the movie played out in front of them. A girl was standing ankle deep in the water on the shores of Mystery Island and she was afraid. Alone and afraid. Someone was after her.

"No, it's not," Hannah whined. "He's going to take her. He's going to kill her."

"It's just a movie, Hannah."

That wasn't Colin's voice. Hannah looked up, startled, and found that she was holding not Colin's hand, but Nick's. He stared at her, blue eyes cold and hard, and when she tried to pull away, he wouldn't let go.

"What's the matter?" he asked. "Why are you so afraid of me?"

The door to the projection room opened and Hannah managed to pull herself away. Claudia's mother walked into the room dressed in black from head to toe—Colin's mother's theater uniform.

"You shouldn't be here, you know," she said, looking down her nose at Hannah.

"I know. I'm . . . I'm sorry. I'll go."

Hannah started for the door, but Claudia's mother blocked her way.

"No. Not here in the theater. You shouldn't be in this town. You don't belong here." She leaned in toward Hannah's face, so close their noses were almost touching. "Get away from the lake, Hannah. Get away from the lake!"

Hannah backed up and bumped right into Nick—or was it Colin? "I'm sorry, I'll go!"

Claudia's mother's expression softened and she reached out to caress Hannah's face. "You look just like her, you know. Just . . . like . . . my . . . Claudia . . ."

Hannah awoke with a start, a gasp stuck in her throat. Outside, the world was completely gray with fog, but it was lighter somehow, as if dawn was trying to break through.

Katie was splayed out next to her, on top of the covers, snoring, with one arm flung across her forehead. Hannah reached for her phone, then remembered it was dead. She tried the bedside lamp, which, of course, did not flick on.

But if the sun was coming up, hours must have passed since Colin had left. Where were the police? They definitely would have been here by now if Colin had made it to town. Which meant only one thing: Colin was dead. Or, at the very least, hurt or trapped somewhere.

Hannah shoved herself out of bed, her heart hammering. She had no idea what time Jacob's parents were due back, but she knew she was never going to make it that long, especially with no way of knowing what time it was now. This was torture, plain and simple. She couldn't take being cut off like this. It was driving her crazy. This was the twenty-first century! It was insane that she couldn't get out of here.

Hannah thought hard. Hadn't some of the pictures she had seen over the years featured Jacob's family paddling in canoes? Did they rent those, or were they still around here somewhere? She knew it was a long shot, since Jacob would have probably mentioned canoes if they were available, but she had to do something.

Shoving her feet into her flip-flops, Hannah walked out of the room and into the hall. The door to Jacob's room was ajar, and he was passed out on his bed. She turned and started downstairs, her flip-flops slapping loudly with every step, hoping to wake up Nick if he was on the couch. Had he ever come inside last night?

She paused halfway down the steps. Nick wasn't in the living room. Slowly she checked the house. He wasn't in the kitchen. She pushed open the door to the half bath, but that was empty, too. Was he still sitting on the porch? What had happened last night? Maybe he'd walked down the dock and tripped and fallen into the lake and the lake monster had gotten him. Remembering how he'd clutched her arm in the woods the night before, she wasn't sure whether to be horrified or gratified by the thought.

Unable to face the lake, Hannah went out the back door and paused for a moment. The morning mist swirled around her and she remembered the presence she'd felt last night. Maybe she should just stay inside. But then a fleeting image from her dream caught in her mind. A girl, alone and scared in the lake, just waiting to be dragged under. And suddenly, the thought of retreating made her hackles rise. She wasn't going to just sit here and be a prisoner—a victim. Not anymore.

Taking a deep, bolstering breath, Hannah tromped through the fog and semidarkness in the direction of the shed. After a few steps, she could just make out its shape. Palms itching, Hannah stomped inside, pushing the door all the way open so that it slammed back against the building, making her jump.

There were two canoes, propped up against one wall.

Why hadn't Jacob mentioned them when the boats had gone missing? Was it because he was afraid to go out on the lake?

Hannah decided not to dwell on the questions, but to focus on the hope that took flight inside her chest. Maybe if she and Katie and Jacob took the canoes and stuck to the shoreline, they could circle the lake and get back to town. If they stayed in the shallows and away from the open water, that thing out there couldn't get them, right? Or, worst-case scenario, if it did try to come after them, they could just bail out of the canoes and run for dry land. Yes, it would take a while to get back to civilization this way—hours, maybe—but at least it was a plan.

She grabbed the first wooden canoe and yanked it out onto the ground. It clattered against the rocks and roots around the shed and Hannah glanced back at the house, expecting to see Katie in the window, but the fog was so thick she couldn't even make out the second floor. Hannah grabbed the canoe with both hands and started to drag it. It was heavier than it looked. Her sweaty fingers slipped right off and she let out a wail as a sliver of metal cut into her thumb.

"Stupid thing!"

She kicked the canoe as she sucked on her thumb. It stung like crazy. When she looked at it again, more blood had already bubbled up.

Tears welled in Hannah's eyes, but she blinked them away.

"You are coming with me!" she said through her teeth to the canoe.

She bent at the waist and grabbed the vessel on both sides, then leaned backward. The canoe slid forward several feet, almost knocking her off balance, but she managed to keep her legs beneath her. She dragged it toward the far corner of the house and past the screened-in porch all the way to the front. At the corner closest to the lake, she stopped and took two deep breaths.

The fog had thinned ever so slightly since last night, so that she could see a bit farther than she had been able to then—almost to the edge of the water. Watching the tiny waves lap the shoreline made her shiver. She wondered if she would even be able to get Katie to agree to her plan—if Katie would go anywhere near the lake ever again. Maybe they'd have to bring in a helicopter to take her out.

The thought made her actually snort a laugh.

Hannah glanced at her thumb again. Blood dripped down her hand and dropped off into the dirt. Forget the canoe. She had to go inside for a Band-Aid. She had to find Jacob and wake up Katie and figure out their next move. Leaving the canoe behind, Hannah headed for the house, intent on walking in the front door, right past Nick if she had to.

That was when she saw the body.

Thumb between her lips, Hannah froze. She recognized the cargo shorts first. Then the skinny legs and the light leg hair. Then the white T-shirt soaked with dark, oozing blood. She staggered forward a step and nearly fainted into the side of the porch.

Nick lay on his back, eyes wide and staring, hair matted and damp, his throat slit and the wound still pumping out blood.

TWENTY-THREE

"No!" Hannah screamed. The word tore from her throat, scaring birds from the trees and echoing across the lake. Tears burst from her eyes with a force she could hardly comprehend.

She was looking at a dead body.

Nick is dead.

Even as she felt the pain of this realization, she felt the underlying thrum of terror. Because it was clear that something— someone—had murdered Nick.

And whatever it was, it was still out there.

Whatever it was, it was *near*.

Hannah fell to the ground at Nick's side, and her knees got soaked with his blood. She clutched his damp T-shirt, shaking with each sob. With her other hand, she reached up and closed his eyes, choking on her own saliva. He was still warm. Hannah turned her head and retched into the grass.

"Hannah, what're you yelling—"

The door slammed and before Hannah could even turn around, Katie was screeching at a pitch that barely seemed human. She fell back against the wall of the house, her hand over her mouth as she stared at Nick.

"What happened?" Jacob said, stumbling out behind Katie.

Hannah staggered to her feet, and her flip-flops slipped in the puddle of blood. She backed up a few steps, then kicked them off and ran up the porch to Katie, who was heaving for breath. Without thinking, she grabbed her stepsister in a hug and Katie hugged her back.

"Nick is dead," Hannah wailed. "I don't know how, but he's dead."

"Oh my God," Katie said. "Oh my God."

Katie sobbed full-body, racking sobs as Jacob walked down the steps to hover over Nick.

"Holy—" he said, and covered his mouth with both hands. He looked green. He hurried back up the steps to face Katie and Hannah. "How did this happen? Who could've—"

Hannah reached out and clutched the front of Jacob's shirt in one fist.

"We have to get out of here," she said through her teeth. "Now."

"But how?" Katie asked, her face soaked with tears. "And where is Colin?"

They all looked out at the lake, an automatic reflex, even though Hannah was patently sure they would never see Colin again—that he was as dead as Nick, as dead as Alessandra certainly was. And what about Prandya? Was *she* somehow behind all this? Hannah didn't know the girl much, after all.

But then her jaw fell open. The mist had pulled back farther and Hannah could now see part of the dock. Nick's Jet Ski—the one Colin had sailed out on the night before—bobbed innocently in the water, tied off to the dock.

"Did he come back?" Katie asked with a sniffle.

"Where is he?" Hannah asked, looking at the patches of dirt and grass and wet leaves around the house—looking for another body. Her brain felt muddled and thick as she tried to comprehend the situation. "If he came back, then where are the police? Why didn't he bring help?"

At that moment, the door burst open behind them. Katie was still screaming when Colin grabbed Jacob around the waist and held the huge, serrated kitchen knife to his throat.

TWENTY-FOUR

"Colin?" Hannah stumbled backward, a splinter slicing into the pad of one bare foot. "What are you *doing*?"

Katie whimpered, flattening herself against the wall of the house. Jacob's eyes were wide as he breathed shallowly through his nose. But Colin gazed calmly at Hannah. His grip on the blade was so tight that his knuckles were white, but his hand was steady like a practiced surgeon's. He wore a light gray T-shirt that was clean aside from a small, dark blood splatter near the hem.

"You may want to look away, Hannah," Colin said in a perfectly conversational tone of voice. "This part could get messy."

"What are you doing?" Hannah repeated. "Colin. What are you talking about?"

"What am I doing? I'm getting rid of him, just like I got rid of Nick," Colin said, like it was so obvious. He laughed and shook his head. "I should have dealt with him weeks ago," he added, nodding toward Nick's body. "I never could stand that loser. What Claudia saw in him, I have no idea."

Hannah felt as if he'd just punched a hole in her chest.

"You?" she blurted, as Katie let out a low, keening moan. "You killed Nick?"

"Of course I did." He almost seemed offended that she could ever have imagined otherwise. "Claudia still had feelings for him. She was going to get back together with him. Just like you still wanted Jakey here. It was written all over your face last night, up at Killer Point." Colin's nostrils flared. "And he clearly had feelings for you, too. I couldn't have him taking you from me. And once I'm done with him and Katie here, you and I will be alone. *Finally* alone. Just like it should be."

He turned the blade. Hannah saw a drop of blood on Jacob's neck.

"Hannah!" Katie shouted.

All at once, it seemed, Hannah saw where Katie was looking— saw the baseball bat leaning against the porch railing right next to Hannah's hand. Hannah reached out and wrapped her fingers around it, flinging it to Katie as Katie shouted:

"Jacob!"

Jacob drove his elbow into Colin's side, and Colin doubled over. He dropped the knife and Katie grabbed the bat, turned around, and swung like an all-star player just as Colin was straightening up.

Crack!

Colin's skull made a sickening sound as the bat struck home. He slumped forward over the porch rail like a dead fish. As he fell, his feet kicked the knife. It clattered across the porch and dropped off the side into the brush.

Katie grabbed Jacob by the shoulders.

"Are you okay? Are you okay?"

Jacob nodded like a bobble-head toy. "I'm f-f-f-fine," he said.

Hannah stumbled down the steps, dropped to her knees, and searched through the mess of plants and leaves until she found the knife. Her hands shook as she picked it up, her palms slick. When she stood up again, Jacob took one look at the blade and staggered backward.

"It's okay! We're all okay!" Hannah put the knife behind her. She didn't know if *she* was okay, but she was acting on pure adrenaline now.

Katie began to shake so violently, Hannah was worried that her stepsister was broken. She reached out her free hand carefully and touched Katie's arm. Katie flinched, but otherwise didn't move.

"Katie, you did good," Hannah said. "You knocked him out."

"He . . . he tried to kill Jacob," Katie said, sucking in air so hard her bottom lip disappeared for a second. "He tried to—"

"I know, and you took care of me," Jacob said, looking her in the eye and squeezing her arm, still trembling himself. "You took care of all of us. You *saved* us."

Katie blinked. She seemed to come to at that statement, like she was waking from a stupor. Her gaze focused on Hannah and she took in a deep breath.

"I saved us."

"Yes," Hannah said. "But now, we have to go."

"Go?" Katie's eyes trailed along the ground until they found Nick's body. She stared at it. "Go where?"

"Katie, look at me," Hannah said. She grasped Katie's hand. Katie did as she was told and Hannah set her jaw. "You're gonna have to get in the canoe."

TWENTY-FIVE

"There's a reason we don't use the canoes anymore," Jacob whispered to Hannah as he helped her carry the first one to the shore. "My dad says they're so old he doesn't trust them."

Hannah glanced back at Katie to make sure she hadn't heard that. "We're gonna have to take our chances," she whispered back.

They got the canoe into the water and Hannah placed the knife, which was lined with dried blood—Nick's blood—onto the floor of the canoe.

Don't think about Nick. Don't think about Colin.

Colin—the murderer.

Hannah's stomach turned and she handed Jacob a paddle. Unlike the rowboat, the canoe didn't have any brackets to rest the paddles in. You had to paddle on your own, digging into the water on one side and then the other, so the paddler could switch back and forth. They were both going to have to paddle if they had any hope of making it out of here alive.

"Why aren't we taking the Jet Ski?" Katie asked, wading toward the canoe.

"No keys. Not in the ignition anyway. I checked," Jacob said. "And it's only for one person anyway." He paused, his face going ashen, and he locked eyes with Hannah. "This isn't going to work, H. This thing will never handle our weight, either. It'll sink if we all try to get in it."

"Sink?" Katie said tremulously.

"We don't have a choice. We can do this," Hannah said firmly as Katie settled gingerly onto one of the two small benches in the canoe.

"We do, actually," Jacob said, handing his oar to Katie as he stood in the shallows. "You guys take this one and get a head start. I'm going to go get the other canoe."

"Jacob, no! We're not leaving you behind," Hannah hissed, glancing back at Colin, who was still out cold on the porch.

"Yes! You are!" Jacob countered, and to prove his point, he shoved the canoe off into the water. Katie screamed, clinging to her paddle with both hands like a battle staff. "I'll be right behind you!" Jacob called.

Hannah glared at Jacob, but she knew he was right. This thing was barely seaworthy as it was. There was no way it could handle all their weight. Jacob turned and ran for the shed to get the other canoe.

"Hannah?" Katie whimpered.

"It's okay, Katie," Hannah said.

"Where are the life jackets?" Katie asked tremulously.

"No life jackets."

Katie moaned. "What about the thing in the lake? Hannah, this is crazy. There's no way we're making it out of here alive."

"I don't know about you, Katie, but I'd rather take my chances getting around the thing in the lake than stay on dry land with an actual homicidal maniac."

Katie fell silent and Hannah knew she'd won the argument. She couldn't indulge Katie's fears right now when she was overwhelmed by her own. Colin was clearly insane, and if he woke up and came after them, she had no idea how they were going to defend themselves out on the open water. Plus, Katie was right—they still had to contend with the lake monster. She had no idea what that thing was, but it was real. She'd seen it. Alessandra had been attacked by it.

Whatever had happened to Alessandra that night, it hadn't been Colin's fault. He'd been standing right next to Hannah when it had happened. He'd screamed just as hard and as long as the rest of them had.

Was that what had done it? Had watching his friend get pulled under by the lake monster pushed him over the edge—made him go crazy? But no. If Nick was right, and Colin had something to do with Claudia's disappearance, then she'd been flirting with a murderer—*kissing* a murderer.

Kissing someone who had just been waiting for his next opportunity to kill.

Hannah shuddered. Her first kiss. The guy who had given her her first kiss had murdered someone in cold blood. Maybe more than one someone. Hannah cleared her throat before the horror could suffocate her. She could cry as much as she wanted to later, once she and Katie and Jacob were safe.

"You paddle on your right side," she said over her shoulder, trying to make her voice firm. "I'll paddle on the left."

"I can't. Hannah, I can't." Katie's voice broke.

"Katie, you're one of the strongest people I know. You can do this."

"How are we even going to see where we're going?" Katie asked, looking around her at the fog that enveloped them.

"We're just going to have to do our best," Hannah replied. "Besides, I think the fog is starting to break up. The sun is peeking through, see?"

Silence. Katie didn't move. Hannah cursed under her breath.

"Look at it this way: We either find a way across this water, or we go back there and Colin tries to kill you. Which is it going to be?"

The canoe was drifting back toward shore. If they didn't do something soon, they were going to be caught in the shallows. Hannah was going to have to get out of the canoe to push off again, or Jacob was going to have to waste precious time helping them. Hannah looked back over her shoulder toward the house to check on Jacob, but the fog had moved in between the water and the shore. She couldn't see anything.

After a breath, Katie placed the paddle halfway into the water and gave a tentative shove.

"There you go!" Hannah cheered.

She put her own paddle in the water and pushed. At first, their work was uneven and spotty and they were going more sideways than forward, but then, slowly, they found a rhythm. Katie began to match her strokes to Hannah's and they started to move. Between Hannah's swim training and Katie's softball training, they had two good sets of strong arms, and the canoe began to skim the water. Hannah's hair pulled back from her face as they picked up speed.

"I don't understand what's happening," Katie said as they paddled together. "Is Colin out of his mind?"

"I don't know. He must be," Hannah said. "It doesn't make

any sense. Why would he . . ." She couldn't bring herself to say the words *kill Nick.* She couldn't bring herself to believe them.

"And what was all that stuff about Claudia?" Katie asked. "Who's Claudia?"

Suddenly, there was a tingling sensation at the back of Hannah's mind. Everything Colin had said on the beach seemed to filter through her thoughts. *What Claudia saw in him, I have no idea.* And *Claudia still had feelings for him.*

Was Colin jealous of Nick and Claudia? Had he liked Claudia? Was that why he liked *Hannah*? Was that why he'd asked Jacob to invite her up here—because he'd seen her picture and she looked like the girl he liked, but couldn't have?

Hannah thought of Claudia's journal, of the boy she'd called *S.B.* That couldn't have been Colin, could it?

"Hannah!" Katie's terrified shout yanked Hannah out of a trance brought on by her thoughts and the nonstop rhythm of her strokes.

"What?"

Hannah whipped around and immediately saw the reason for Katie's panic. The canoe was filling with water. Something bumped her ankle and she looked down to see that the knife was floating there. Her feet were covered by three inches of lake.

They were going under. And fast.

TWENTY-SIX

Hannah stared across the lake toward the far shoreline. The fog was so thick, she couldn't see the parking lot of the Dreardon Lake docks. But she *could* hear car doors slamming and a truck beeping as it backed up. Someone's laughter carried to her briefly across the water, but then it was lost. Hannah thought about screaming, but what good would it do? If she couldn't see the people and their cars, they wouldn't be able to see her, either. With the way sounds echoed around this water, they'd never even be able to tell which direction the screams were coming from. She glanced over her shoulder to search for Jacob, but saw nothing aside from the fog.

Please let him be out on the lake behind us. Please don't let Colin have woken up and—

Hannah refused to finish the thought.

She grabbed the knife and placed it on the bench next to her to keep it from nicking her legs. The water was up to her ankles now. They weren't going to make it. And if the canoe went down, Katie would certainly panic and flail like she had the other day.

They could both drown.

"Hannah . . . ?" Katie asked. She sounded desperate.

"We're going to the island," Hannah said, making a snap decision. "Mystery Island." She shoved her paddle into the water and turned the canoe, her arm muscles straining with the effort. "It'll buy us some time . . . give us someplace to hide. Maybe some fishermen will come close in their boat and we'll be able to flag them down."

"Maybe?" Katie's voice was like nails on a chalkboard. "What about Jacob?"

"Jacob . . . Jacob's just gonna have to fend for himself," Hannah said. It was the only plan she had. "Now paddle!"

Katie did as she was told, but with the canoe rapidly filling with water, it was getting harder and harder to inch it forward. Hannah's shoulders quivered and sweat ran down her brow, pooling above her upper lip. Katie started to cry quietly as the canoe grew heavier and heavier and their progress slower and slower. They had gotten themselves close, but they were still a good fifty yards from the island's rocky shoreline.

Hannah dropped her paddle and said, "We're going to have to swim."

Then Katie began to cry in earnest, her shoulders shaking with every sob.

"It's okay," Hannah said in a soothing voice, refusing to let herself think about the lake monster, about Alessandra, about the blood. "I'm going to put you in a lifeguard's hold and get us both to shore." Hannah was so physically spent and emotionally exhausted at this point, she wasn't entirely confident she could do it. But she wasn't about to tell Katie that. She grabbed the knife, turned it blade-side out, and held it between her teeth.

"Nick's blood is on that knife!" Katie wailed.

Hannah glared at her. She knew Nick's blood was on the stupid knife, but what was she going to do? Leave it behind? It was the only weapon they had.

"I'll take it," Katie said.

She reached out and grabbed the knife's handle. Her hands shook as she gripped it.

"Thank you," Hannah said.

The canoe sank beneath them and Katie reached for Hannah with one hand, clutching her and digging her nails into her flesh.

"It's okay, Katie," Hannah said. "I promise it's okay. Just . . . try to keep the knife away from me."

Katie nodded mutely. Hannah locked one weak arm around Katie's chest and started to tread water as the canoe dropped away entirely. Katie's legs and arms thrashed and Hannah held her tighter, keeping one eye on the bloody blade.

"If this is going to work, you have to stay calm. You have to stop moving," she said in Katie's ear as she began to inch toward shore. "Just trust me, okay? I'm not going to let anything happen to you."

"But you hate me," Katie said, going limp. Her voice was such a quiet whisper Hannah barely heard her.

"I don't hate you," Hannah replied. Swimming with one arm was so maddeningly slow she wanted to pull her own hair out. "Besides, if I let you drown, your mother will definitely divorce my father and then my dad will hate me forever. And that's not happening."

Katie actually snorted a laugh, and Hannah thought, *Everything's going to be fine.* At least for the moment.

The water was cold, and slimy weeds tugged at Hannah's legs as she pushed herself forward. She tried not to think about the other things living beneath the surface. Of Alessandra and how she'd perished. Of the other people who had taken their own lives here. Somehow she found an extra reserve of energy and swam with every ounce of it until her feet hit the bottom of the lake.

"Put your feet down. You can stand," she told Katie, releasing her.

Katie spluttered and threw her arms out until Hannah reached down and hauled her up. When Katie finally stood, she was shaky, her wet hair plastered across her forehead, the knife clutched in one hand. She half walked, half ran out of the water, stumbling up the wet rocks of the beach. Hannah followed more slowly, breathing in through her nose and out through her mouth in an attempt to catch her breath. She turned around and saw the two paddles floating on the surface of the water. The canoe was completely submerged.

Where were the police? Had Colin even . . . ? But no. Of course not. He'd never even gone to town, had he? The realization was like a stab. Colin had probably put-putted a few yards along the shoreline, docked, and waited for them to go to bed. Then he'd crept back through the woods, lured Nick into the mist somehow, and murdered him.

He'd murdered Nick. In cold blood. Had Nick been scared? Had it hurt very much? Had he known what was happening?

Had *she* been standing there, on the porch just a few feet away, when Nick had died?

Oh, God. She *had*. The shadow she'd seen lurking in the mist—that had been Colin.

Suddenly Hannah was overcome with emotion. It built up inside her head, then exploded. She doubled over from the force of it, crying hard and snotting down her face. Poor Nick. He was just a kid, like her. And he'd come out to the cottage to try to warn them and she'd basically thrown him out so Colin could kill him in cold blood.

"I kissed him," she said out loud, the words broken.

Katie put an arm around Hannah's back. "Shhh, Hannah. It's not your fault."

"I . . . I kissed him, and he *killed* Nick! And he tried to kill Jacob," Hannah said, shoving the back of her hand across her nose. "And—" she said, horrible realization hitting her. "He probably killed Prandya! I kissed a murderer."

Hannah thought of the way Colin had looked at her on that trail, the way her heart had skipped around like a kid with a jump rope when he'd brought his lips to hers. She turned around and vomited into the weeds. There was nothing left in her stomach, though, so all that came out was spit and tears.

"Are you okay?" Katie asked quietly, once Hannah was finished.

Hannah stood up straight; managed a nod. "No," she said. She reached out, took the knife from Katie, and pushed it into the waistband of her shorts. The steel was cold against her backside, but it was also comforting to have it near her somehow. Besides, she couldn't look at it anymore. "We have to figure out a way to town. We need the police."

"Maybe we should walk to the other side of the island," Katie suggested, pushing her hair off her face. "It seems like more people fish and stuff on that side. We might have a better chance of getting rescued."

Hannah didn't hate the idea of putting the island between them and Colin, either, just in case he woke up and figured out where they'd gone. Every bit of distance would help.

"Let's do it," she said.

They started up the slope and into the woods. It was only then that Hannah realized she'd kicked off her flip-flops back at the house. Katie was barefoot, too, and they both winced and cursed as they stepped on sharp branches and rocks. Otherwise, neither one of them spoke. They just kept moving, cutting as straight a line as they could across the small island. At some point, Hannah realized they were close to the spot where she'd found the mountain of rocks and the lockbox. The box with Claudia's diary. She couldn't think about that now.

Finally, the lake came into view again on the far side. The mist was so thick on its surface, Hannah couldn't see more than ten yards offshore.

Were there people trying to fish in this? Was anyone out there?

Crack.

Hannah and Katie both froze.

"What was that?" Katie asked.

Hannah's breath was short. "I don't know," she whispered.

Snap.

The mist in the trees undulated.

"There's someone out there," Katie whispered, and clutched Hannah's arm. "Maybe it's Jacob?"

"Oh, God," Hannah whispered, her eyes wide as she looked at Katie. "Colin?"

And then Alessandra emerged from the fog, thick, viscous mud streaking her haunted face.

TWENTY-SEVEN

Hannah staggered backward and tripped over Katie's foot, her butt hitting the ground hard, jarring her spine. She felt the tip of the knife nick the back of her thigh, but barely cared.

"No no no no no," Katie blubbered.

But still Alessandra came. She reached out a hand toward them, her eyes bloodshot. Katie screamed an ear-piercing scream.

"You're—you're dead!" Hannah stammered. "You can't be here! You're dead!"

Alessandra stopped. She reached up and ran her hands down her face, clearing some of the mud away. When she sighed, Hannah felt a brief blip of hope.

"Calm down," Alessandra whispered. "I'm not dead. I'm not a ghost." She glared at Katie. "I just tripped on the hill and it basically became a mudslide. Can you please stop screaming?"

It wasn't until she spoke that Hannah saw what she was wearing. A dirty pair of jeans and a tank top—completely different from the bathing suit she'd had on when she'd been attacked. Hannah pressed her lips together. She squeezed Katie's shoulder and Katie turned into her, crying, but quietly.

"What is going on, Hannah? I don't understand what's happening."

"Alessandra," Hannah said. She was cold and wet and her butt throbbed where she'd collided with the ground. Her chest still hurt from gasping for breath—from the panic and fear—and she could still see the look on Nick's face as he lay dead in the dirt at Jacob's house. But somehow she kept her voice steady. "What are you doing here? *How* are you here?"

She thought about pulling the knife out and checking her thigh, but she didn't want Alessandra to know she had it—not yet. Not until she figured out if the girl was friend or foe.

Alessandra sighed again and pushed her hair back from her face. "I'm here because I lost my tennis bracelet the other night when I swam out here," she said. "Have you guys seen anything? And also do you have any food on you? I didn't eat breakfast this morning. A granola bar? Anything?"

Hannah gaped at Alessandra. It was like the girl was speaking Greek. Backward. And in pig Latin.

"Alessandra, what are you *talking* about?" Hannah asked, shivering. "We thought you were dead!"

Alessandra blinked and seemed a bit thrown. "Colin didn't tell you?"

"Tell us what?" Hannah asked, frustration and fury building inside her.

Alessandra looked behind them as if she was waiting for Colin to emerge from the trees. "Perfect. This whole thing got entirely screwed up."

"*What* whole thing?" Katie demanded.

"I'm really sorry," Alessandra said. "It was all a joke. Colin and Raj's idea. Nick didn't want to have anything to do with it, but he did come pick me up on his Jet Ski that night, which was nice of him."

Hannah's heart gave a pang at the sound of Nick's name, so casually mentioned. Wait, Nick had known Alessandra was alive? He'd been so freaked out by the story. Was that just an act?

"I'm sorry. What was all a joke?" Hannah asked.

"Everything," Alessandra admitted, blushing. "There is no lake monster."

Hannah's jaw dropped. "But I saw it! More than once."

"That was an old inner tube Raj messed with to make it look like a creature from the deep," Alessandra said. "He was pretty much behind that whole part of it. Almost drowned himself trying to make it hover out of the lake long enough for you to see it."

"Oh my God," Hannah said, shoving herself up off the ground. "Oh my *God*! You guys are evil."

"Is this place even nicknamed Drowning Lake?" Katie asked.

"Yes. That part is true." Alessandra raised one hand, as if taking an oath. "A lot of people really do think the lake is cursed. That was how Colin came up with the idea. We made this whole plan the night before you guys got here, and Raj enlisted a bunch of his wrestling buddies to help with the stuff in the lake."

"What *stuff*?" Katie demanded.

"Like when you thought something was pulling you down during the race with Jacob," Alessandra said to Hannah. "And then the scraping under the boat and you getting thrown in," she added, glancing sheepishly at Katie. "That was all them. They've all been staying over at Raj's place so they could get to the lake quickly. Colin or I would text them when you were going in the water and they'd strap on the scuba gear and swim out."

"I don't freaking *believe* this," Katie said.

Hannah narrowed her eyes. "So, the other night you were . . . ?"

"Acting." She paused and shot them a proud sort of look. "Did I mention I'm kind of the star of my drama club?"

Hannah's stomach was sour. She and Katie stared at each other.

"Raj was under the water with my scuba gear and some pig's blood from the butcher in town," Alessandra explained, at least having the courtesy to look apologetic. "After you guys ran off, we swam out here. But Raj, like an idiot, only brought his little crappy Jet Ski, so he went back and sent Nick to come get me. It was a whole big thing. Anyway, I didn't realize until last night that my grandmother's tennis bracelet was missing, so I came back out here to look for it. Futilely, apparently," she said, glancing around at the ground at her feet. "Seriously, nothing? Gum? Mints? Candy?"

"So you staged everything?" Hannah shouted. "The drowning? The blood?" Suddenly her brain went weightless. "So wait, is Nick actually alive? Was that all staged, too?"

Alessandra's brow knit. "Nick? What do you mean? What happened to Nick?"

"We woke up and found him dead!" Katie shouted. She seemed to be coming back to herself a bit. "That's what happened to Nick!"

"What?!" Alessandra blurted, clutching her stomach. "What the hell are you talking about?"

"His throat was cut," Katie snapped. "Colin did it. And then he attacked Jacob."

"What? No. Colin would never—"

"He did, Alessandra," Hannah said. Any brief hope that Nick had just been pranking them was fading. "Colin's insane, and he's still out there."

Alessandra was shaking her head back and forth, back and forth. "And Jacob?" she whispered.

"He's okay. We think," Katie said, glancing at Hannah. "He was coming after us in another canoe, but we got separated in the fog."

Alessandra turned away, her hand over her mouth, and when she turned back again, her eyes were full of fear.

"Why kill Nick?" she said quietly. "Why would he—"

"He said it had something to do with Claudia," Hannah said. "Do you have any idea what he was talking about?"

Alessandra was silent for a moment, and it looked to Hannah like she was thinking something through—like she was trying to figure something out. Then she breathed, "Claudia."

"What?" Hannah said. "What about her?"

"Who is *Claudia*?" Katie wailed, throwing up her hands and letting them slap down at her sides.

Alessandra looked away, her eyes distant. "What if that was him?" she said under her breath.

"What if what was who?" Hannah said.

"Who is Claudia?" Katie repeated.

"We don't have time for me to explain right now." Alessandra reached into her back pocket and pulled out her phone.

"Is that working?" Katie asked.

Alessandra nodded, her hands trembling as she turned it on. "I forgot to charge it last night, so it's almost dead, but I think I can make a call."

She pressed down on the screen and held the phone to her ear, her arm shaking. "Prandya, yeah. It's me."

So apparently Prandya was in on the joke, too, Hannah thought, her anger growing. *She probably hid her kayak somewhere and just paddled home yesterday when no one was looking. She* has *been at her house this whole time.* Hannah felt, for the first time in her life, that she could truly punch someone.

"Sorry, I know it's early," Alessandra continued. "We're stranded out on the island and we need you to come get us. I only have my Jet Ski." Pause. "Yes, right now. It's an emergency. Me, Hannah, and Katie. Listen, Prandya . . . Nick's dead. Colin killed him."

Hannah heard Prandya's *What!?* through the phone.

"I think he might have had something to do with Claudia, too."

Hannah's stomach twisted.

"I'll explain later. Just come. And call the—"

Alessandra pulled her phone away from her face and looked at the screen. It was black.

"It died."

"Can somebody please explain this Claudia person to me?" Katie demanded.

"Claudia was a friend of mine who disappeared the night school ended," Alessandra told Katie, then looked back at Hannah. "Remember when I told you that you looked like her a little bit?" Hannah nodded, her throat completely dry. "Well, she was going out with Nick, but a couple of weeks before she disappeared, he caught her kissing some summer guy in the park. He wouldn't tell me who. I think it might have been Colin."

"But Colin's not a summer guy," Hannah said.

Alessandra's face screwed up in confusion. "Yes, he is."

"No. His mother manages the theater in town," Hannah protested. "He said his grandfather owns it."

"His grandfather does own it, but Colin and his mom only come up here for the summers to help out," Alessandra said. "Colin's from Indiana. They get out of school like a month before we do, so he always gets up here in mid-May."

Hannah's brain reeled. Colin had never actually told her he lived here year-round. She'd just assumed.

"I should have realized it when he saw your picture and convinced Jacob to invite you here," Alessandra said. "I noticed how much you looked like Claudia, and he couldn't stop talking about how beautiful you were . . ."

"So he has a type?" Katie asked. "You think he goes after blue-eyed girls with brown hair and then murders them?"

Hannah started to tremble.

"Oh my God. Vicki," Hannah breathed. "Nick tried to tell me, but I ignored him."

"Who's Vicki now?" Katie said.

"Colin's girlfriend from home, he said." Hannah pressed her eyes closed. "Nick told me to look her up on the internet. He said it was an *interesting read.*"

"How much you want to bet she looks like you, too?" Alessandra said.

"What if she's also missing?" Hannah added, feeling sick to her stomach.

"This is bad, you guys," Katie said. "If this is all true, then Colin is basically a serial killer."

Snap!

The noise made Hannah jump.

"Come out, come out, wherever you are!"

Hannah's blood went cold as Colin's voice carried across the island.

"He's here!" Katie hissed.

Alessandra grabbed Hannah's wrist, her fingers like ice.

"Run!"

TWENTY-EIGHT

Hannah ran. She ran like her life depended on it. She ran like she'd never run before. Behind her, Katie tripped and fell, then scrambled to her feet and took off again. It was a good thirty seconds before Hannah realized they weren't running for the far shore as they should have done, but moving inland—traveling uphill. It was Alessandra who was leading the way, and a sliver of dread suddenly ran down Hannah's spine. A tree branch snapped back and hit her in the face and she tripped blindly, going down on her knees. A sharp pain took her breath away.

"Alessandra! Stop!"

Hannah rolled over, clutching her kneecap, and her leg brushed up against a hand.

A scream wrenched from her throat.

"What? What's wrong?" Alessandra asked, hovering over her.

There was a hand sticking up out of the mud. A stiff, gray hand. Part of a body.

Alessandra cried out and Hannah scuttled back on her hands and knees. Rocks tumbled everywhere and Hannah realized through blurred eyes where they were. The rock pile she'd seen before. The one near the lockbox. This had been the rock pile. All the rain and the mudslide Alessandra had told them about must have dislodged it.

Wincing as her knee spasmed in pain, Hannah dragged herself to her feet and clung to Alessandra.

"It was a grave," she croaked. "The rocks were marking a grave."

Whimpering, Alessandra took a couple of steps forward, dragging Hannah with her. She paused, looking down at the hand, and let out a wail.

"It's Claudia."

"What?" Hannah said.

"It's her. That gold ring . . . that's her mother's ring."

Alessandra stopped, doubling over at the waist to catch her breath.

Hannah remembered a fragment of the line from the diary: *Mom let me wear her vintage gold ring . . .*

"Oh, God," Hannah cried. It *was* Claudia. "We should have gone toward the shore—tried to flag someone down."

"My Jet Ski is this way. Besides, who are we going to flag down in this fog?" Alessandra shot back. Her eyes were wide and wild, her teeth almost bared.

"There are people fishing out there!" Hannah whispered.

"But they can't see anything," Alessandra replied. "They can't—"

There was a rustling nearby, and Alessandra fell silent. Hannah reached out and grabbed her arm. She glanced around at the trees and her heart all but stopped. She and Alessandra were entirely alone. Entirely. Alone.

"Where's Katie?" Hannah said.

"She's right—"

Alessandra turned around and brought her hands to her forehead. "She was right behind you."

"Oh my God," Hannah said. She took a few steps back in the direction from which they'd come, carefully avoiding the ruined grave. "Katie!" she whispered, tears stinging her eyes. "Katie!"

There was a twitter and a screech. Animals. Birds. Maybe. Or was it Colin? Was he out there in the fog somewhere, watching them? Taunting them? Or was it Katie? Was she hurt and couldn't respond?

And then came the voice again.

"Haaaaannaaaah! Come out, come out, wherever you are!"

Hannah jumped and Alessandra made an awful sound at the back of her throat. Colin sounded like he was right on top of them.

"Hannah, come on . . . I just want to talk to you!"

Hannah and Alessandra locked eyes.

"*Does he not know you're here?*" Hannah mouthed.

Alessandra raised her shoulders.

"Come on out! If you do, I won't drown your sister here," Colin called out.

Hannah's stomach crumbled. She leaned her hand on an oak tree to catch her breath, the rough bark cutting into her skin.

"I'm on the beach on the west side of the island." Colin's voice was deadly serious. "I'll give you two minutes and then she's going under."

Hannah turned and started for the western shore—the shoreline closest to Jacob's house. But Alessandra grabbed her arm.

"What're you doing?" she whispered harshly.

"I can't let him drown Katie," Hannah replied.

"What if he's bluffing?" Alessandra asked.

Hannah's pulse was going crazy. "What if he's not?"

"Come here." Alessandra tugged on Hannah's wrist, but Hannah resisted. "If they're really down there, we'll be able to see them from the top of the hill. Come on!"

Hannah did as she was told. There was no way she wanted to sacrifice herself to that monster if he didn't actually have Katie. She and Alessandra sprinted uphill until they came to an outcropping of rock. Alessandra dropped to her knees and then her stomach, and Hannah did the same. They inched to the edge of the rocky shelf and peeked over.

The fog had pulled out about ten feet away from the shore. Colin stood in the water, blood dripping all over the back of his neck. He was soaked from the knee down, a tear in his jeans, and his T-shirt was wet along the hem. Hannah barely noticed any of this, however, because dangling from one hand at the end of his arm was Katie—unconscious, limp, and pale. A ribbon of blood trickled down from her nose and over her lips.

"What're we gonna do?" Alessandra asked.

In the distance, Hannah heard a boat's motor roar to life, then another. She could only hope it was Prandya and her family, coming to save the day. The fog made it impossible to tell.

"The fog," Hannah whispered, an idea springing to life inside her.

"What?" Alessandra asked.

"Hannah! You're down to a minute!" Colin called out in a singsong voice. She saw his smile and her insides revolted. She couldn't believe this was a person she'd found handsome just yesterday. Someone she wanted to know better; someone she wanted to be near. Now, he was threatening her sister's life on top of everything else. And he was taunting her—mocking her— like this was all a game. Well, fine—if he wanted to play, she would play.

TWENTY-NINE

"You have ten seconds, Hannah, and then I'm holding her under," Colin shouted. "Drowning is not a fun way to die . . . or so I'm told. The body really fights it, hard, and the victim has a lot of time to contemplate the fact that they're going." He paused—chuckled. "That's eight seconds, Hannah. Seven."

Hannah crouched behind a huge boulder, the tiny pebbles around it cutting into her knees. She ducked as low as she could, terror coursing through her veins. Her plan was crazy. Totally insane. But all she could do was pray that it would work.

She heard a splash as Alessandra stepped boldly out of the tree line.

"Ali? What are you doing here?" The confusion was plain in Colin's voice. "Where's Hannah?"

"I haven't seen Hannah, Colin. What the hell are you doing?" Alessandra asked.

Hannah held her breath as she listened to the exchange, and every muscle in her body quivered. This had to work. She had to buy them time—enough time for Prandya's family or the police to get here. This was the only way.

"This has nothing to do with you," Colin told Alessandra.

"What about Claudia? And the fact that you tried to frame Nick for her disappearance?" Alessandra shouted. "Does that have anything to do with me?"

Hannah hesitated. Technically, she was supposed to be submerging herself in the water right now, but she wanted to hear this. Colin had attempted to *frame* Nick?

"I don't know what you're talking about," Colin said after a brief hesitation.

"Oh, please. Let's not act like we both don't know what happened," Alessandra said bravely. "That note they found at Claudia's house. The one that said *I miss you. We need to talk. Meet me at our special place. N.* The cops went straight to Nick, of course, because everyone in our class knew they'd been going out, so it wasn't hard to make the leap. But the handwriting didn't match Nick's and he was with his baseball buddies that whole night, so they cleared him. Too bad you didn't know they had an all-nighter planned, huh, Colin?"

Silence.

"What I don't get is, how did you know that was what she called him in her diary?" she asked. "What'd you do, sneak a peek when she wasn't looking?"

He definitely did exactly that, Hannah thought, chilled to the bone. Colin was the one who'd read Claudia's diary that day when she came home and it had been moved. And he probably went back and stole it after he murdered her. That and all the other personal stuff of hers he buried on the island. Maybe that stuff was evidence, and he hid it near the body, hoping the cops would never find it.

"She was going to go back to him," Colin said through his teeth. "She never gave a crap about me. She was going to go running right back to him."

"What did you do to her, Colin? What did you do to Claudia?"

Alessandra's voice broke, and Hannah suddenly realized they were running out of time. Either Alessandra was going to crack, or Colin was going to realize how much Alessandra had on him and he was going to go after her.

It was now or never.

Hannah pressed her lips together and lowered herself down into the water, which quickly closed in around her up to her neck. The drop-off here was steep, and within two steps the lake was about four feet deep around her. She took a deep breath, held it, and dove.

Beneath the surface, Hannah opened her eyes. Everything was gray and murky and her retinas stung. She turned left, blindly, praying that she was headed in the right direction. She prayed she'd be able to hold her breath long enough. She prayed that the fog would keep her hidden and Colin wouldn't spot her. She prayed that she'd have the swim of her life.

Weeds slipped over her skin and tugged at her ankles, slowing her pace slightly. She let out a bubble and tried not to panic. Her lungs were starting to burn, and she longed for a breath, but she forced herself to keep going, and suddenly—heart slamming against her rib cage—she saw the fuzzy outline of Colin's legs. They were much closer than she would have thought and she brought herself up short.

Telling her lungs to quiet, Hannah turned her body slightly and swam around behind Colin. She wished she knew what was going on above the surface, but she could hear the muffled sound of voices shouting at each other. She knew Alessandra was keeping him talking; keeping him distracted; keeping Katie alive.

This is going to work, Hannah told herself. *It's going to work.*

Suddenly, surprisingly, Hannah felt an odd little thrill down her spine. This guy was evil. He had murdered Nick. He had probably murdered Claudia. He had come up with the idea for Alessandra to fake her own death, for his friends to release that blood in the water, for them to taunt Hannah and Katie with a fake lake monster. Colin was an out-and-out sociopath.

He had made Hannah and Katie believe that there was something to fear in these waters. And now there was. *Hannah* was the thing to fear. *Hannah* was the thing lurking beneath the surface.

Feeling the power of that, Hannah reached out, grabbed Colin around the ankles, and yanked as hard as she could.

He hit the water with a grand splash. Hannah emerged and sucked air into her aggrieved lungs, but she didn't have time to savor it. She fumbled the knife out of her waistband as Alessandra dove for Katie, who was just coming to after hitting the water face-first. Before Colin could get his knees under him, Hannah jumped on his back and brought the knife around his neck, holding it against his throat until she drew blood.

"Don't move or I swear I'll do the same thing to you that you did to Nick."

Colin laughed. "You don't have it in you."

Hannah pressed the knife harder, gritting her teeth as blood dripped down the blade. Colin made a choking noise.

And then the prow of a boat suddenly cut through the fog.

"Everybody freeze!"

It was the police. Two officers had their guns trained right on Hannah and Colin.

Hannah released him and put her hands in the air, holding up the knife.

"Well, I guess now we'll never find out," she told him.

It was all she could do to keep from laughing right in Colin's stunned face.

THIRTY

"Now the sun comes out," Katie said, squinting up at the sky.

"I hate fog," Hannah said, pulling her police-issue blanket tighter around her shoulders. It was at least eighty degrees out and she was shivering. She and Katie were sitting on the back of an ambulance, parked in the lakeside parking lot, their legs dangling toward the ground as they waited for their parents to show. "I'm going to hate fog forever."

"But if it wasn't for the fog, you might never have saved me." Katie knocked the side of Hannah's knee with her own. "So it's not totally awful." Then she sat up straight. "Jacob!"

Hannah's heart leapt as Jacob stepped out of a squad car that had just pulled into the parking lot. Katie jumped off the back of the ambulance and ran to him, throwing herself into his arms. Hannah watched them kiss, and even though it didn't feel great, she didn't much care. Jacob was alive—he was fine. He'd gotten the canoe across the lake without any leaks and made it to town while they were fighting off Colin on the island. The cops had told her this, but she hadn't really believed it until that very moment.

Alessandra had gone back out to Mystery Island with the police to show them where Claudia's body was buried. Hannah could see the lights on the police boats flashing in the distance.

An officer with a stern face and wiry gray eyebrows approached Katie and Jacob, breaking up the quiet, tearful reunion they were having. Together the three of them walked over to Hannah. Jacob wrapped Hannah in a hug as Katie climbed back up to sit next to her again.

"You're okay?" Hannah asked him.

Jacob nodded. "Okay enough."

Hannah gave him a small smile. She knew exactly what he meant.

"You?" Jacob asked, squeezing her arm.

Hannah nodded. "Same."

"Kids," the officer said. His voice was the low and rumbly kind that made him seem like a sweet old grandpa. He nodded at them, then looked over his shoulder. "There's someone here that wants to talk to you. Now, you don't have to talk to her, but—"

Suddenly a streak of black cut across the parking lot and Colin's mother was right in front of them. Her face was haggard and her hair was pulled back in a tight ponytail, highlighting the dark circles under her eyes.

"I'm so sorry," she said, looking at Hannah. "I didn't know. I didn't want to know . . ."

"Ma'am, I'd appreciate it if you'd take a step back," the cop said, holding his arms out to shield Hannah and the others.

"It's you," she continued, ignoring the officer. "You look just like her. Just like Vicki. And just like Claudia. Ever since Vicki dumped him, he hasn't been right. And then she disappeared and I just . . ."

"She disappeared, too?" Hannah asked, a knot between her heart and her stomach.

The police officer's eyes widened.

"Yes, but I hoped coming up here this summer would fix things . . . give him a new start . . . but there's obviously something . . . wrong with him," Colin's mother continued.

"Understatement," Katie said under her breath.

"What did you say?" Colin's mother snapped.

"I said, *understatement*," Katie replied venomously. "Your son is a *murderer*. Nick never did anything to Colin, and now he's dead!"

Katie started to cry and leaned her head against Hannah's shoulder. Hannah wrapped her arms around Katie and shot the officer a look until he led Colin's mother away.

"You say another friend of your son's disappeared?" he asked her on their way across the parking lot.

"It's okay," Hannah said to Katie, stroking her back. "It's going to be okay."

Even though it wasn't. She knew that all three of them were going to be seeing Nick's dead body in their dreams for years to come. How would anything ever be okay again?

"Well, kids, your parents are going to be here in about thirty minutes and they're all anxious to see you," another officer told them. "Your father said they hadn't heard from you since he got a text on Saturday; is that right?" he asked Hannah.

"We lost power," Hannah said. "And there's no signal out there. We couldn't call them or text."

"One of my men went out and inspected the house and said it looked like someone had taken an ax to the electrical box," the officer said, checking his notes. He glanced over his shoulder at a police cruiser, where the authorities had been keeping Colin in cuffs ever since their rescue. He sat in the back of the car, his head down, and looked as if he was muttering to himself. Hannah couldn't believe it. *He'd* cut their power? How elaborate was his plan?

The officer took a breath and looked at them, his eyes kind. "I'd say you kids are lucky to have gotten away with your lives."

Katie sniffled and rubbed gently under her nose, which had stopped bleeding only after the EMTs had stuffed a wad of gauze up there.

"Thanks, officer," she said.

He tipped his hat and walked off, skirting right around the front bumper of Hannah's RAV4. It was weird to see the car sitting there, innocently waiting for her and Katie to return.

As Jacob stared off across the lake, Hannah tightened her grip on Katie, and Katie tightened her grip right back. It was hard to believe that just a few days ago, the two of them had driven into this parking lot, fighting. It seemed like a million years had passed. So much had changed since then. Thinking about everything they'd been through—all the fights and conversations, the near-death experiences and the things they'd done to save each other—Hannah's heart welled.

"Katie, I have something to tell you," she said quietly.

Katie sniffled again and looked up. "What?"

Hannah managed a small smile. "I think we can officially call ourselves sisters now."

Katie smiled unsteadily back at her. "I think so, too."

Dear Diary,

I've never thought about keeping a journal before, but in a weird way it feels like I kind of have to now. Like I owe it to Claudia or something.

It's been a month since Nick died, since we found Claudia's body, since Jacob's parents closed up the house and put it on the market. School's started up again, but nothing feels the same. Katie and I talk about Dreardon Lake all the time, and Jacob fills us in on what's been happening since we left.

Colin told the police he did hide Claudia's stuff on the island because it was evidence, and that he didn't destroy it because he "could never destroy anything of Claudia's." Um, except for CLAUDIA HERSELF. They also found Vicki buried in a park near Colin's house in Indiana. Now he's sitting in jail somewhere, awaiting trial, and one day we're all going to have to testify, which is going to be awful, but I'm not thinking about that today. I'm not thinking about the killer, because today was about his victims.

This morning Katie, Jacob, Theo, and I drove up to Dreardon Lake to be there for Claudia and Nick's memorial. I told Theo he didn't have to come, but he insisted. We're kind of, maybe, sort of . . . I don't know . . . going out now? It started when I got back to Ohio from that weekend, and told Theo everything, and he was so supportive and sweet. All I know is I like having him around, and it ended up being really good that he came along. He kept things light during the car ride, when the rest of us could only think about Nick and all the things we could have done differently. He also kept things light when Katie ran that red light and almost took out a fire hydrant making a left-hand turn.

The memorial was as sad and horrible as you'd imagine. All their friends were there—Alessandra, Prandya, and Raj included. Plus, Raj's wrestling-team buddies who helped with the pranks. Every one of them apologized—again—for going along with Colin's plan to scare us. It was both nice and weird to see them, but I didn't talk to any of them for long. It was only a month ago, but it feels like another lifetime. Sometimes it even feels like a dream.

The worst part was seeing Nick's and Claudia's parents, though. I can't describe how destroyed they are. When Claudia's mother saw me, she went white, and that's when I started to think it was maybe not such a good idea for me to come. So Theo and I bailed.

We walked up to the Dreardon Lake docks so I could show him where it all happened. He's heard enough about it by now that he was curious. When he saw Mystery Island he shuddered and reached for my hand. He said he could see why the whole lake creeped me out so much—even before we got trapped at Jacob's house and found Nick's body, and then Claudia's body . . .

When I first got home, I researched Dreardon Lake online. Just as Jacob had told me, it was true that some careless campers had started the fire that burned down half of Mystery Island. And it was right after that, weirdly, that the drownings started happening, as if the lake was angry. I hadn't really taken any of that seriously. Not after I found out how Raj and his friends tricked us. But I now know the difference between silly ghost stories and real, true danger. I know too well.

Theo and I didn't stay on the docks too long. It was getting a little chilly—the leaves are already starting to turn, can you believe it?—and the sky started to cloud over in a way that brought back too many memories. Theo asked if I was ready to go and I said, "Yes. Definitely."

And I didn't tell him this—I can't even believe I'm writing this—but as I turned away from the lake, I could have sworn I saw something large and gray rise up out of the water.

But when I turned my head again, it was gone.

That's all for now, Diary.

Xoxo,

Hannah

PS Katie and I are STILL grounded. Dad and Mylin let us go to the memorial, but after that, we're basically stuck at home until October. Can't say I didn't warn her.

ACKNOWLEDGMENTS

Thanks so much to Aimee Friedman, David Levithan, and everyone at Scholastic Book Clubs and Fairs, who support my crazy little stories. Special thanks to all the readers, teachers, and librarians who seek out creepy books like these. It's because of you I get to write them, and I do so *love* writing them! Thank you, as always, to my awesome agent, Sarah Burnes, and to my friends and family, especially Matt, Brady, and Will, who make it all worthwhile.

Don't miss another creepy read by Kieran Scott!

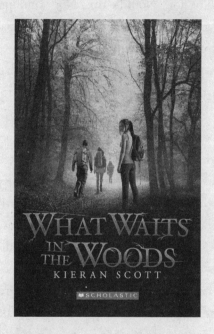

Turn the page for a sneak peek . . .

ONE

Callie Valasquez wasn't ready to die.

Not here. Not now. Not like this. Not standing in the middle of the pitch-black forest clutching a roll of toilet paper. No. That just seemed wrong. She was only sixteen.

But it was going to happen. Especially if that thing—that snorting, breathing, hulking thing—managed to pick up her scent.

Callie stood perfectly still. She tried as hard as she could to keep her breath shallow, but the terror gripping her heart kept making her want to suck in air, to cough. Her knees quaked and her stomach twisted itself into horrible, ever-tightening knots.

Why had she used that strawberry shampoo this morning? The sugary scent wafted from her thick, dark, meticulously straightened hair. Or could the thing out there smell her coconut body wash? Or maybe the chemical odor of the olive-green nail polish she'd applied to her toes in the kitchen after breakfast, thinking it was oh so hiking-appropriate? Callie looked down at her bare, throbbing toes in her new Teva flip-flops.

Maybe it was her feet. They'd been pretty rank when she'd peeled off her sweaty socks and carefully applied first aid cream and Band-Aids to her lovely new blisters. Oh, God. Could it smell her feet?

Another snort. This one even closer than the last. She could feel the thing's presence just behind her like a pulsating warmth. It was so large it radiated heat. She imagined a huge brown bear with a snout as wide as her father's hand. A wild boar, awful fangs glinting in the moonlight. A mountain lion, crouched low and taut, primed for the kill. Her instincts told her to run, but her fear kept her frozen. That and some vague notion from a movie she'd once seen as a kid that the best policy in this situation was not to draw attention. Bears couldn't see you unless you moved. Or was that dinosaurs?

What was she even doing here? Was being part of the popular crowd in the tiny upstate town of Mission Hills, New York, really so important to her that she had to risk her life? Just because she had some insane need to prove that she was no longer the nerd she'd been back in Chicago, now she was going to die?

The moment Lissa Barton and Penelope Grange had noticed her in the cafeteria that second week of school, when Callie had been the shy new girl, she'd latched on to them like a life raft in a storm. And that moment had led directly to this one.

Callie had never been camping in her life. Had never felt the *need* to go camping. But this was apparently what people did for fun in upstate New York—at least, what her new friends did for fun—so here she was, having loads and loads of fun.

When her boyfriend, Jeremy Higgins—yes, Callie had a boyfriend now, another upside to being newly popular—had picked her up this morning, she'd been so nervous she started up a kind of mantra—*four nights, four nights, four nights.* That was all she had to get through.

Yet here she was, evening one, about to get eaten alive.

She vaguely wondered if the thing would maul her friends after it was done with her.

"Hey, Callie!" Jeremy shouted from their campsite, which was probably forty yards from where she was standing. "Are you okay out there?"

There was a surprised snort and, suddenly, the thing took off into the woods. Callie whipped around in the direction of snapping twigs and crunching leaves, but saw nothing. Just some low, weak branches crushed in the underbrush nearby. She heaved a breath, bent at the waist, and pressed her hand to her heart.

"You're okay," she whispered to herself, tears squeezing from her eyes. "You're okay, you're okay, you're okay."

She was going to live. *Four nights.* By Sunday, she'd be back in her dad's car and they'd be driving to the airport to pick up her mom after her summer in São Paulo. Then, next week, she and her mom would go to New York City for a back-to-school shopping trip. Callie was going to live to see her mother again. To finish writing at least one of the ten short stories she'd started since June. To read the rest of the *Black Inferno* series and finish painting her new bedroom now that she'd finally settled on that pretty aqua after three misguided attempts in the purple family. Everything was going to be fine.

Except.

Callie stood up straight and turned around. She had no clue which direction she was facing. She'd lost her bearings when she'd whirled to spot whatever it was that had crept up on her. Was the camp in front of her, behind her? Where was the skinny, muddy trail she'd taken to get here?

A low mewl escaped her lips. Callie brought her hands to her head, the soft triple ply of Penelope's toilet paper soaking up her sweat. She thought about shouting out for help, but she didn't want to look like an idiot. Lissa and Penelope had already spent half the day teasing her for not breaking in her hiking boots, for packing her makeup bag and a change of earrings, and for forgetting to bring her water bottle, which she knew for a fact was sitting on the kitchen counter where she'd thought she wouldn't miss it on her way out the door.

She didn't want them to think they needed to babysit her every time she had to use the bathroom, too. If that was what you could even call what she'd just done—squatting next to a tree. Ew.

If only she'd had her phone. She could text Jeremy and he would come find her without alerting Lissa and Pen to her total lameness. But she'd left it in the pocket of her hoodie, which was tossed uselessly on a blanket by the fire.

"Callie," she muttered to herself. "Think. You're a straight-A student. You survived getting lost on the Chicago L by yourself when you were ten years old. You can figure out which direction to walk to get back to camp."

It was funny, really. Until now, she'd always thought of herself as a survivor. Her parents had been letting her walk home from school with her friends in Chicago since she was eight. At twelve, she'd flown to Brazil, alone, to visit her grandmother, and hadn't freaked out or cried once.

With her friends back in Chicago, she was the leader—the one who could navigate the map at Six Flags, order the exact right number of pizzas for a party of fifteen people, *and* figure out the tip. She hadn't even crumbled when her parents had told her that her dad had gotten the job at Cornell Law and they were moving to New York, leaving behind the friends she'd had her entire life and the only neighborhood she'd ever called home.

But it seemed upstate New York survival skills were entirely different from Outer Loop Chicago survival skills.

Callie looked up. It was past eight o'clock on an August night. The sky was deep ink blue beyond the tangled canopy of branches and leaves, and every last tree trunk looked black in the darkness. Black and exactly the same.

Okay. Forget pride. Pride was stupid. It was time to shout for her friends.

She opened her mouth just as a hand came down on her shoulder.

ABOUT THE AUTHOR

Kieran Scott is the author of several acclaimed YA novels, including *What Waits in the Woods*, *Pretty Fierce*, the Cheerleader Trilogy, and the He's So/She's So Trilogy. She also wrote the *New York Times* bestselling Private and Privilege series, as well as the Shadowlands trilogy, under the pen name Kate Brian, for Alloy Entertainment. She lives with her husband and children in New Jersey and enjoys working out, baking, and camping. Visit her online at www.kieranscott.net.